THE STAR STRUCK DANCE STUDIO

OF YUCCA SPRINGS

the
star struck
dance studio
of
yucca springs

by

Mary Lou Sanelli

SEATTLE
2019

Chatwin Books
www.chatwinbooks.com

For my mother, who would have loved this.
"A novel means you are a *real* writer," she said to me once.
I didn't agree with her, of course.
But none of that matters now.

Contents

One 1

Two 27

Three 38

Four 57

Five 64

Six 74

Seven 87

Eight 100

Nine 130

Ten 140

Eleven 161

Twelve 179

Thirteen 217

Fourteen 241

Fifteen 258

Sixteen 266

Acknowledgments 310

One

"A star danced, and under that was I born."
~William Shakespeare

So help me.

MY MOTHER REACHED OVER AND GRABBED MY WRIST TO say that it would take me half my life to find the one thing I really wanted. "And the other half trying to keep it," she said, emphasizing the word "keep" while closing her eyes as if she were in pain, and her whole body went still. I knew she was mad. Not at me. At everything. At *life*. We were sitting at the supper table. I was eight years old.

"Do you hear me, Lucy?" she said with a worried look on her face, "do you?"

I shrugged, afraid to say anything. There are only a few moments when a daughter is allowed to see so clearly into her mother's view of the world and how she views herself within it, and how she fears her daughter might have to view herself within it, too. I sensed this. Even if the opposite was dying to leap off my tongue. "Yes," I said, struggling to sound as if I believed her.

I didn't believe her.

I felt as though I already knew what I wanted, and once you've found what makes you happy, it's impossible to believe anyone's soured opinion of it. I sat quietly because

I knew she wouldn't believe me, or couldn't. It's easy to be a pessimist when your own dreams have not come true.

Today, I understand the stress and the disappointment that took hold of her that day and that what she was trying to say had less to do with any single want for ourselves, and more to do with husbands—hers, and my own someday if I wasn't careful—and how I could end up with the wrong man if, desperately wanting to be loved, I let him choose me.

How could she feel otherwise?

In a town small as Yucca Springs, a girl can grow up believing that sex *is* love and that once you love someone it will last, especially when her mother, the nonna I was named after, was quick to see "potential" in any boy who caught my mother's eye, nagging her endlessly about what she said to the boy, what he said back, and how he said it. And so, with no other prospects, hopes, or expectations after high school—which is discouraging, even to kids used to so little—my mother fell for my dad, married him a week after graduation (guess why?), and spent the next fifteen years trying to keep him from sleeping with the neighbor ladies.

This is why I pretended I believed her. And a small part of me thought, *maybe she does know.*

But the other part, the sensing part, knew better, even if I didn't yet have the words for how or why I knew, I knew. So help me.

See, I was only five when I found the one thing I wanted, and it had nothing to do with men or marriage, I knew that, too. But when a mother has no faith in marriage left, it's easy to fill in all the regret with forewarnings, and regret was in good supply in my mother's heart by then. "I don't want you to fall for the first man who looks at you with a twinkle in his eye," she warned, and without saying another word, she excused herself from the table.

Now, as far as my keeping the "one thing" forever, well, at the time, forever seemed so far away I figured it would never come.

Until it did.

And I'm here to say some things can never be foreseen. One day you are marching confidently towards your future, and then suddenly you can imagine yourself running away from it. But you don't run. You stay. And if you are patient, forgiving, especially of yourself, and find at least one friend in the world to share what you are deeply feeling, everything you feared would bring you down can become exactly what you need.

You'll see.

Young, so young.

One hour before my first ballet class, I sat crossed-legged on the floor, dressed and waiting, arms locked around my middle as if to keep hold of myself. Calm as a carrot one moment, and the next I am a fizzy pop ready to burst out of the can, which is so unlike most days in Yucca Springs. Usually it feels like all the fizz in the world is somewhere, anywhere else.

"Please, let's just *go*," I sighed, eyes on the clock.

"Oh, for Pete's sake," my mother said as soon as she found me, her eyes settling on my pink-slippered feet. "You can't wear those outside, Lucy."

A tiny shoot of independence rose up from deep inside me. I shook my head *no*.

A smile spread across her face. There was no predicting when this smile would come, but when it did, we both knew arguing was useless. "Why, you stubborn little bugger," she'd say, or something like it, and I'd wrinkle my nose. "You get that from me, you know." She reached out to pull me off the floor, squeezed my cheeks until my lips puckered, and when she called me "bell'angelo" her mouth opened a little wider. This always happened when she spoke Italian. "Let's go see if the Star Struck is all it's cracked up to be."

"It will be," I said.

She nodded slightly, making no remark. I could always read her nods. I think all kids can read their mother's nods. This one said that no matter how it went, how good or bad my new "experience" was, we would be fine, mom and me. And though she did her best to hide it, she was upset to see how eager I was to go. "If you don't like it, come straight home," she said, the loneliness of beginning a new phase of life in her tone, I heard this and I wanted to be able to comfort her, to convince her that even though I wanted to go I wasn't *leaving*. "I'll pop us some corn and we'll watch TV."

This was our life. Night after night, everything exciting happened behind the blue wavering light of TV, overshadowing any natural light or any real motion, while outside the world got on with its destiny, sometimes silently and sometimes loud as a heavy desert wind before lightning filled the sky and thunder shook our eaves. And though destiny is not a word I normally use, it sounds too make-believe, I did fear that watching too much television would get in the way of my own.

Now or never.

On the desert, trees are worn scrawny by the heat, and unless there's a westerly, the air is stark still, so, generally, we hear something long before we can see it. On that afternoon, we could hear the Star Struck long before we reached the door, piano music swirling in the air, definitely not country music, for once.

I panicked.

Ever-tuned to the look on my face as well, my mother squeezed my hand. "Well?" she said, swinging open the door, "it's now or never." She let go of my hand.

I think the beginning of my future began with that release. I yanked my Scrunchy tighter. I took one step. Two steps. Once inside, the first thing I remember were two big blue eyes staring down at me, bluer than any berry on any Juniper tree. "Hello there," a voice said, and my first thought was, *Oh! My teacher is so pretty.* And that night at the dinner table, probably with macaroni in my mouth, I told my mother just how pretty my new teacher was. Without a twinge of guilt I said, "but not the old-fashioned kind of pretty with a perm piled on top of her head." As soon as I said the words, I sensed my mistake, but I had surprisingly little ability to control my insensitivity sometimes.

Sadly, I think the same can be said of me now.

"What's wrong with a perm?" she said, brushing away a curl that had fallen over her forehead, the hurt visible in her eyes even though her perm was supposedly more modern, bendy, a "loose wave," she called it.

"Nothing," I said.

"So now I'm old-fashioned, is that it?"

As gently as I could, I steered the conversation away from my teacher and I never mentioned her beauty to my mother again. As the years passed, and her hair wasn't kinked into ringlets anymore, I hoped she'd forgiven my comparison, though I'm pretty sure she never did.

Anyway, I looked up into these two big blue eyes and I heard her voice say, "My name is Miss Stephanie. And you are?" as she knelt down to look me in the eye. I was dazzled by how light she seemed, but not as a feather. And she was flexible as a Slim Jim. Even more, she didn't stand up after I told her my name, she *rolled* up, "like a cat after it's been sleeping in the sun," I heard someone say. And no one missed how flat her stomach was. I heard gasps. My next thought was how my mom's stomach had always seemed like a normal grown-up stomach until I saw one as level as the sidewalk. Don't worry, even I knew not to compare my mother's stomach girdled between Vanity Fair underpants and an underwire bra to Miss Stephanie's. No, I made sure stomachs never came up.

"Lucy," I said, thrilled to tell my teacher my name, thrilled to be asked.

"Lucy," she repeated. "Pleased to meet you. Now, go on in to the studio, I'm right behind you."

Flustered and a little afraid, I whispered in a voice that didn't sound like mine, "okay." I saw that Miss Stephanie was a whole new level of something, like looking up at the Bighorn Mountains, bigger than anything else around, but never scary. This thought came to me like a flash of warm light and once it did, I wasn't afraid anymore.

Today, whenever I think about how many people are moving to Yucca Springs who don't bother to see how beautiful our wildflowers are, who call our fields "vacant lots," I like to remember how Miss Stephanie arrived to town to nurture us, not to exploit. I felt that right away. Instead of itching to build a subdivision or drill for gas, she yearned to plant a garden.

And I am one of her many seeds.

The point of everything.

As soon as I stepped up to the barre, Richard, the only boy who danced with us from day one, the only boy at school who didn't say, "I'd *never* take ballet, ballet is for girls," pulled me over to whisper, "You could balance a margarita on her tummy!"

Pretty amazing, I thought, coming from a five year old. I think this was the moment our friendship began, the moment *we* began. By the time class was over, we both seemed to understand that dance would not only become the point of everything in our tiny world, but that it already had.

Before class began, my mother stepped into the doorway to nod goodbye. I looked back at her, but for only a second. But a second, I learned, is long enough to stab the air to pieces. A second is long enough for a daughter to wince, long enough for a mother to feel that wince, and long enough for her to shoot back another nod before sneaking out the door, a nod that I could read like a flashcard. "What? I'm not good enough for you now? Is that it?"

I clearly have never forgotten this exchange. It's as if I need to remember how I winced at my mother's saggy jeans, her scuffed Keds, her stomach sticking out. And whenever I do, I could just die. Richard says I've punished myself long enough, and not to be too hard on myself because I was so young at the time, and I want to believe he is right. But every once in a while, I still think about how I knew from the beginning that Miss Stephanie could show me things my mother never could, and how I just didn't know how to hide my feelings about that. It was like I'd been a flower-beetle living under a Mesquite burl, and then Miss Stephanie came along and dug up the burl, and suddenly there was all this movement and light.

As soon as my mother reached the sidewalk, I caught her studying her reflection in the window glass and I felt like I could bear anything except the way she looked at herself right then, as if she wrestled with every competitive-womanly-demon and, one by one, lost every fight. But as soon as Miss Stephanie clapped her hands twice and told us to make a circle (after one girl pointed at Richard and said, "but he's a *boy!*"), I'm even sorrier to say I forgot all about my mom. And when Miss Stephanie's voice rang out, "Each of you is budding with possibility! You will make magic in this room!" all I could think about was that I hadn't known much magic in a room before. My parents had been fighting since I could remember, and there is not a lot of magic in a house full of fighting. All I could remember about being in a room was sitting on my bed wishing they'd stop yelling at each other, even after my mother said to me, snippily, "like *that* will ever happen," for the hundredth time.

I pointed my toes (we hadn't yet learned to say *tendu*) and I tried hard to feel something as magical as my own *possibility*, and eventually I did feel it, big and bright as a Mariposa Lily. And if I had found the nerve to share what I was feeling with Miss Stephanie, I would have yelled at the top of my lungs, "Yes! There *is* magic! I can feel it!"

I know there are people who'd say it's ridiculous to think we can remember so far back, but I do, I remember everything about my first ballet class. Still, if I had tried to explain all this to my mom back when she was just as sure it would take me half my life to find my "one thing," well, it probably wouldn't have come out all that nicely.

Now, to update how I feel about how hard it can be to *keep* it?

Well, as it turns out, she was right about that all along.

The genie is out of the bottle.

But not everything went smoothly during our first class. Something else happened. A "mishap" is what Miss Stephanie called it, "an unfortunate mishap."

One girl, Lisa (and I'll get back to Lisa), was so upset her body shook and she started to cry. I took a few steps back. I felt like I already knew all I wanted to know about tears. When her mother rushed in to swoop her up, one of her pink slippers nearly fell off, but she kept struggling to keep it on as if, even in her misery, she wanted to keep its possibility from totally slipping away. She clearly *wanted* to stay, but she couldn't find the nerve.

I didn't realize it at the time, but now, when I remember the look in her eyes, it helps me to see how quickly we must make a choice sometimes when our balance starts to slip.

~∘∘∘~

That evening, I twirled around our living room in three folds of scratchy crinoline, too good to be true. When my father came home, he took one look at me, eyed me with a squint, and yelled, "Peggy, that's money we ain't got!"

I froze as if struck by lightning. The air turned bristly as my tutu.

"That's money you haven't spent on beer yet," my mother said, walking into the room so close to where he stood before turning her back to pinch a leaf off one of her aloe plants, as if showing my dad what she'd like to do to his head. Turning to face me, she said coolly, "So compare *him* to Miss Stephanie, why don't you?" before walking back to the kitchen with her hands on her hips. "Now *there's* a culture clash for you."

He shrugged and sat down on the couch. "Yeah, well, culture won't put the goddamn food on the table, will it?"

It was the stupidest thing I'd ever heard anyone say. Mom still made fun of it years later. Somehow I found the nerve to walk right up to him and repeat the words I'd memorized off a poster that hung at the Star Struck over a cardboard box full of left-behind socks, slippers, backpacks, and missing barrettes. "Ask me why I want to dance, and I'll tell you it's like asking me why I want to breathe." I sounded less sure of myself than I'd hoped for, more like Julie Andrews in *Mary Poppins* than in *The Sound of Music,* but I didn't flinch.

Suddenly, he looked over my head and stared into space with that faraway look he got sometimes, and his eyes got big. "What the ...?" he said under his breath, but I could hear him. His mumbles were louder than his talking and swearing put together. It must have seemed like I was bragging about how much better than him I wanted to be.

A picture comes to mind, clear-cut as all the pines they felled to make way for Paradise Acres up Hillcrest Drive. My dad was always saying how the wall around the subdivision was a border between the "rich folk" and the rest of us. "There are two kinds of families around here now," he said between swigs of beer, "the ones who can afford to eat out every night at the Paradise Grill, and those of us who think Del Tacos is a big deal once a month." But I could tell that the border he spoke of had less to do with his lack of money, and more to do with his lack of confidence. And how a father might see his daughter differently once she becomes someone who highlights the disappointment he already feels in himself. To have your child say, "I'm a baller*iiiiiii*na!" well, he must have known I had to look right past him into a place he'd never found, and it made him jealous of me.

Imagine it, a grown man jealous of his own daughter.

What's more, a daughter sees herself differently once she realizes she has the power to make her father's eyes grow so big. And once the genie is out of the bottle, there's no going back. And whenever anything like this happened, when there wasn't much else he could say or do, he stormed out and slammed the door. Mom and me were used to it, the swear words, the jingling keys, the slam, and finally, our shared sigh of relief.

A few years later, when Miss Stephanie said, "Each of us is born with a path inside of us," pointing to her new hand-stenciled sign in big block letters, "the point is to *take* it," it made me think back to the first time I stood up to my dad. I must have longed, even then, to chassé down a path much wider than his.

It wasn't until our second class that Miss Stephanie demonstrated a chassé, raising her arms to frame the right side of her body, arms in fourth-position (though in Pre-ballet we call it "reaching for the stars") and off she flew, convincing us of the magic she'd promised. My mother said she could hear our claps from across the street. "Never forget," Miss Stephanie added in a voice that sounded like she was about to share a secret, "a chassé is like a skip, but it is so much *more*."

I nodded my head, spellbound.

"Breathe in through your nose," she said next, so we all breathed in. "Exhale through your mouth." She went on, "A skip is like a single white Prickly Poppy, while a chassé is a bouquet of poppies gathered in a tall red vase set down in the middle of a posh white tablecloth."

Posh. The sound made me gulp. "And the bouquet works to bring the table together, see," and she flew across the room before coming to a willowy finish, "but it's lovely enough to stand alone."

I bit down on my lower lip. *I can do this,* I thought. *I've done this. I've chasséd.* Hadn't I? Just? Across a warm stretch of soft sand only days ago?

Before everything turned cold again.

Family for a day.

An hour after my dad stormed out the door, he was back again, looking nervous.

"What's this?" my mother said, "Pappy & Harriet's run out of beer?" Mimicking her stance, I stood with my arms crossed high.

He looked straight at me and said, "Your mom ain't never seen the ocean, kid. I think it's time to take a little road trip."

I had no idea where we were headed, but anywhere was good enough for me. We drove west on Interstate 10, no one talking or fighting, and it made me feel hopeful to ride in the back with my parents holding hands upfront.

Mom's face grew eager as we approached the sea, her eyes tearing up at the sparkle, her head shaking back and forth in wonder of such waves. I thought the curved sweep of sand looked as if the ocean had taken a huge bite out of the land, and if we didn't back up quick, the whitecaps would lap up the sides of our truck.

Soon the three of us were standing ankle deep in the waves, happy to be out of the car. Each swell whooshed up with more power than the last, and there were shells everywhere. The only shells I'd ever glimpsed came from snails, and I personally have never cared for snail shells. I picked one up and held on to it.

Tossing back her new Farrah Fawcett haircut, mom ran into the waves and back to safety, and then dad and mom ran in together with all the affection of a happy couple, and when she leaned in to kiss my dad's cheek, my legs went soft with aching for them to always be like this. It was such a strong pang that it made me think everything was going to be okay with the three of us after all. I suddenly felt sick of the desert behind us, tired of the sweltering heat and the fighting, fighting, fighting. Maybe the sea would cool everything down and wash us clean of all that. A début! A new beginning!

That's what I wanted.

And the feeling was so hopeful, I skipped across the sand, I *chasséd*! I think smooching parents can make a child believe most anything.

But as soon as I heard my father yell, I knew he wasn't even close to as loud as he could get, or would, once his temper gathered steam. To myself, I whispered, "big surprise." I dug my toes in deeper and yelled as loud as I could. "Big surprise!"

At once, they turned to look at me as the wind filled my dad's open shirt and blew my mother's skirt against her shins. In a few moments, they turned back to look at each other, and when mom yanked her hand away from his, I knew how hard they'd go at it. My stomach sank knowing how bad the drive home would be. Really bad. I stood looking into the rise and fall of the waves and listened to the surf, trying not to hear or see or feel anything but the melting sand under my feet which I thought, under the circumstances, made perfect sense. I put the shell between my thumb and first finger and cracked it into pieces.

Mom ran back to the car and slammed the door. When I climbed in, she tried to smile at me and pretend nothing was wrong because pretending was what she always did after the worst fights. I knew she was trying to protect me, but I turned that fake smile into anger against her. "So, it's not just Farrah's hair you're copying, that's her smile, too!"

"Not now, Lucy," she said. All the way home, her eyes never met my dad's.

An hour went by like that. I stared out the window.

"Mom?" I said, softly the first time, louder the next because I knew she needed to pee as much as I did and that she couldn't hold it in much longer. No one is *that* good at pretending.

Windmill after windmill went by and I started to make promises to myself, the way you do when something bad is happening and you think you can make a deal with God after paying no real attention to him since the last time you felt utterly hopeless. *Please God! Please God! Please! One more mile and my bladder will burst!*

Finally she yelled, "Goddamnit, Fitzy, pull over!"

Turns out, the best memory I have of that day wasn't of the sea, or the shells, or even of skipping lightheartedly across the sand, but when mom and me bolted from the car and ran into the weeds. When she lifted her skirt and I pulled down my shorts, we squatted shoulder to shoulder and made the loudest splash. "Monsoon!" I cried. We laughed our heads off because it felt so good to be alone again, together, which was always the better way for the two of us.

She was still laughing as we pulled up our underpants, and then, just like that, tears spilled down her cheeks. Her emotions were like that sometimes, it took so little to trigger the opposite. (Like mother like daughter, I think now.) I noticed that her sobbing was different than how she usually cried, and I could tell by watching her face that she was sick of the crying, sick of the fighting, plain old sick of my dad.

As if she knew what I was thinking, we both turned around to look at him still behind the wheel, staring straight ahead. "He'll calm down," she said, burying her nose in my forehead, and I said I'd believe it when I saw it. I was always saying things like this, even though she'd get real quiet after I did. "Would you tell me something, please?" she finally said, so softly it made me swallow hard. "Why on earth should I walk back to that truck?"

"Maybe you shouldn't," I said.

"Maybe I *won't*."

I didn't believe she meant it. I knew she thought she meant it, but I wanted her to prove it to me, prove that she was stronger than him, that her will was stronger than his.

We were lost in our own thoughts for a while. The weeds swayed, the silence lingered.

Dad leaned on the horn.

And when mom started to walk back to the truck, I hated her for it immediately. My look was worse than a wince this time. I yelled, "I'm so embarrassed of you!"

Those were long miles back to the desert.

Who would do such a thing?

But *before* our day at the beach was over (and my parent's marriage was over, no matter who won or lost that fight, it was over), I didn't have to stop and think about how to make my feet step-together-step. Adrenaline pumped through my legs as if I'd been chasséing my whole life.

But that's not exactly how it went in class.

Miss Stephanie called out "next" and fear shivered through me. It felt like the floorboards under my feet shivered, too. I kept moving further and further back in line until there was no one left to sneak behind.

With no more excuses, it was time. Slowly, I slid forward. I felt a lightness come over me. And before I knew what was happening, I chasséd. When I finally came to a stop, I suddenly remembered Lisa's sobs and I think her tears came to me to show how fear has as much to do with pushing us forward as it does with holding us back. And when Miss Stephanie raised her chin higher than usual and cried, "Well done!" I felt as if I could hear the rhythm of my own joy come to life.

On our way home after class, I was so revved up, I held my mom's hand and sort of pulled. I was usually more in a hurry than she was, but that day, even more so. "Ballet has changed my life!" I cried.

She stopped walking, looked down at me and said, "Yeah? Well, it's changed mine, too. My life is significantly better. I now have forty-five minutes to myself once a week."

Never one to mince words about how much she loved time to herself, not to me, not to Miss Stephanie, not to any of the other moms who invited her to sit down in the waiting room, it still stung to hear her say it. Right up through Ballet I and II, when her time alone stretched to an hour twice a week, then to an hour and a half three times a week, she sat across the street on the wooden bench in front of Big Ralph's Star Market, smoking her cigarette and staring up at the wide open sky as if it held all the answers to life here on earth and in heaven.

Oh, that's another thing troubling to a ballerina. She smoked. She smoked all the time. "In my day," she said, "no one held on to a cell phone. Cigarettes were the number one way to feel stylish."

Anyway, other than to bring her cigarette to her lips, she hardly moved an inch until it was time to make her way to the intersection of Twenty-Nine Palms and Cherokee Trails which lead straight to the door of the Star Struck with its huge banner flapping over the sidewalk, a pink blaze of fabric with black and white lettering, just in case anyone drove by without noticing.

I mention the banner because once I hit my teens, Miss Stephanie and I began to disagree about it. "I think it's good to remind people that dancing is a positive escape from the humdrum of everyday life," she said, sort of defending herself as much as the banner.

Applying the confidence I'd been taught, I said, "We don't need to remind them," thinking about the odds of anyone really being affected by a banner. "We need to *show* them."

"Point taken."

Soon after, we added regular in-studio performances to raise funds for our annual stage recital. Sometimes we just need to say certain things to the one person who taught us to say them. I was thrilled when Miss Stephanie started our first informal performance by saying, "I want to thank Lucy for reminding me that no one dances because of a silly banner."

"Which sounds like something she'd say," my mom said, a little jealous again, this time of how Miss Stephanie always seems to say the right thing.

So when someone snatched the banner and its pole as if nipping the head off a dandelion, and then gouged a bigger hole into the wall as if digging for every last root, it turned our studio into a buzz of suspicion for days. "Who?" Miss Stephanie shouted, "would *do* such a thing?"

After a week of outrage, she announced that she would be *damned* (too loudly for one of the more prudish moms who said, "language?") if she would waste one more minute worrying about such a small, petty person.

But anyone could tell she was still fuming inside. She walked back and forth across the studio with both arms crossed under her chest tightly, as if to stop herself from feeling all the anger inside until she could contain it. Finally, she announced, "You know what? I've been dying to update that banner anyway, good riddance."

She never did update it, though. And I knew it continued to bother her deeply that someone would disrespect the Star Struck like that. Eventually she asked one of the dads, likely the one most behind in payment, to spackle over the hole.

This should have been our first sign that something was seriously amiss. In Yucca Springs, people don't just walk by and rip down your business-related resourcefulness, even on Saturday nights after the bars let out. I don't know why no one, not even the officer who came by to "take a look" suspected anything more than a silly prank. Why no one assumed by how deep and jagged the gouge was that the thief was not laughing when he stole the banner, but dead serious, now makes me wonder if we all see only what we can handle and excuse the rest just so we don't have to turn a small but vicious act into something much bigger.

Even today, if I let myself think too hard and long about these questions and then look up, the sky feels less open, less wide, less blue.

And I'm reminded that the way forward is so easy to lose.

It could have been worse.

Did I mention how the other moms would run haphazardly across the middle of the highway to fetch their daughters from class, but my mom never varied her route? She'd stand, check her watch, stub out her cigarette with the tip of her sneaker, maybe bend over to brush a little ash off her toe, boost her handbag to her shoulder and walk to the corner to wait for the light to turn, look both ways, then cross. I remember complaining about how unfriendly she looked when she came through the door. "None of the other moms like you!" I cried.

She wasn't the least put off by my claim. "Now you listen to me. The most important friendship you'll ever make is the one you have with yourself. Anyone else, if they don't break your heart, is a bonus. I don't waste my time looking for friends." By the look in her eyes I knew she was finished talking about it, despite the look in my eyes that said, *but I want you to have friends!* I thought she wanted more friends, she just didn't know how to go about making them, and that other moms didn't talk about having friends because they had friends. I would go so far as to picture them bringing jello molds to our house, handing them over to me on the way through the door before they'd say things to each other like, "now isn't that the truth," or "you know how it is, men, can't live with them, can't live without them," even though we never had a potluck. Not once.

Out of the corner of my eye, I'd watch my mom walk into the studio and barely acknowledge the other moms, take a seat on a folding chair, and pull a magazine from her purse before staring blankly at it in her lap (the same magazine, year after year, the same *People*) until I'd gathered everything into my dance bag and off we'd go.

It could have been worse. She could have been constantly late, rushing into the studio with a made up excuse or apology, neither of which Miss Stephanie ever believed.

Or she could have forgotten to pick me up altogether, forcing Miss Stephanie to delay class until she could track my mother down. She had to do this a lot, remind parents she wasn't running a babysitting service. Once she located Mr. or Mrs. Late-Again on the phone, she'd sound calm, but I could tell she was thinking, *get your butt over here right now!* I loved it because I'd never known anyone able to pull off being two different people at once. I loved it so much that, without thinking yet again, I said to my mother more harshly than I intended, "When *you* don't like someone, you're mean to their face."

"Good for me," she said.

No, the worst thing my mother ever did was fill the waiting room with whiffs of stale smoke. Needless to say, I didn't really have a whole lot to worry about in those days. My parents annoyed me, sure, but I'm beginning to think that annoyance is the bare-minimum expected between parents and kids, so I guess I considered myself lucky.

Hearing myself say this now, all I can think is *luck is luck*.

And it can change in a heartbeat.

Not a local girl.

I was growing more and more fascinated by another facet of Miss Stephanie's personality—how little she seemed to care about what other people thought of her.

People in Yucca Springs gossip. People everywhere gossip. It's the number one form of entertainment for a lot of people, not that they'd ever admit it. Gossip spills out like monsoon clouds raining down. It's always been like this, so I admired Miss Stephanie for not giving in to it, and she even sometimes seemed to enjoy knowing people were talking about her. People were always on the lookout for new tidbits about Miss Stephanie. People *noticed*. If she strode too far—dress too tight, skirt too short—they talked. Worse, she was "different," that is, single, thin, and supporting herself, and she wasn't a local girl. She wasn't born in Yucca Springs, but had come all the way from San Bernardino. People talked a lot about that too, as if they had the right to send her back.

"You could almost get the impression that marriage isn't in the cards for her," I heard the teller say to my mother as she counted out singles, "though she sure *dates* plenty." I was so mad, I had to step away from the counter. What a blabbermouth!

Though, she did have a point.

We could always tell when Miss Stephanie had a date. The moment class was over, she'd shoo us out and tell parents not to worry about paying, which, under normal circumstances, would never happen. Minutes later, a handsome man would appear, unable to budge himself from the doorway while we all looked him up and down. It's not something I remember any of us ever talking about, but if he kept looking at the floor instead of at us, we detected shyness as a good move on his part. When a father or brother or a date is reluctant to stare, a sense of relief is what we feel because we are young girls, nearly naked to the civilian eye. Men don't know where to look. It's awkward for them.

Or, at least, we hope that it is awkward for them.

At first, anyway.

So while it's true that Miss Stephanie never married one of the men who came around, it was this, combined with her penchant for clothing that never hid the fact of her semi-professional training at California State University, that continued to grease the gossip mill. I still think that had people been asked to pay for all the years of entertainment Miss Stephanie provided *outside* of our annual recital, she could have saved enough to buy a big house in the hills off Redondo Drive rather than live in the two-room apartment above the Star Struck, shakily close to the rumbling edge of Route 62.

Even if she did say once in private, when I was sixteen, in the way she does when she's about to say something important—lifting her chin until the tendons come to life under her jaw— "Lucy, I didn't love any of those men."

I stared at her.

"And it doesn't bother me what people say, so don't let it bother *you*."

But deep down I believed, and still do, that Miss Stephanie wasn't completely ignoring the gossip. How could she be? How could anyone?

Like the time (oh, I love this story) she dealt with her least favorite dance mom.

Recital was only minutes behind us when Mrs. Leone, mother of two pre-teen girls (one in Ballet I, one in Ballet II, but only by an inch), said backstage in a voice loud enough for everyone to hear, "So, Steph, mind if I ask you something?"

"Fire away."

"Now that this is over," she said, lifting her arms full of cast-off tutus, "do you plan on getting married?"

Everyone turned to look at Miss Stephanie. "Now why would I want to do *that*?" I heard it the way my mother would hear an actor speak on one of her shows, all ears to hear what the other woman, in an even fancier dress, would say next.

Except Mrs. Leone didn't speak. Her face fell as she wiped the sweat from her brow with her forearm, but she didn't say a word.

A man's voice piped up. "You got that right," he said, in a tone that suggested a private joke between him and the whole idea of marriage. I couldn't see who it was, but "oops" popped out of his mouth next with a quick switch of attitude and you could tell he regretted his joking right away. Once it was clear the voice belonged to Mr. Leone,

Mrs. Leone turned away in a huff, nearly dropping her bundle of tutus as she walked to the end of the stage, a self-conscious drag to her step, as if she were waiting for him to step-up and make Miss Stephanie see everything wrong with what she'd just said, while, in the same breath, realizing he wasn't capable of saying such a thing. Ever.

One tutu fell to the floor. The zipper hit the wood with a crack. "Give me that!" she said, swiping it from the hands of her daughter who'd rushed over to pick it up. "Come on girls, we're going home!"

"I've always believed," Miss Stephanie whispered to my mother, her voice more relaxed, "that backstage is where the real drama is."

Mom and Miss Stephanie had grown to be nearly friends by then, as close to trusting another woman, younger and prettier than herself, as mom ever got.

"I think you're right," my mom whispered back. "I mean, marital drama doesn't do a thing for me. Unless it happens to someone else."

They laughed and laughed and I thought my mother could not have thought of a funnier thing to say if she had copied a real live comedian.

Déjà vu!

Now, should you ever drive through Yucca Springs, you'll see how Richard (who kept right on dancing, even though people's eyes bugged out whenever he insisted on wearing a tutu like the rest of us) likes to prop open our door with a big yellow cement shoe.

I'll get to why the shoe is yellow, bright as the center of daisy, and how, not too long ago, another yellow shoe rushed into our lives like a flame, setting fire to our hopes and dreams.

But for now, I'll just say that Richard found the shoe at the Cactus Nursery, but I'm the one who painted it yellow, and if you crane your neck to the south, you'll see it. You will just have to pass the Calvary Baptist Church, Desert Electric, Desert Prosthetics, Desert Septic Systems, Gonzo Tacos, Papa's Smokehouse, Bear Arms, the Aztec Mobile Home Park, the Apache Mobile Home Park, the Blue Star Mobile Home Park, Blue Star RV, the Feed Barn, AAA Tire & Muffler, Bill's Diesel, Desert Cigarettes *CHEAP*, and the 7-Eleven first.

Wait. Déjà *vu*!

Dad said the same string of names the morning we drove to the coast. The three of us played a game of who-can-name-all-the-business-without-looking, only because he knew he would win. Except we were on our way out of town so he listed all the names in the opposite direction.

"Well, who would know better than a man who's always leaving?" my mother said in a tone that could have taken all the fun out of it, squashing my dad's good mood before we even left town.

But it didn't faze him. I knew he must have worked hard to memorize all those names ahead of time. That's how much he needed to win. "And I win, 'cause that's just the hoop-dee-do out the *left* side of the car," he said.

My mother rolled her eyes, and I remember thinking how on *earth* she could roll her eyes at my dad as much as she did and still stay married to him for as long as she did. But she did, she rolled her eyes at him all the time.

I caught her eye and we smiled, rolling our eyes together this time.

And now that I'm dealing with difficult, unimaginable, unpredictable things all the time, I understand how an eye roll is just what people do sometimes when someone does something annoying, or says something small, but it sheds light all the same.

Such an illumination will roll anyone's eyes.

Two

Twenty years later. How the time flew by.

Dear Lucy,

*I might as well tell you the bad news first, like when
we had no choice but to rehearse your first solo on a
lacquered floor after our roof sprang a leak, and my
first thought was: how will I tell Lucy? I had to turn,
physically turn, your pout toward the door, and off we
marched toward the high school gymnasium.*

*There's just no easy way to say this. I won't be
returning to the Star Struck come September.*

*Now, you might believe that I have grown tired of
the Star Struck. But in that belief, you'd be wrong.
There are many reasons a person decides to move on.*

You know how much I love teaching, it's true.

*What is also true is that time catches up. And lately,
it's as if I can hear my own footsteps resonating behind
me. If I were you, Lucy, I'd find a way to choreograph
this sound to your advantage. Transitions carry a
strong echo.*

I'm about to tell you about a photo my sister snapped of me while I was standing on Mission Beach and I was just about to ask why our mother was in the photo when I realized how crazy that would sound. The image just about blew me over. I was not ready to believe it. I felt my knees buckle. For the rest of the day I couldn't quite regain my footing. No image has ever put me more in touch with the truth.

My work now is to choose a new director. And I choose you.

Yes. You.

The last time I saw my friend who is also a choreographer, she'd been working with a company somewhere in Seattle, I think she said. The look in her eyes was weary. We joked that creating an ensemble piece is like giving birth for other women. If we remembered the agony, we might never go near a studio again. Always more passionate about the process than the performance, we compared recitals to Olympic skiing because we also maneuver through a hundred hurdles to reach the end. I tell you this not to scare you, Lucy, but to prepare you. Because there will come a day during recital season when you imagine yourself packing a bag and fleeing in the middle of the night!

After my friend left for Seattle, I could have called to see how things were going, but it was more fun to hear about it once we were sitting in our favorite café, when everything she said was likely a little more exaggerated than what she'd actually been through, but I think that's the point of Chardonnay.

But only one glass, Lucy, not two, and not as a habit. Promise me!

Drugs and alcohol are the enemy.

And there are other potential enemies to be leery of.

For one, too much internet. This may be the most valuable thing I can tell you. Facebook is nothing like a coffee break. If anything, it is the opposite. You aren't taking a moment of quiet time to let your own creative thoughts trickle in. It does not bring solitude and silence, two key elements for any creative process. It is your job and your responsibility to listen to your own mind.

For another, parents. Not all of them mean you harm, but it only takes one. Bless their hungry little hearts that desire so much. Who think their kids are headed for Broadway, even with two left feet and no sense of timing whatsoever. The internet has fooled everyone into believing accomplishment is a speedy pursuit. Paste a smile on your face whenever a mother says, "my Monique was born to dance!" Don't dare say what you are thinking, "Monique is not so unique, we'll just have to wait and see." Because they are one soul, mother and child, not two. Not in pre-ballet, anyway. The first rhythm we hear is the sound of our mother's beating heart. Can you imagine any duet more in sync? But that doesn't make hiding her chubby little graceless clunk in the back line any easier.

Forgive me for being so direct. But directness is the number one reason we are called directors.

I know, I know, it's silly to sound so serious about a dance recital. But when you are in the thick of it, trying to keep the big picture in focus, you have to make the hard decisions, ones you pay for dearly when you try to sleep at night. You may even find yourself walking around at 3 a.m. noticing every surface that hasn't been dusted in months, the laundry piling up, the dishes stacked in the sink. I barely had time to grocery shop, let alone take in the colors of spring. The white spikes of yucca are a wondrous gift rising from the desert floor. But in all my days in Yucca Springs, did I ever just stare at one for minutes at a time?

No, I did not. There wasn't time. I'd lost myself in the Star Struck.

But I'm convinced we all lose ourselves to something. My sister lost herself in her children, my mother in the church, and so many women lose themselves in their husband's dream of success. But too few of us lose ourselves in our own good work. Losing myself in dance? I never question it for long.

And because you feel the same way, Lucy (I knew this about you from day one), you must also realize how lucky we are to know what we are meant to do from a very young age. So many people search their entire lifetime for work that brings meaning into their lives. I would have held you in my arms right then and told you to trust this feeling always, but, of course, this kind of favoritism is out of the question for a dance teacher.

You were just so intent, though. I had to laugh.

I know there are teachers who continue running a studio into their golden years. I've often wondered if they have more inner acceptance of aging than I do, demonstrating that age is not about how our body looks, but about how it feels.

Or, possibly, what they have is more independent income. I don't know.

It's not that I won't continue to dance. I will, but I want to dance for the pure joy of it, not as a teacher of technique, discipline, and style.

But here's the thing, I love technique, discipline, and style. Together, they are my calling. Otherwise, what? Study essential oils? Strap myself to a Pilates reformer? Become someone who believes garlic and turmeric and coconut water will keep us alive forever?

No, I don't think any of that is for me.

So I've agreed to teach adult ballet right here in San Diego, in a studio just up the street from my sister's home. To be honest, I came to apply for the position, given how hard a time I've been having lately with the thought of living by myself forever.

Remember when your mother tried giving up smoking cold turkey and she nearly went crazy before going back to her cigarettes? She showed me how hard it is to walk away from something you love all at once. I remember her telling me how she'd limit herself to two cigarettes a day. I wish you could have been a fly on the wall. You'd understand then how hard she tried to stop.

I will teach my new students the basics of technique, but I won't get hung up on it. My work now is to teach mature people how to dance from the heart. The heart is the muscle I want to focus on now.

And I know people talk endlessly about whether passion is teachable. But I believe passion is contagious, or else why would any of us teach? If we are not carriers of passion, what good are we, really?

And luckily, no one comes to an adult class with a strong desire to make dance their life, or with parents in tow.

But when you live in a town as small as Yucca Springs (and I know people would rather say it's "peaceful," but you know what I mean), reinventing yourself is not the easiest thing in the world. People think they know who you are and they prefer for you to stay that way. Add this to something I read—that, under a town's watchful eye, a woman is remembered for the worst thing she's ever done; men for the best.

How unfair!

I don't want to be one of those women thought of as eccentric or lonely or "local color". Attention of that kind is worse than ridicule. I suspect that every one of the people who thought of me as an outsider considers themselves to be a good, upright, decent, caring person. But, together, they have looked at me and said things in ways that are cruel in their insensitivity. It's a huge relief to walk around my new city without anyone noticing. I know I acted as if I didn't care about the gossip, but despite myself, I did.

Oh, Lucy, this letter has turned out to be much longer than I meant it to be.

It's just that what I want to say can take a while. It's like when I build a dance. At first, I put it all out there. Then, as it begins to take shape, everything becomes less, and my only choice is to scale back to the first thing about the music that moved me.

Oh, that's it! That's what I've been trying to say all along. It is all about choice.

Remember when I moved you into Ballet II, even though your mom thought the added expense was too much, seeing as how it was my decision and not hers. I told her we didn't have a choice. Our only choice was excelling right in front of us. And she was you, Lucy. Y O U! Embracing your talent was the only choice we had. It startles me that I found the nerve to sit your mom down and say what I did, but neither of us could limit you, Lucy. Holding you back wasn't our mistake to make.

And as much as I like to think our dear Richard is capable of running things, between you and me, he isn't. You are better organized, generally. And without A-1 organization, no matter how solid the choreography or well-intentioned the director is, the whole year will be nothing but chaos.

Richard has an amazing eye and sharp sensitivities, which makes him a good teacher, choreographer, photographer, and faithful friend, but how many times have we told him to put the seat down after he uses the toilet? And he still leaves it up. Every. Single. Time. And, see, it's not so much that he fails to put the seat down. It's that he doesn't remember he put it up in the first place, and this is not the kind of detail-oriented direction a studio needs.

One more thing.

No, two.

You will have to remind yourself OFTEN that dance has always been more about a way to live than a way to make a living. Also, remember that choreography is a lot like life. If you shift one thing, everything else shifts, too.

In the meantime, make sure the mirrors are Windexed and the floor is wet-mopped and that no one wears street-shoes into the studio. You know how Mrs. Powers likes to think of herself as THE fashionista of Yucca Springs, showing off her new Payless heels by strutting in without removing them. Watch her like a hawk. Nothing is worse for pirouettes than those tiny ruts she leaves behind that I've had to sand off one too many times, thank you very much.

Now, Miss Lucy, it is time for you to take the leap! It is in the leap that our highest possibility unfolds.

With all my love,

Stephanie

Nothing changes, if nothing changes. It's true.

The late-afternoon sun played across the words of Miss Stephanie's letter, more confiding than how she talked to me in person, which, of course, I loved. But to hear myself referred to as *Miss* Lucy? I wasn't at all sure I was ready to sound so adult. I sat down on the floor. I felt off-kilter.

And for the next few days, I didn't quite recognize my life, or Miss Stephanie's expectations for it. And my nights felt like a dream, as if what was being asked of me, *handed* to me, would disappear as soon as I swung my legs over the side of the bed.

But soon enough I began to see Miss Stephanie's letter as just another one of her nudges to the small of my back. My first solo, she literally had to shove me onto stage. I froze in the wings. I couldn't go on. Except she knew that I could, and she made sure that I *did*.

"I don't want to drop the 'miss' from your name, though," I told her. "Or add it to mine."

"These are your choices now," she said.

It took about a month to make the full transition from student to teacher, but once I did, I made a call to Eileen the real-estate agent and my mother's first real friend in Yucca Springs. No one was more taken aback by this friendship than my mother. There's nothing wrong with being alone most of the time, but to be with someone her own age once in a while made my mom happier, anyone could see it. They paid special attention to each other. It was Eileen who helped my mom open her heart up to Miss Stephanie. It was Eileen who sat with her near the end with all the patience in the world.

So, naturally, I thought of her when it was time to sell the house, the house my mother had rented on Sage Avenue until I was nearly fifteen, until the landlord offered it to her "dirt cheap" rather than updating the plumbing, the electricity, or re-shingling the roof. "Well, why not?" she said. Then she took me by the hand, walked me outside and pointed at the "DEAD END/NO OUTLET" sign at the start of our cul-de-sac. "If I buy this house, Lucy, I want you to remember one thing. Those words were never meant for you."

My mother was the only single woman who owned a house on our street. And I suspect she always knew that I would leave it behind to move into the apartment over the Star Struck because Eileen's rubber gold-embossed card was the only refrigerator magnet she ever saved, "Yucca Paradise Properties: *Nothing changes, if nothing changes.*"

Refrigerator magnets have special meaning for me now.

Preparation.

"I love that Miss Stephanie took the time to write a real letter," I said to Richard while tidying up the studio.

Miss Stephanie was always reminding us what is appropriate for digital communication and what is not, which didn't have a lot to do with dance, but she must have felt it was important to remind us anyway. DARE TO BE YOURSELF! is the first pre-made sign board she hung, to which our reaction was, *huh*? For days, I scratched my head over those words. But once I figured out what they meant, it made me feel better about the fact that I wasn't obsessed with social media like everyone else.

"I'd rather talk to people," I confided to Richard. "And all the bragging bores me to pieces." Still, Facebook was not something I wanted to criticize too strongly around Richard, devotee of the digital world. But I couldn't stop myself. "As *if* everyone smiles all the time. Who do you know who smiles all the time? Keeping up with everyone everyday takes too much time and who has the time?" I shook my head. I knew he didn't agree with me, but it was the kind of outburst I liked to share with him just for the satisfaction of hearing his side of things. When he didn't say anything, I said, "Not that watching YouTube isn't inspiring, but it can leave me feeling..."

"Inadequate?"

I stared at him. I knew he was only joking, but now that the studio's success or failure was up to me, I felt vulnerable—about everything. If the whole world was a portal, how could I compete? Or keep up?

It seems funny to me now, but that was my greatest concern at the time.

Easing along the mirror with my squeegee, I remembered our last recital. Richard had a new phone and was obsessed with taking pictures of me pulling up my tights and obsessively reapplying lipstick, things I do backstage when I'm packing a hundred extra pounds of pressure. *Click. Click. Click. Click. Click.*

You have to make the hard decisions. Miss Stephanie's warning echoed in my ears. "Stop it!" I yelled, and grabbed his phone away. "Even Mikhail Baryshnikov didn't have so many pictures taken of him! If there is òne thing I learned after losing my mom, it's that the moment is all we have. And you are not in the moment, you are too busy recording it. And for who? Who will care later as much as we do now?"

But he wouldn't listen. No one would listen. My students kept snapping pictures like addicts hooked on their own faces. "You *could* just look in the mirror all day," I said, trying to sound clever, but I ached for them. Instead of buoying each other up, they were all, "Let me see that. Oh, no, I look awful! Take another!" Like a dam breaking, one of Miss Stephanie's expectations for me sprang into action. I yelled, louder this time, "Chuck the phones. I mean it!"

Seconds later, no one seemed to care so much what they looked like—they were having too much fun stretching, laughing, marking through the combinations, no one posing or pretending.

The sheer repetition of reading Miss Stephanie's sign board every day must have fixed a lot of truth in my mind about who I was willing to be to fit in.

And who I was not.

I think she had begun preparing me even then.

Three

*"Dance is the only way to run away without
leaving home."*
~Twyla Tharp

A good story, after the fact.

IN THE ABSENCE OF HIGH SCHOOL, ANY POSSIBILITY
of college—since neither of us bothered to apply—or
marriage, Richard and I kept right on dancing into
adulthood. We thought it would secure us to a more
creative and trouble-free life.

That was our hope.

It still is. Though our troubles got bad for a while—
really bad.

"Well," my mother said once, "trouble makes for a good
story, after the fact." And when I didn't answer, she said,
"No, really, there's a lot to learn from trouble, you'll see." I
felt that I didn't yet know enough about trouble to object,
but there was something so definite about her tone that I
feared one day soon I would.

What makes me want to kick myself now is not only did
Richard and I not realize what real trouble was before it
fell on us like a ton of bricks—so crushing we hardly knew
what hit us—we had a trouble-free life, and we took it for
granted. I've never seen something so tender and innocent
as an early photo of Richard and me holding hands in the

wings. We thought life would stay like that. We believed it would. I dare say we even believed all of our hard work entitled us to it.

But neither of us carried on any sort of family mantle by choosing to dance. In my family, dancing is what made me *different*. The same could be said of Richard, tenfold. We both grew up listening to people nit-pick anyone "different" apart.

"He's a sissy, that boy is," my father said when I was about ten, his latest crack about Richard. The blood rushed to my cheeks. He never seemed to understand that people could live in a world so unlike his.

"Richard is my best friend!" I screamed. He opened his mouth to answer, then smacked it shut again. My mother had warned him about making fun of Richard, that was a rule. I pulled my backpack up close to my chest and turned my face toward the window.

"Now that teacher of yours," he said, whistling through his teeth. "There's a sight for sore eyes. Where'd you say she's from again?"

"I didn't!" As soon as we slowed down enough for me to jump out, I hurried out of the truck.

"What happened?" my mother said, as soon as I was inside.

"I would have walked home if I knew you were sending him!" I cried. I slammed my bedroom door, locked it, and tried to hum over the rise of her voice. "Lucy! Open the door. We're trying to make things *work*."

I knew what that word meant. My dad had found steady work again and steady work meant that she'd make it *her* work to try to get along with him. And when I wasn't mad at him or embarrassed by him, I was tempted to try myself, until he'd make fun of Richard again, sometimes to his face. Richard would clench his hands and plaster a frozen smile on his face, but he never stuck up for himself. He said that some grown-ups just aren't worth it. I blinked at him for a few seconds because that is not an easy thing to swallow about your own flesh and blood.

I knew something was going on as soon as a new photo went up on the fridge—my dad standing at the base of a windmill, staring up, his head sheltered by a hardhat, open-mouthed as if he was about to yell at someone out of view—but it wasn't the towering steel that made him look so small, or me so uncomfortable, it was that I could tell by his expression that he'd never find his place in the world anywhere near those swirling white blades.

I had also noticed a new return address on my dad's paycheck, American Recovery and Reinvestment Act, and saw how eagerly mom waited by the mailbox for it every other Friday, ready to launch into a yelling match with the mailman if he didn't deliver it.

By now, there were thousands of turbines spreading over the San Gorgonio Pass turning one of the windiest places on earth into a giant wind funnel, gathering the cool coastal air into the heart of the Sonoran Desert, like a mountain lion gathering her cubs. "I could maybe give it a go," my father said half-heartedly to my mother who wouldn't take no for an answer when the call finally came from the Wind Turbine Company.

Only years later did she admit to me that her boss at work was the brother of one of the higher-ups of the WTC, and that she'd asked "as a special favor" if he'd put in a good word for my dad. "People in high places are necessary sometimes, Lucy. We had a hundred bucks left to our name." But she said it in a way that seemed to suck all of the air out of the kitchen, and I sensed something she'd done was way worse than having no money.

A few weeks later, I heard her say to someone on the other end of the line "Fitzy?" in that way you ask a question when you aren't really asking one. "Are you kidding? He's lost out there as a mule deer wandering into town." What I heard between the lines was that my dad wouldn't be working on the windmills much longer—like the wind rushing through those broad steel blades, he'd be on his way out of town again soon. *Whoooooosh.*

In secret, I knew part of the reason my dad was lost was his fear of heights. He wouldn't even change a light bulb. Instead, he'd stand at the bottom of the ladder and make me climb up. But the larger part of the secret that doomed him to failure was that he couldn't read. No one ever talked about it, but I knew. Kid sense, I guess. My mother filled out his application and, other than the traffic signs and business names he'd memorized, he got by without reading. He tried to keep it a secret, but the jig was up.

"I really should teach him," mom said.

"I think we both know how that will go," I said, and the switch from her wanting to help, to agreeing with my opinion, took all of about two seconds.

Today, it scares me just to look at that stretch of Route 62 where the Coachella Valley windmills keep right on multiplying. Some people call it a burial ground, on account of the birds. But I think of it as the place that scared my dad in a way he had not known he could be scared. "Bye bye," I always say to myself, once those whirling blades are in our rearview mirror.

Thinking back on all this while finishing our weekly tidying up, I asked Richard, "Have you ever noticed that no matter how often those companies call it clean energy, they always make such a big awful mess?"

Richard stopped sweeping and leaned his broom against the wall with a w*hack.* I was surprised it didn't splinter. He walked over and grabbed my cheeks between his hands and brought his nose close to mine until I went a little crossed-eyed for a second. "Hmm. I wonder just what mess we are referring to?" He was just being Richard, always a little malicious whenever I insist he help clean. But the smile that crossed over his lips told me something he'd never had the nerve to bring up before, and instead of just saying what he wanted to, he mocked me, and it stung a little to be made fun of like that.

We scoffed whenever the mayor talked about "environmentally friendly" development because no one had made more of an environmental mess or more rivals around town than the natural gas people. "Fracking fuckers," my dad called them, "taking advantage of people who can't afford to put water tables before putting food *on* the table." It was the one time I remember looking at him attentively after he spoke, instead of away.

But—and this is the point Richard was trying to make—no one had made more of a mess of my personal life, either. I think he was afraid I might go down that road again, or he would, because the truth is, engineers, natural gas or windmill, are the only new blood in town. And they are generally handsome, arriving with payoffs that dazzle people who are just trying to get by.

And I'm no exception.

Mr. Methane, Richard's name for him, waltzed into town to convince all the good people of Yucca Springs that fracking doesn't affect our drinking water. "Like hell, it don't," people said, but they took the money anyway. He was one of those men who demanded attention because of the way he looked, and I suppose the reason he was hired was because it had become routine for him to get what he wanted just by lifting his chin and flashing his teeth. And it's one thing to be blinded by a man's smile, but quite another when he wears clean Carhartt work jeans and a pressed white shirt. Oh, the shiver I felt the first time I set eyes on him, like touching an electric fence.

But that was only part of it. I'd graduated high school nearly three years back and was still a virgin, if you don't count Jason Lombardo's index finger, and I don't—despite the fact that I had a dream that night that my whole body was weightless, released into a soft white cloud. I never talked about it, but I was starting to worry that my inexperience showed somehow—that's how obsessed I became with it—and that kind of exposure felt like too much pressure on top of everything else. So I formed a plan. The next man I found handsome enough to have sex with I would just get it over with.

This plan was a little too extreme for most to consider. Even I, who thought of myself as modernized, was a little shocked at my behavior. And if the affair had ended after only one night, he would have been easier to forget, but it didn't end after only one night. He was staying at the Hat Rack motel on Twentynine Palms, but no way would I go back there again. So several times more, six, to be exact, I let him in the back door of the Star Struck.

I'd lead him up the narrow stairs to my apartment that I still thought of as Miss Stephanie's apartment, which made me feel a little sleazier than I wanted to because I could hear her voice in my head, telling me the man was no good, and why I should ask him to leave. But, like many warnings people share, I didn't listen straightaway. I knew Richard disapproved of him too, and truthfully I didn't much like him myself. For one thing, if I tried talking first, he'd put his hand over my mouth and say, "shhh, don't talk." I've never liked being shushed, but I let it go because we both wanted the same thing, this was clear from the beginning. For another, his kisses were not how I'd imagined they would be. They weren't soft. They weren't sweet. They were rough and scratchy and they left a sensitive red ring around my mouth, like an allergic reaction. And his hands smelled of rotten eggs. But once my panties were off, none of that seemed to matter.

And then without asking why, Richard subbed all of my classes the day I found out my "plan" had left town without so much as a goodbye. I couldn't face the mirror. I couldn't face myself. "I don't know what on earth I was thinking," I moaned to Richard.

"Well that's not exactly true, is it?" he said.

My father's side of the mantle.

After dad left the windmills, he found work on an oil rig and shortly after, a woman in Texas to move in with. It was around this time that I was also trying to accept the fact that, before he drove off, he seemed prouder of his new radial tires than he was of me. Climbing into his truck where three 16-ounce beer cans sprawled across the passenger seat, he said, "Now aren't they just about the sweetest damn things you ever seen?"

The next day in class, Miss Stephanie took me aside to say something I'll never forget, as if she'd already heard about my dad's leaving—I'm sure she had. On my behalf, she had subjected herself to his wandering-eye more than once in order to praise my abilities, going out of her way to brag about my technique, as though complimenting me was the most basic thing in the world and that he should do more of it himself.

He'd never do more of it himself, but I loved her for trying anyway.

"Remember," she said, taking both my hands in hers, "we can't expect support for reaching for our dreams from people who have never reached for their own."

Again, some people might have taken offense to a comment like that made about a family member, but Miss Stephanie isn't someone who pretends to care about men like my father. She cares about the kids they are supposed to stick by and support, but don't.

So, I formed another plan. The one time he did come back home to get the rest of his tools, "before your mom sells them on eBay," my goal was to shame him. I ran out to greet him with my recital program in hand. When he tried to hide the fact he couldn't read it, I said, "read it."

Mad at him, I'd learned to tell people that he'd left town for better money. Everyone seemed to approve of better money and, if you were a man, wherever you needed to go to get it. I was vague about the rest because I still thought I could keep people from believing the worst about my dad, even though I believed it myself—he'd left us for good this time.

All I ever wanted was for him to be proud of me and say so, but if I was expecting a dad who hugged me and said

I was the best little dancer he'd ever seen—and of course, that *is* what I wanted—I was sadly mistaken.

So I decided to pick on his sorest weakness.

He grinned without opening his mouth, stared at the front of the program, then at the back, running his fingertips over the text as if reading dots of Braille. I knew he was bluffing when he said, "Yep, that's my dancin' girl."

That's it. That's all he said.

Half an hour later, he climbed back in his truck, waved blindly, and stepped on the gas, leaving me alone with what practically felt like a genuine compliment.

Later that night I couldn't sleep, I kept thinking about how on earth could I be his dancing girl? Only once did I ever see him dance and my memories of that day are not good ones. I was maybe ten at the time. We'd been invited to a neighbor's barbecue because my dad was home for once, and also because "no one invites a single mother to a barbecue," as my mom said.

"But aren't *we* a family?" I said, meaning just the two of us.

"Well, you'd think so, wouldn't you?"

When he didn't want to go, my mother's voice was final as a whistle, "Get your lazy butt off that couch and get dressed!"—so loud that the wrens at the backyard feeder flew off. I walked outside and sat on the back step. The wrens were circling the top of the feeder but they didn't land, as if they were waiting to see which way the fight would go, same as me.

"And you better not drink too much!"

"Since when do I drink too much?"

My mother's eyebrows pulled clear up to her forehead.

She bought him a new shirt to wear to the barbecue, blue with silver snaps. Unbuttoned at the neck, his curly chest hair shot out of the V. I'd rarely seen him in anything but a faded T-shirt. I liked the change and told him so. "Your old man cleans up good," he said, obviously pleased with himself. But when I started to tell him why I liked it, he made that face, the one that gives off a kind of disinterest in what you think or might say next. It hurt, him snatching back a rare good moment between us so fast it hadn't even had time to land on me yet.

No sooner were we at the barbecue and his empty Budweiser cans started to line up—three drained before the hot dogs were even hot. Someone turned up John Denver's "Thank God I'm A Country Boy," and he shot up. He could easily have fallen over and brought the whole table down with him, but something made him stay upright. Grit, I bet. He started dancing, such pitiful movement, the worst dancer you'd ever want to feel sorry for. Everyone could see his cheeks getting red as clay, and my cheeks were getting red, too. I could feel how hot they were. A few people laughed. "Please," I whispered, "please *stop*."

I kept waiting for my mother to stand up and drag him off, but I don't remember her looking half as embarrassed as I felt. It took me a long time to figure out why this was—even longer to forgive her for it—but now I see that she was probably just happy to see him doing something other than flirting, freeing her up to enjoy herself.

Why I didn't turn away and run home, why I stood there tormenting myself, I don't know. It's been years, but the memory of that day has yet to die down. People still bring it up, "remember the time your dad was dancin' his fool-head off?"

As if I could forget.

My mother's side of the mantel.

On my way upstairs from the studio one night after a long stretch of teaching—taking the stairs two at a time after turning off the lights—it occurred to me that maybe the real reason my mother let me take ballet had nothing to do with time *to* herself, but with lost hopes *for* herself. The thought made me stop running. I stood in the darkness and started to see my mother in a whole new light. Maybe I hadn't strayed nearly as far from my mother's side of the family after all.

The longer she is gone, the more supportive some of the not-so-supportive things I thought she said feel to me now. So much about her got by me then.

Like, there was a time when she said we couldn't have two dancers in the family when I told her how some of the other moms took tap once a week. "Oh, well," she replied. "I'm a single mother and the assistant manager of the Dollar Tree, but if you don't think that's enough learning curve for me, maybe I should quit all that to take a tap class, what do you say?" It took me awhile, but after a few years it occurred to me that we couldn't *afford* to have two dancers in the family and this was just an excellent way to deal with a selfish child when a perfectly good explanation fails.

I have another clear memory of something she said. When I objected to her working late—you know, how kids will spread the guilt around to get something they want—she said, "Lucy, I'm the breadwinner now, and that's something I never thought I'd be able to hear myself say, so quit your grumbling." She was especially proud of the fact that she was left in charge whenever her boss had the urge to drive off to Vegas. "I've been entrusted to make daily deposits in the bank," she said. "Now, promise me you won't tell anyone." She put her hand on my shoulder and repeated, "Promise?"

"Okay," I said, a little frightened by the image of a bad person conspiring to steal her money or harm either one of us in any way.

"You just never know what crazy person is out there looking for trouble."

All I thought at the time is that I'd finally learned why her shoulder-bag needed to be so big. A lot of other moms carried clutches, so this felt like something important to understand. But whenever her warning comes back to me now, my heart leaps into my throat.

We'd lost track of my dad by then, until an envelope arrived from someone we could only guess was his new girlfriend. There was no letter, only a torn out page of newspaper with a Post-it stuck to it that said, "Thought you should know."

Underneath the Post-it was of a huge plume of smoke burning on an oil rig off the coast of Galveston and a headline that read "5 Killed in Gas Rig Explosion." "Was dad one of them?" I asked. She gave no answer in a way that confirmed he was. I stared at the smoke until all the anger I had at him sort of melted away in the flames.

But in no time it came back.

I guess any thread between us was too weak to hold onto—that's how it felt, like my dad and I hadn't practiced loving each other, so I had no muscle memory of how to miss him. When I told my mom this, she hushed me softly as I cried, and I hushed her softly as she cried, and we wept until we were spent.

Finally, I stood, took the newsprint from her hand, walked over to the trash can like I'd thrown away the same page a hundred times, squashing it under the coffee grounds and eggshells. I sat back down on the step and we both stared up at the stars so far off until I had to lay my head in her lap, I was so tired. It felt like everything about our family had led up to that fire, and led away again, like a cloud creeping across the sky.

"You've always been a lot better at being sensible about him, but life is hard when you don't have a man close by to lean on," she said with a sigh so heavy, I sat back up to hug her.

"Mom," I said, pointing at the sky, "those stars are closer than he ever was."

She made a *shh* sound again and looked away. She rocked back and forth, buried her head in both her hands. I peeled one of them off her cheek and held it tight. After a while she said, "It's not that simple."

I sat there, but I didn't say another word. It wasn't the time to bring her back down to reality. I decided that whatever make-believe she was building up in her mind about my dad right then, I would pretend to agree with, if that's what she needed. I'd learned this. But no way would I let go of her hand.

Later, we heard from the oil company that there was some kind of check coming, one to my mom and one to me.

"To me?" I said, shocked.

"That's right. And I don't want you to spend it all at the Star Struck once I'm gone."

The thought of that check cleared the air somehow. Even if I didn't understand why.

Even if my mother said it was too little too late.

Even if all I can remember in the weeks after he died is how many hours in the studio I put in trying to dance away my sadness and confusion. Until it finally came to me and my heart began to pound.

I was drawn to the Star Struck because we all need a safe place to shine when we are young—if not in our father's eyes, at least in our own.

From both sides of the mantel.

I think it's safe to say that from both sides of the mantel I did inherit a healthy distrust of city officials.

An officer showed up at the studio one evening just as we were making headway with our pivot turns. Miss Stephanie stopped the music, told us to take five—I remember thinking *five of what?*—and her eyebrows squinted together like two little wings in the air. She raised her water bottle to her mouth, set it back on the top of the speaker with a bang and said, without so much as lowering her chin or her voice, "I'm sorry officer, but if you are here to tell me to turn down the music again, remember this is a dance studio and you are going to have to tell whoever is complaining, and I suspect I know who is, that we hold classes in the evening when he should be home with his wife and children," emphasizing the word "he" in a way that made us all look down. Even the officer stood there looking trapped and a little afraid, squeezing his hands together and releasing them over and over.

Everyone in town knew Mr. Lawson—whose law office was next door to the studio—was carrying on with the new librarian at the Desert Hot Springs Library. There are no such secrets in Yucca Springs. "This was true long before the internet," my mom said once. "Things haven't changed all that much. A big man in a small town can still get away with just about anything."

The good part about Mr. Lawson's two-timing, to me anyway, was that it reduced the gossip about my dad's cheating to the bottom rung. The bad part was that Mr. Lawson was otherwise engaged during daylight hours, so he worked in the evening when our jazz class was in full swing, likely to the sound of Lesley Gore's "It's My Party," a timeworn favorite of Miss Stephanie's and perfect for both beginning and intermediate-level pivot turns.

"I could maybe talk to him," the officer said, but you could tell how nervous he was because he was new in town, meaning his grandparents weren't born in Yucca Springs. Mr. Lawson, on the other hand, was a local man, meaning if he went to the high school football game, he'd be yucking it up with all the other old-timers about what went on under the bleachers in their day.

The air seemed to hiss between the officer and Miss Stephanie. I closed my eyes.

"Well," Miss Stephanie said, "you wouldn't want to *maybe* talk to him, would you? Because then you'd actually have to involve yourself and no one wants *that*." And without so much as another word, she began to count to eight again, but only after staring the officer down until he tipped his hat and backed out of the doorway.

In my ear Richard whispered, "She's like Ginger Rogers meets Andy Sipowicz."

I thought it thrilling to see Miss Stephanie play chicken with her eyes like that, like a Saguaro flower—soft to look at, tough as nails. I wondered how it was even possible to have such nerve. Was she ever afraid? Whenever she held her ground like that, I felt I had the same distrust of authority down deep.

But what did this mean exactly?

I loved it in my teacher, but inside, I wasn't sure I could be as brave, or that I even wanted to be. I was so young. I still wanted everyone to like me. I felt torn.

"Now, class, observe. A floor roll," Miss Stephanie's voice rang out as she dropped down to the floor in one seemingly-effortless transfer of weight, turning our attention away from the officer, "is like learning to handle the ups and downs of life, up one moment, and down the next." Even the way she lifted herself was reminiscent of a bird in flight. "Then right back up," she said. "It's all a matter of breath, balance, and a few flops. And the rare times we get it just right."

I put my hand on the floor and lifted myself up on one arm. Miss Stephanie touched the small of my back. Her fingers were trembling. So she *was* afraid? A little at least.

Later, when I asked Richard how we can ever be sure of anything, he said that even when we are, it doesn't mean much because we will still have to start from scratch when a new challenge comes up. "Just be yourself," he said.

When I told him my biggest bewilderment was who "myself" *was*, he said, "Then just be one self until it's time to be the next."

Hardly a day goes by when I don't remember him saying that.

Negative example.

My mother eventually surrendered to her own smoke-plume, Emphysema.

When I think back to when she told me she was sick, and how my first thought was, "does this mean you won't live long enough to see the first recital I direct?" I could just kick myself. When I told this later to Miss Stephanie, she laughed and said if she thought about it, she could probably recall a dozen reactions of her own that were just as obsessed.

The strongest images I have of the last year of my mother's life are not ones I'd choose to remember if I had any say. It took me years not to see her struggling to speak more than a few hoarse words, before it sounded like she'd cough herself to death.

But before all that, she was always there for me. I see that now. I'm finally able to appreciate how difficult it must have been for a free-spirited woman to play her part around town, as if her character had been cast for her in grade school. I'm sure it drove her crazy—as crazy as it did my dad—but I'm proud of her for sucking it up.

And my dad? He's more of a stretch for me. But Richard said that a negative example is better than no example at all.

"You think so?" I said.

"Not really," he said.

~⚬⚬⚬~

As for where my grandparents fit into all this, well, I never knew them, but they didn't dance, even for fun. This is clear to me not from their bodies, soft as jello in every picture I have of them—big people can be excellent dancers, I've seen it a hundred times—but from the fact that there is no joy in their eyes, none whatsoever. And not because no one smiled in photos back then, it goes deeper than that.

My mother said life was a lot harder back then, so it wasn't their fault they had so little to smile about. What I think is that if you've found something you love to do, and you find a way to do it, there is light in your heart that shows in your eyes, regardless of whether the rest of your life is dreadful or not. But nothing in my grandparent's eyes even comes close to lightheartedness, not even in the Christmas Polaroids.

And I am all too aware of the disappointment and judgment that took its place, reminding me of the kind of person I don't want to be.

Cheese!

"A small town thrives on its recitals!" Miss Stephanie announced in rehearsal once. "Oh, sure, the coaches like to think the spotlight belongs only to the football team, but people will talk about a brilliant recital for years to come."

"You remember when we danced to 'I Want to Dance With Somebody'?" I said to Richard, just the other day, in fact.

He flinched, clearly still troubled by what happened to Whitney in the end. *Feel,* I thought, *feel with every bone in your body, Richard, it's what makes your dancing so alive!*

Richard's dancing *is* alive.

"You're amazing!" I yelled on one occasion over the roar of the audience. I was in the wings, trying not to bump into him as he came flying off stage. He was on fire that night.

"I *know*!" he shouted back before running out to take another bow. How can I relate the effect Richard has over an audience? Imagine a dancer having so much quality that, for three whole minutes—or the recital will go on too long even for the most supportive parents—he totally grabs you.

And the golden rule of performance is that it has to grab you.

Even more, he knows how much he needs to respect his audience, no matter who they are or what they believe, before he can receive respect—even if there is one person, and there's always one, who simply refuses to watch Richard, who won't allow himself to treasure a man, any man, like Richard.

But Richard isn't thrown. He's too busy letting everyone think there is no limit to his flap-heel combination, and then skillfully showing there *is*. "The energy in that boy could replace oil, gas, and windmills put together!" Miss Stephanie cried.

Still, come May, we are already competing with prom and the Healthy Hearts 5K Run, so when Richard sticks out his chin and yells "cheese," we smile.

Even if we are already at the breaking point, we smile.

Even if we feel like the pressure is crumbling our confidence, we smile.

Because a smile, we know, is not a magic pill, but a hedge against losing our balance.

And we need our balance. Here on earth and on stage.

Four

"Show me a person who found love in his life and did
not celebrate it with a dance."
~Shah Asad Rizvi

Just about enough.

No one was ever able to pin down who stole the Star
Struck banner, but in the days after, I often wondered if it
was someone we hadn't thought of yet. "Someone with a
bone to pick with Miss Stephanie," I said to Richard who,
ever since reading that Hitler had applied to art school in
Vienna where a Jewish professor rejected his application,
has no trouble imagining everyone as a ticking time-bomb
about something. He grew quiet for a moment. "Joey," he
said finally, letting the name hang in the air.

The memory flooded in. Richard catching the roll of
paper towels I flung over the top of the stall, trying to
wash off what Joey had drawn on the back of the door
before Miss Stephanie caught sight of it. Richard's eyes
getting wider when Miss Stephanie, narrowing hers, asked,
"Richard? What are you doing?" as soon as she saw the roll
of towels in his hand—Richard never cleaned voluntarily.

"Nothing," he said, trying to sound normal as I
gathered up the towels off the floor.

Miss Stephanie swung open the door hard on its hinges
and stared with her hand over her mouth before whirling

around to fetch a spray bottle from under the sink. "That boy!" she cried. The tone of her anger scared me. The idea that she could be putting any one of us in danger by bringing us together under one roof was something she hadn't realized until then, I think.

And from the moment Joey drew the penis—did I mention that it was a penis he drew on the door? And not just any penis, either—the Star Struck was no longer the uncomplicated place I could count on. Fear had made its way in. I wanted to cry out, "No!" because I already spent too much of my time trying not to feel afraid of what people would say and do to one another. If a fight broke out between my parents, I'd run outside. If a fight broke out at school, I didn't stop to watch. I ran as far away as I could.

For weeks, everyone went out of their way to avoid that stall. And eventually we stopped talking about Joey's disgusting drawing, in the same way that we eventually stopped talking about the missing banner—out of relief. But we'd all been affected by the incidents, much more than we wanted to believe. Every once in a while, Miss Stephanie would wonder aloud again about who stole the banner, though I could tell she regretted it as soon as the words slipped out. Then one day she said, quietly, as if to herself but loud enough for Richard to hear, "I think Benjamin's father was involved."

Like Joey, Benjamin was a new student, a senior, who'd signed up for Tap I. Smallish, calm, and polite, he wore tinted contacts that made his eyes shine blue as sapphires, something a lot of us hadn't seen before. I liked the way his eyes flashed like jewels when Richard explained the difference between a stamp and a stomp. His family moved to Yucca Springs from Cathedral City (Cat City to the locals), but he never said why. Even Miss Stephanie couldn't get the reason out of him, though she made it her business to size-up every new potential student—her eyes probing, her wheels turning.

But after Richard met Benjamin's father, he said it was an easy guess as to why the man packed up his family to move thirty-five miles north. "Cat City is the back porch of Palm Springs where the first African-American and openly gay mayor was elected. That's too much broadening for a mind as narrow as his," he said.

"I see your point," Miss Stephanie said.

I saw it, too. My own dad didn't like to go anywhere near Palm Springs—not to be confused with Palm *Desert*, golf cart capital of the universe, no, this is not a mistake you want to make. If for some reason he had to drive through it, his face would scrunch up and he'd say something mean to make it sound like Palm Springs was weird and dark, and the road out was like heading his pickup toward the light. Richard said my dad sat on his opinions the same way he sat on the couch, on the far right side.

At twelve, Richard was already assistant tap teacher, since he was about the only boy in town who'd openly admit, no matter what company he found himself in, how much he loved to dance—if you don't count square dancing. As he got older, young men would drift in and out of his class, but most of them didn't stick around once Richard let it be known that he was all about teaching and nothing else. Benjamin, he said, would have stayed with it if his father hadn't yanked him out of class by the collar, another horror that left us shaken for weeks.

"The humiliation in that poor boy's eyes!" Miss Stephanie cried. She'd yelled at Benjamin's father, trying to stop him, "Now you wait just a minute, who do you think you ..." but before she even got to "are doing?" the man threw up the back of his hand, causing Miss Stephanie to turn around and round up every one of us, shuffling us into the bathroom quick. My heart starts to beat faster just remembering how scared Miss Stephanie looked, like the man could be packing.

The worst part for Richard was more personal—his own father wasn't much better. He never once showed his face at one of our recitals. His mother would come just before curtain and sit alone in the back. But even from backstage, I could spot the pride in her eyes, a twinkle that faded as soon as the house lights came on and she shot up to leave. But for the length of Richard's solo, she was spellbound and I understood enough about love by then to see that for those three minutes, she and Richard shared the same breath.

Mastering the splits.

It was the summer after Richard graduated from high school that his parents left Yucca Springs for San Mateo, California to live closer to their older son, John. Richard jokes that the place has something fishy in the water that makes everyone look and think the same, but the move left him with a more serious feeling of abandonment he couldn't shake at first. But as time went by, he experienced a freedom he admitted he didn't want to shake. "I'm glad they're gone. Well, him, anyway," he said, referring to his father. The corners of his mouth slid down, as they did whenever he talked about the man. "And if that makes me sound like a horrible person, I don't care."

"Are you kidding?" I said. "I was always listening for my dad's truck to start up. I couldn't wait for him to leave."

On a silent level, I was convinced that Richard was still clinging to the notion that he and his father would make amends, although he never seemed to want to talk about it. And I tried not to push.

Sadly, neither parent ever returned to Yucca Springs to see Richard dance again. But they did get old, and with age the heart can soften sometimes, at least I think Richard was hoping so. Then, suddenly, his mother died. "A stroke," John's email said. *Email!* I don't know which was worse for Richard—his mother passing, or the fact he found out about it in his inbox. He said he didn't think he could face his father and brother without his mother as a buffer, especially after John wrote yet another email to say that he didn't think it was a good idea for Richard to come to the service because their father was convinced no one "like him" would be there.

"That's what he thinks," Richard said, but he didn't go to the service. What he did do was play Sade songs in class for an entire month. Songs too sad and slow to dance to, but everyone swayed along, trying to be sympathetic.

They were the quietest tap classes I ever remember.

Yet, all through the worry and stress that both Joey and Benjamin's stories caused, I sensed something else, something positive, happening all around us, too. We were like any other group of impressionable young dancers, but something in the air had shifted until I think there was a loosening of all sorts of tightly held attitudes, feelings, and ideas. I've thought about this a lot since those days—it wasn't only our technique that was expanding, it was everything, it was our whole world. It might have been something impossible for Miss Stephanie to advertise in her promotional flyer, but every day made me feel the most remarkable truth about becoming strong and flexible—that it can have the same effect on your mind. Like mastering the splits, I was stretching beyond resistance. Slowly, my awareness unlocked, along with my hips.

At first, I only sensed the unlocking.

Then I felt it in everything I did. Heard it in everything I said.

I was simply more open.

⁓

One morning, in the quiet hours before classes began, Richard was sweeping the floor again, this time with a funny look on his face. "Richard, are you okay?"

"Yep."

"You don't look okay."

"I'll tell you later," he said, in an airy way, or trying to sound that way. He went back to sweeping, using something that resembled a broom. (The nagging I once had to do to get him to help. Now I have to make room in the closet for all the up-to-the-minute cleaning tools he feels the need to collect.) He kept sweeping, and I kept expecting him to tell me what was on his mind, but he didn't. So I stood there, knowing he couldn't contain himself for long.

He dropped the broom and came running over. His voice went up, "I've signed up for a self-defense class in Palm Springs every Wednesday for a month!"

"Great!" I said. "I'll sub your class." Immediately, I thought of showing the movies *Stomp, Shall We Dance,* and *42ⁿᵈ Street.* It would be hopeless for me to teach tap any other way. Only Richard knows me too well.

"No need, they'll take Saturday's class."

Already thinking how wonderful it would be to have the studio to myself, mid-week, after my last ballet class, I smiled.

"So, you're free to come with me."

"Me? Why do I need a self-defense class?" As soon as I said it, I knew how ridiculous I sounded, especially to Richard who gave me his you're-talking-to-someone-who-knows-you look I was used to getting from him. "Considering you live by yourself next to the interstate and have been known to be a little too accommodating to certain trespassers, I'd say that's a pretty dumb question."

Again, I knew what he was referring to and I will always be sensitive about it. "I have not," I said, trying to sound unruffled, but it came out as defensive—worse than when he told me everyone was hooking up on Tinder, and I pretended I knew what on earth he was talking about.

"How many men have you dated since then, anyway?" He hesitated but only for a second, "or, for that matter, how many have I? We live like nuns. It'll do us both good to get out of town once a week. Plus ..." he hesitated again.

"What?"

"You can pay for the gas."

I got on with wiping the smudges off the mirrors, which was fine because there was no use objecting, no use at all. There is just no arguing with Richard when he is determined to have his way.

Not that this distinguishes him from other people, really.

Five

*"I don't want people who want to dance, I want
people who have to dance."*
~George Balanchine

Worlds away.

It's not that I didn't notice all the men at the WorkOUT
Gym checking Richard out as soon as we entered the
double glass doors, I did. Richard is fit, boyishly handsome,
and excitement makes him even more so. Even before we
climbed out of the car, a man who was climbing off his
Vespa winked at him.

But something even more obvious came into view—I
was the only woman around. In Yucca Springs, men didn't
go to the gym unless they wanted to play basketball. But
here, men were walking toward the door hand in hand.
"Can you imagine?" Richard said, leaning in so close our
foreheads bumped. I knew he loved teaching at the Star
Struck, but as a teacher, he simply wasn't able to take
certain risks.

In no time, he was flirting, too. He flirted with the
man who took our money. He flirted with a man in tight
short-shorts who leaned over the counter to watch the
other man take our money. He flirted with the janitor who
said "gracias" after Richard complimented his Mets cap.
He excused himself to use the bathroom, and when he

came back, we walked into the gym together and sat cross-legged on a blue wrestling mat. The man next to us moved in closer. "Nice shoes," he said of Richard's soft yellow-leather loafers.

"Thank you," Richard said, clearly eager to show them off, turning back to me to scrunch up his nose. For a second it looked like he was about to laugh, but I could see what he felt underneath was more serious. With a lift and drop of his shoulders, he said nothing, as if there was nothing more to say so why bother. I put my arms around him, but he stiffened in my clutch.

"What?" I couldn't imagine what I'd done.

He fixed his eyes on mine.

"You've been acting about as straight as Nathan Lane, so I don't think there's any confusion that I'm your girlfriend, if that's what you're worried about."

He sat up straighter, and put his hands on my shoulders to shove me away. The man next to us clicked his tongue.

Richard was so cold to me all of a sudden. I remembered something about friendship I'd heard Miss Stephanie say to my mother once—there are always a few injuries nearer to the surface than you'd ever think. "Is that right?" My mom replied. "Well, I think I've got more than a *few*."

Then it came to me. The one other time I'd compared Richard to Nathan Lane was during the first week I was in charge of the Star Struck, and I suggested he tone himself down during registration week. I worry he still holds it against me.

He'd come through the door, looking gorgeous and strong in white hot pants, a muscle T-shirt, and the same glowingly-yellow loafers, causing the mailman to say, "that boy sure likes his clothes tight and his shoes bright." I think that awful try at poetry made me more nervous about the parents' reaction to Richard's clothes than it should have. I liked that Richard had the nerve to stand out and dress in creative ways no one else in town would dream of, but being financially responsible, all I could think was *the parents will just die!*

At once, he noticed my expression and came right out with, "What?"

"Do you think, um, maybe you could tone it down a little?" I said, trailing after him as he walked through the studio.

He turned around to catch my eyes. "I can't believe you just said that," he said, and that was all. We managed to keep everything civil, but I must have made him really angry, even if he pretended otherwise.

Did he defend himself further? To make me sound even worse, I can't remember. Probably. Even more probably, I'm sure the relief showed on my face when he said he'd dress "more boring from now on like *you*." That's when I said the crack about Nathan Lane. I was going for a joke, but my joke fell flat, coming off more like name-calling.

I felt horrible, like the worst friend ever, disrespectful and unaccepting. The next day I apologized. He accepted, kindly enough, but he never strode through town in hot pants again, not that I know of. I'm ashamed to say, I got what I wanted. He still wore his yellow loafers, but only under jeans—boot cut, not skinny. I wondered if he'd been hiding something else, too—that he thought maybe, just maybe, deep down, I was like all the other prejudice people in his life. This thought still bothers me.

"Listen up!" the instructor yelled over the chatter, clapping his hands together for emphasis. His voice didn't sound like an animated little girl's voice anymore, like it did when we first sat down and he ran over to say, "I just came over to see if you need anything?" Meaning, he just came over to see if Richard was available.

"Let's get started," Richard said softly—at least I thought no one heard him, turning to fake strangle me— "before I kill someone with my bare hands."

So he *had* been thinking what I was thinking. But he squeezed my neck in an affectionate way. There. Done. Forgiveness. I remember hoping we'd always find a way to recover ourselves like that.

"Choose a partner!" the instructor yelled. Everyone started to size each other up. I noticed how Richard's cheeks began to tingle red, and his eyes darted around under lids smudged with gray eye shadow he must have put on when he was in the bathroom, the sight of which tore my heart open. The only other time he wore makeup, that I knew of, was during recital week. He's the only one who ever bothered for dress-rehearsal—the rest of us didn't think it worth the effort. Mostly, I saw what a huge part of Richard he held back at home, and what that must feel like on a daily basis. I was worried he'd want to move to Palm Springs. I felt a stab of sadness at the thought.

Richard practically jumped into the arms of one young man, who'd run up to him animated and smiling, leaving me alone to choose a partner until the man who'd clicked his tongue volunteered—not because he wanted to, but we were the only two left. Just like in high school, I thought, when no one wanted me on their team, because I'd rather practice stag leaps on the sidelines when everyone else was shooting hoops.

When the demonstration was over, and we'd practiced punching the padded mugger, it was time for us to go at each other. "Project confidence! Use body language!" the coach yelled. Everyone started moving right to left, facing each other, arms up, boundaries clear, assertiveness firm. But when I looked over at Richard, his cheeks had turned two deeper shades of red. Even his forehead was red, which doesn't happen unless he is totally beside himself.

From the moment the whistle blew, I found strength in my arms I never knew I had, "from all the hours of holding my arms above my head," I said smiling, pleased with myself—raising my arms into fifth position to show what I meant, before tussling my partner to the ground in two seconds flat. Splat. After which, he gave me a nasty look and the C word escaped from under his breath. I felt my chest contract. "What did you just say?" I said, challenging myself not to swallow it, I was so mad. "I don't know why I thought coming here would be different. I'm glad I flattened you."

Later, I would tell Miss Stephanie excitedly, "For once, I found the exact words I wanted to say exactly when I needed to say them, without having to wait until three in the morning to hear them rush into my brain!" When I was younger, I thought there'd be so many more of these confident comebacks, but I haven't found this to be true.

Richard's nose was pressed against the chest of his partner and he was struggling to stand, but brute force without panache is just not Richard. The coach shouted, "We're not disco-dancing here, pretty boy!" and I thought that sounded so disrespectful. "Too much hip action!" he yelled again, and I could have stabbed him in the eyes with my fingers until red came out, like when you jab at a sweet potato in the oven. "Use your core! USE YOUR CORE!"

"For fuck's sake! My core what?" Richard yelled back, letting go of his partner with a push, and standing in defiance with his hands on his hips.

I had to say something. "Your center, Richard. He means your center!" I spun around to face the coach. "We're dancers. Dancers don't say *core*." I turned around to look right at Richard and recited what Miss Stephanie had told us a thousand times at least, "Your *center* defines your power. Your *center* is the beginning of all physical strength!" It was like giving him permission to come back to himself. He turned back to his partner and went at him. *Slap, slap, slap, slap, slap.*

The coach yelled, "Stop sissy slapping! Pretend you're coming out of a bar and some homophobe down from Idaho calls you a mother-fucking fag!"

The slur flew through the air and landed on Richard sharply. Another spear thrown into the center of his world. He started to punch. *Punch, punch, punch, punch, punch.* There was cheering from the crowd. Someone yelled, "Kick ass!"

"Strike!" The coach yelled. "Strike. Strike. Strikkkkkkkke!"

In less than a minute, Richard leveled his partner. Flip, flop, it was over.

"That's what I'm talking about!" the coach beamed. "And now I need to know, Richard. Doesn't it feel great?"

"Yes!"

"Doesn't it feel powerful?"

"Yes!"

"To know you can take control of the enemy like that?"

"Yes, sir!" Richard yelled, and saluted.

"Now, are you ready to do it again?"

"Not on your life!" And with that, he dashed—well, skipped—over, grabbed my hand, and off we ran back to the car where, as soon as the doors were shut, we crumbled into laughter. Between snorts Richard said, "I wish I didn't have to admit this to you, but the first thing I felt when that guy tumbled over was how much I missed Yucca Springs. Gay men are so competitive."

On the drive home, we grew more serious. We talked about our students: the ones with will but no talent, the ones with plenty of talent but no drive, and we went on like that until, before we knew it, the lights of Yucca Springs came up. Oddly, we felt like survivors seeing shore for the first time in days. It surprised us a little, I think, to feel as happy to be home as we'd felt to leave it behind. I wondered aloud if maybe we were a little too afraid of the world beyond our valley. "Am I turning into my mother?" I asked. Richard swore I was nothing like her because dancing made us risk everything in ways other people would never have the guts to pull off, which put us both in danger of going inside the Star Struck and turning up the music even though Mr. Lawson's lights were still on.

I unlocked the door and the wood floor shone in the moonlight. "Hello," I said, comforted, as if someone met us at the door with ice tea. I thought about how there are far more costly and impressive health clubs with studios now, but none with the soul of the Star Struck. It may be silly to say that a dance studio has a soul, but I believe the best ones do. We walked to the middle of the room and stood staring at our space (I think Richard used the word "bubble"), not moving at all, just staring. "Every time I've been away for even just a few hours, I come back here and I can feel the nest Miss Stephanie made here."

"So she wouldn't have an empty one?" Richard said, trying to see what I saw by asking the question, his eyes searching the mirror, as if waiting to see his younger self appear.

"I get that now," I said. I didn't add how often I looked
for the very same image of myself.

"And you know what this nest needs?"

"What?" But I knew what he was getting at.

"Music." And with that, no amount of looking over
at Mr. Lawson's lights would stop us. He whipped out
his mini iPod. I gave my scrunchy a yank. And, oh, how
we danced that night—we *soared!* Every move we'd ever
mastered: isolations, turns, leaps. We were our best, not
only technically, but by being together. I remember feeling
that distinctly.

Growing up, I heard my mother say all kinds of things
about Miss Stephanie, but the most convincing thing she
ever said was, "as long as she keeps dancing, she'll never get
old like the rest of us." It wasn't true, of course. We all get
old, but as loose and lithe as I felt just then, I understood
what she meant.

Pulling off his T-shirt, Richard ran over and whipped
open the door. Minutes later, the door slammed shut,
which seemed a little odd because no Santa Ana blew,
but we ignored it. I looked out the window to see that
the moon had slid way over in the sky, and the hour had
passed into midnight. It was time for us to say good night.

Later, I lay wide awake thinking how quickly a day can
turn around, and turn around again, and turn around yet
another time.

Until you find yourself right back under the same soft
covers.

<hr />

I hold back tears remembering how naïve and happy we
were that night.

Now. Honestly, I'd be perfectly happy to get swept up by all the best memories of the Star Struck indefinitely, and not let the worst of them reappear at all.

If only it were possible.

For good.

After the shock of my dad's death had faded, mom started up her sorry thoughts again, wondering where she'd gone wrong and what she could have done better—saying things like, "You know, I did learn a lot about marriage from your father, like what I'd never put up with again. So at least we had *that*." I guess we both felt the less either of us complained about him, the better. We were raised to believe that one of the worst sins you can commit is to talk badly about the dead—even if they deserve it.

The next morning after breakfast she said something— something I've forgotten until now—out of the blue that had nothing to do with what we were talking about, nothing to do with what I'd just said. "Truth is, Lucy, you can remember the good things all you like. You can remember the good things until the cows come home," this sounded funny because she knew about as much about cows as I did, which is exactly nothing. "But you can never forget the worst thing that happens because it changes everything..." she sighed, pausing to turn toward the window and lay her palms on the screen, "for good."

Something about her tone scared me deeply. I remember making up some excuse to run outside.

At the far end of our driveway, I was still afraid. I hadn't ever realized until then that you can try to run away from your mother's regrets and fears the same way you can try to outrun your own but they sneak back in unexpected ways, at unexpected times, often disguised as something safe to latch onto. Like when you try to avoid the poison oak when you walk up Black Canyon, but the older vines send out lateral branches that can be mistaken for tree limbs you try to push out of the way.

This knowledge circled overhead like a large hawk, its shadow sweeping.

Six

"A dancer needs enough money until she needs some more."
~Josephine Baker

Resonance.

The mailman shoved the new Capezio catalogue through the mail slot and it landed with a plop on the floor—one of the most heart stopping sounds of the year, a little like the earth giving way.

Still in my nightgown, I gently lifted it, careful not to leave smudges on the glossy cover or dog-ear the pages or, heaven help me, rip one out. As Costuming Director, Richard has a "no nonsense" attitude about being the first to reject all the shapes, sizes, and sparkle he can never see the point of, and we could never afford even if he did. Even so, *"This,"* he'll say, holding up the catalogue with a possessive look in his eyes, "is mine." I let my hand rest on the cover for a second before opening it to peek at two young dancers like statuettes cast in *relevé*.

"Lucy?"

"Richard?" I said, hiding the catalogue behind my back. I don't know why I played the game. It was like trying to hold on to the wind. He lowered his chin, extended his right arm, wiggled his fingers. I handed it over.

"It hardly matters anyway," I said. "We'll be lucky to scramble something together from Big Lots this year."

Most students had returned after Miss Stephanie left, but not all, and many times I thought of asking around to see where, or if, they were taking class. I never did ask, though, remembering something else my mother said while sitting in her favorite chair in front of the TV. "Never ask a question you don't want the answer to," in response to me asking, "are you okay, mom?" She had seemed extra worn-out that evening, and that worried me more than I had let on. "Just tired," she said, which led to a brutal coughing spell, her chest trying to free itself of all the gook. When I said that I understood because class that day had wiped me out too, she snapped. "Yeah, ballet is rough," with, of course, a roll of her eyes.

I wanted to cry. I knew she was pretty uncomfortable by then, but she could still surprise me. If it wasn't her sarcasm, it was something else. I'd come to terms with the fact that she needed someone to take her pain out on, and that someone was me. Who else? And once I knew she was sick, I tried not to let her comments drag me down any further than hurt feelings.

Which I had a lot of.

"Okay, sure, whatever," Richard said quickly, flipping through the pages, already distracted. Feeling a little sorry for myself, I went upstairs to get dressed.

It was a lot to handle on my own, but at least once a day, money worries gnawed at me. The cost of tights and slippers and toe shoes was one thing, but there was the rent, the high school auditorium to pay for, the lighting tech, the skyrocketing cost of liability insurance. Every time I went to the bank, my mother's voice rang out, "You'll end up broke and then what?" At one point while brushing my teeth, I was on the verge of tears.

Miss Stephanie had warned me about the dark side of running a studio: money issues, the upsetting things people will say without thinking, the fatigue, the sleepless nights. We were talking on the phone. "But it's worth it. Because as your students rise to their fullest potential, you'll be rising to your own," she said, and I thought how she's always saying things like this—she's famous for them. But if I were to imagine a word bubble above my mother's head, it would have read, "If it's alright with you, Steph, I think I need to barf. Where's the can?" I smiled to myself.

Just before we hung up, Miss Stephanie added with a trace of skepticism in her voice—as if she didn't quite believe it was entirely possible herself, but worth trying anyway—"Try to enjoy it, Lucy. All of it, even the stressful parts. One thing that always helped me is to think of recital season like Christmas for other women, only we have a hundred kids to please, twice as many parents, and grandparents who, rest assured, pay the tab nine times out of ten. If they don't like what they see, the disapproval they pack in one sidelong glance will scare you to pieces." She laughed. "But relish it, because now becomes then so much faster than you ever dreamed it would."

The heat rose in my cheeks.

I'd been searching for a theme for recital and in her advice, I heard it. For days, I held on to the idea—*Now Becomes Then: Faster Than You Ever Dreamed it Would.* I didn't want to share it with Richard, though, or with anyone, not yet. Everyone would chime in and want to give their two cents. We all have a stake in recital, and everyone starts to obsess about it. I wanted to cherish my idea privately a while longer.

When I finally did share my idea with Richard, he flat out rejected it. "Too depressing," he said.

"It's a reminder," I said.

"Of what?"

"To relish the process, the journey. To relish *life*, since we'll all leave the limelight eventually," I said, trying to tweak his compassion.

"Precisely. And that's why it's depressing." He walked away from me. Obviously, we were not going to agree right away, nor either of us persuade the other.

In a few moments, he walked back with a list of reasons for disagreeing with me, and I argued each and every objection, but, I admit, my enthusiasm was easier to feel than it was to explain. But the good part of being challenged, was that it did allow me to picture my idea more clearly. Debating made me even more sure my idea was a good one, except Richard didn't see it that way. "Perhaps you should not be so controlling," he said, opening the door as if about to leave again.

"Don't," I said. I knew how everything can change in an instant between people, even between people who love each other, and the level of his disapproval made me nervous. I could never rest easy if Richard thought less of me.

"I'm going to walk out this door and never come back if you call our recital—what is it you called it again? Then is now? Now is then? Either way, it's terrible." As soon as the words were out, he let go of the door, walked over, and we both sank to the floor with our arms folded tight over our knees. I scooted in closer, and laid my head on his shoulder. We'd been through recital stress so many times. It could undo us for a while, but it always brought us closer together in the end.

Struggling with what to say, I said, "I'm sorry, but I really do think it's a good theme, even if I don't know how we'll flesh it out yet. But it's always just a feeling at first, and it comes together eventually, you know that. And sure, it's scary, but what isn't? Scared is how I feel most of the time anyway."

This got his attention. "Me too," he murmured.

We sat quietly. And with each passing second, what became clear to us both was how the number one reason why I couldn't let go of my idea, was that Richard's dislike of it didn't outweigh my belief in it. "Whatever," he said, finally, in the dismissive way people say the word when they are pretending something doesn't bother them when clearly, it does. We continued to sit there until slowly he resigned himself—nodding once, twice, to himself, and then at me. "What*ever*," he said again.

Only this time he didn't sound bothered, but willing.

Nothing about people is ever just what we think.

My mother had another way to describe recital season. "Blood, sweat, and tears," she said, after her favorite pop group. When I asked her why she thought they called themselves that, she said, "Because of everything rotten they've been through, probably. And everything rotten they'll go through again."

This was right around the time my father left, and I have this clear memory of her singing, "You make me so very happy, I'm so glad you came into my life," so I'm not exactly sure who she was singing about. But to be honest, my mother having no love affairs whatsoever? I'm afraid that was part of the fantasy I once believed, hell-bent on blaming my dad for everything that went wrong. But finding myself within earshot of too much gossip to the contrary over the years, I've overheard enough to make me question my mother's faithfulness, as well. I considered asking her straight-out if she ever cheated with the man who agreed to hire my dad for the windmills, but I never found the nerve. Even if true, who's to say the guilt didn't bother her as much as being cheated *on*.

Anyway, she must have been about thirty when I found her in the kitchen singing that song at the top of her lungs, spooning mouthfuls of ricotta straight out of the tub into her mouth so the lyrics were squishy sounding. Still, her voice was lovely. I had walked in the front door and made a beeline for the kitchen, but she never heard me come in. I didn't know what to make of my mother who had never sang before, not in front of me anyway. I caught my breath and ran to my room. In complicated ways I'd not faced before, every part of me was confused at once—I didn't know why, and I'm afraid I burst into tears. I wasn't sad. I was happy to hear my mother sound so alive for once. It made me see how much more like her I was—or she like me, I'm not sure which, but it was a feeling I had longed for, in one way or another, all my life. I sat and stared out the window until the sun dipped below Old Greyback Mountain.

With an unsteady voice, I talked to myself. "You just have to figure out how to deal with the fact that she has become Peggy Maglietta, *gifted singer,* right before your very eyes," I said.

Even though, to her dying day, she swore that she had just been making macaroni and cheese to the sound of her own rusty voice.

But I'd heard differently.

And every day after, I might have pretended it was the same old kitchen we shared, with the same wooden spoons standing upright in the same blue mason jar on the stove—but in my mind, nothing about the room was simply a kitchen anymore once it had been my mother's stage.

Years later, when I shared this story with Miss Stephanie, she said it was a good lesson for a budding choreographer—to see how nothing about people is ever just what we think. "And I find it fascinating how for some, it's only when they think no one is watching that they can be their most passionate selves. And for others...we need a stage." The pause in her voice was unmistakable, so whatever support may have been her intention, it felt cut off by the word that sprang into mind: *showoff*.

When I was around ten, I had come down with a bad cold and still insisted on going to ballet. My father yelled, "Give it a rest, kid. Can't you go one day without being a showoff?" Stunned, I couldn't answer. The word felt shameful. My mother laid into him, but later I heard them through the air vent, sharing the same "show-offy" suspicion. And though I thought the word had gone its own way, there it was again, stirring up my insecurities. Miss Stephanie must have detected the uneasiness in my voice when I said, "But that makes us sound like show-offs."

"It does, doesn't it?" she said. "And I'm sorry, but that just isn't true, no more than a visual artist is a showoff when they want to share their paintings with the public. So I'm thinking I will rephrase it. How about this? I think it takes a very confident person to become skilled, secure, and brave enough to take command of a stage."

"I like that better," I said.

It didn't solve everything about the sound of the word "showoff," but it did help how I wanted to feel about it in the future. When you are a performer—either today, tomorrow, a month from now, or years down the road—the word will come up again. It's inevitable.

And it always catches you by surprise.

Someone's at the door.

Richard was still sitting on the floor of the waiting room, legs in the shape of a "v" around his precious catalogue, when I came back downstairs to finish picking little-girl undies and dust bunnies off the dressing room floor. "So it's come to this," he said, clicking his tongue. "Polyester everything. It doesn't stretch, doesn't absorb sweat, and it definitely doesn't breathe. It suffocates the skin. It's spun petroleum, a byproduct of crude oil. Why don't people care about that? And the more you wear it, the greater your risk of absorbing toxic chemicals. I miss breathable fabric and I want it back!"

I stopped what I was doing to take in what he'd said, but only for a minute. I appreciated how he was always in "the know" about fabric—always a history lesson when the subject of cloth came up, but I was eager to finish cleaning so I could pick out music for *Now Becomes Then*. I was hoping that the stack of LP's, tapes, and CD's that Miss Stephanie left behind, plus every download Richard and I had collected, would give our playlist the historical quality it needed.

Flipping through the LP's, I found *Dance of the Periwinkle*. All I had to do was close my eyes to see my five-year-old self, tiny bun sprung out of the top of her head. I played the song again. I was about to play it for the third time when I heard a loud knock on the door. The past felt so real, I expected to see my mother out the window, handbag over her shoulder, "let's get a move on" written on her face.

"Someone's at the door," Richard yelled, giving a little shrug and turning a page without so much as looking up to see who it was.

I can safely say this would not have been the case had he bothered to look up. He would have jumped at the chance to talk to the boy, any boy, looking intently at the class schedule taped to our window.

———✐✐✐———

As soon as our visitor, Charles, was gone, I told Richard what I'd been thinking the entire time we answered questions about our ballet and jazz classes, before Richard, seeing how Charles was not only the first African-American, but the only male potential student either one of us had welcomed into the studio in a while, jumped up to say that there was room in tap class, too, plenty of room. "It's as if he wants to be a mirror image of young Michael Jackson," I said.

Richard turned to look at me, but he didn't say anything.

"And I know you think I said that because I'm a small-town hick," I said.

"No, I think you said it because he has a fluffy halo of glossy hair with one curly strand suspended over his forehead."

I smiled.

"*And* you said it because his cheeks are creased into dimples and his nose is wide and more natural looking than the reconstruction that went under the knife one too many times."

Outside the window, we watched Charles walk away. The muscles in his legs bulged under his low-riding shorts as he kicked a stone down the sidewalk. Richard sighed, cocking his head the way an admirer would, like he had just heard something wistful whispered into his ear.

I laughed, but my own thoughts were elsewhere. "How many years has the world been dancing to Michael Jackson. Twenty?"

He gave me the same look he gives students when they finally grasp a step. "Longer. Since 1972."

I took that in.

"But wait. Let us not forget child sexual abuse."

"Accusations, I believe. But even if true, we can still love the music even if we don't endorse the man, or his actions. We can't pretend the best dance music ever just didn't exist."

"Addicted to drugs, prescription and otherwise. I don't think that's a message people are going to like around here."

"You mean the same people who pick up something from Walgreens and Rite Aid, not to mention that creepy kid with the backpack who hangs out by the Community Center, for every little ache, pain, and worry?" I stared out the window again. "I bet he can dance, too. Wait. Is that a racist thing to say? Even if I mean it as a compliment?"

"He probably won't even show up. He'll end up driving to San Bernardino for classes."

"Why would you say that?" Which prompted us both to turn and look at the couch Miss Stephanie bought ages ago—reliable softness after hours on our feet, but dated and slumped. Richard said it made our lobby look like a retirement home.

To change the subject, I said, "Remember how Miss Stephanie used to call the people who asked a string of questions but never bothered to show up, tire-kickers? She said she felt like sending them over to the Chrysler dealership."

To change the subject even further, he said, "How's about this year we, meaning you, try and relax more."

"Try and relax? If you have to try, you aren't really relaxed, are you? Besides, as soon as something goes wrong, you'll be the first one hollering at me to fix it."

"Well, you are the director," he said, sliding into a perfectly balanced split, laughing at me so I'd laugh at myself.

Later on, this image of Richard would come back to me again and again, not because Richard can do the splits without warming up first, which may not sound related, but it is. His flexibility became the perfect metaphor for his resolve. No matter how devastated and disappointed he was to become, he was determined to find his way back to a more grounded place.

⤚◦◦◦⤙

After about a minute of humming "Thriller," Richard declared, "Charles has talent."

I asked for proof. "How do you know?"

"You can see it in the way he walks. The writing is on the wall, or like, *off* the wall. So, if we are going to do this, are we talking Michael alone...?" He rolled up from the floor, catalogue tucked under his arm, "or all the way back to The Jackson 5?"

"All the way back," I said. Then I ran up behind him and put my arms around his back tightly.

In mind, I could see it—the audience hushed by a young man seeming at the center of the universe, except he doesn't feel that way inside, but the opposite, vulnerable and sad as he tries to find privacy in a life of fame. With Charles narrating. "Do you think Charles will be offended? That he'll think we're nothing but small-town, small-minded people, the kind of people who would say, 'hey, buddy, you moved here, so you *have* to play Michael Jackson.' I mean, doesn't that make us sound…"

Before I could say the word again, Richard dropped the catalogue. The floor trembled. He looked down at his feet and waved his hand over them, as if brushing cobwebs off of another era, until slowly, the illusion of gliding backward while seeming to move forward came back to him. It was a move no one did smoothly without a lot of practice, and it took me longer to get the hang of it again. I had to study Richard's feet hard before I moonwalked across the floor.

And there it was, the moment when recital week becomes the reference point for everything else—when it's just so easy to believe that there is nothing more important going on in the world.

"This means two things," I said. "One, I won't have time left over to worry about money. And, two, while Charles is reciting the story, we'll have time to change costumes without having to ask Mr. Neville to play piano between numbers."

Richard tossed his head in his most exaggerated way. "Mr. Neville playing Cat Stevens again? That morning *has* broken."

I clapped my hands, so relieved. He made me laugh and forget myself. I stepped back to let him moonwalk past me.

Seven

*"Dancing is a perpendicular expression of a
horizontal desire."*
~George Bernard Shaw

I see a star.

DAYS WENT BY AND NO CHARLES.

I went through a slump thinking he wouldn't come back that lasted right up until the afternoon he did, a whole week later—ten minutes early for ballet, staying right on through tap. Still, I didn't want to spring my idea on him until we were sure he'd stay with it because, apparently, he was also on the football team. Time-wise, this could be a problem. But other than the game against Bakersfield, when the bus didn't roll back in to town until after eleven, he never once missed class.

At fifteen, a dancer can choose to stay in teen classes after school, or dance later in the evening with a hand-full of various-level adults. "How young we are, while considered old on the dance calendar," I remember Miss Stephanie saying once, staring at her feet. When I got home and repeated this fact to my mother, she said, "I don't mean to downplay your enthusiasm for everything your teacher says, but you are *ten years old.*"

Charles was seventeen. Luckily, adult classes fit his football schedule.

"I worry that once the team gets wind Charles is taking ballet, they'll tease him to death," I said to Richard.

"They'll poke some fun, sure. But he'll be fine," Richard said. "I see the way people look at him. He's no victim. Besides, NFL stars have been taking ballet for years to prevent injury."

I took what he said and thought *true*.

But that was then.

Now, I remember those words and they burn like a strap, like the time my father pulled off his belt and lashed out—he never struck me again, my mother saw to that.

"So, you'll be staying with us then?" I asked Charles, after his third ballet class, feeling sure enough by then of what he'd say.

Slinging a gym bag over his shoulder—there was something in the way he threw it that made me see, would make anyone see, even his teammates, that he was no victim, just as Richard had said—he said, "Yes, ma'am. It's cool," on his way out the door.

"It was like hearing the Bolshoi is cool," I said to Miss Stephanie. "But that didn't bother me half as much as being called *ma'am*."

She laughed. "Sooner or later, every woman has got to make peace with that word. I've adjusted my reaction to it." She paused. "Well, I try anyway."

"Into what?"

"Something less upsetting. I tell myself that what they are really trying to express is acknowledgement of how much wiser we are."

"Can you really do that?" I said, bouncing my body gently onto the couch.

"Theoretically," she said.

The next morning as I was trying to convince Richard that Charles was straight because, well, he played *football*, Richard asked if I had ever bothered to read the newspaper. I had to admit that even when I did, I'd skip the sports section. After a week of getting to know Charles better, I had to fight back the urge to say "told you so" with a ten foot pole.

"Such a pity," Richard said. "One year out of college and his body will turn into one you don't ever want to see in tights again."

"I guess we'll just have to show him that there's more to life than football and more to adulthood than conventionality." A spark sailed up my spine. Our eyes met. I was ninety-nine percent sure I meant dancing.

But not a hundred.

"I see." Richard's eyes lit up. Richard can always spot when I have feelings for someone, good or bad. "How long has it been, anyway? Since, you know?"

I sighed, but there was nothing I wanted to say. I turned to leave the room.

"Quick. Come downstairs," Richard whispered, after knocking on my door. Tap class was over and the studio was finally quiet.

Already in my robe, I opened the door. "Now?"

"Now."

At the bottom of the stairs, we walked into the studio together where Charles was sitting on the floor lacing up his Nike's. "Charles?" I said. "Can we talk to you for a minute?"

"Yes, ma'am," he said.

I took a breath. "Richard and I have noticed what a natural you are," I said.

We had noticed. Charles cut through the repetitiveness it takes most adults to learn a new step, and went at it his own way, and not with attitude—nothing like the kids with a lot to prove once their parents drag them out of Los Angeles, and their need to show us how small our studio is becomes huge. No, Charles was just comfortable in the spotlight. We saw it a couple of times his first week, more the second. "I see a star," I whispered to Richard.

"*I* see ticket sales through the roof."

Charles beamed, clearly pleased with our compliments. And he didn't take our idea as anything this, that, or the other about his skin color, other than its necessity in order to play Michael.

And with that, a new part of our life was set into motion.

Unfortunately, I'm referring to the trouble part.

＊＊＊

Where to begin?

"At the beginning," I said aloud to buoy myself.

"ABC" for Pre-Ballet—tiny hands fanning the air and yanking at their fanny elastic.

"I Want You Back" for our two seniors—off to college and the army the next year, so a duet was theirs without question, objection, or jealousy.

"Rock With You" for Tap I, leading into "Off the Wall" for Tap II—both classes stomping down the aisles, surprising both sides of the audience at once.

"Bad"—Richard's solo, which I, and everyone else, predicted he'd choose.

Advanced and Beginning Jazz had fun with the choreography that I had even more fun setting to "Shake Your Body Down To the Ground," though the costumes I found at Walmart were a bit of a problem, until Richard thought to sew elastic shoulder straps on the one-sleeve-shirts I thought were such a great idea.

"Never Can Say Goodbye" for Ballet I, though at first I had my doubts. "I don't know if little girls can pull off such heartache," I said to Richard, forgetting how perceptive kids really are.

"I'll Be There" was perfect for Ballet II ensemble work, as well as soloing frames.

"Thriller" would have been the obvious choice for a finale, which is why we didn't choose it. Instead, we chose "Don't Stop 'Til You Get Enough"—Richard's steps leaving the stage in quiet retreat rather than letting the curtain fall as we hold hands, a real departure from tradition.

Miss Stephanie was thrilled that I took her idea to heart.

As I was saying, I had feelings.

There was the first time Charles stayed late at the studio to rehearse. Then there was the second. He was even more beautiful in the evening light, so much so, I felt swept-up. At one point, I became so flustered that the things I said sounded awkward and silly because I put too much effort into trying to sound strictly professional.

But there is no need to string this part out, or even put any more emphasis on it. Because if you are thinking what I think you are thinking—that a scandal the size of Mary Kay Letourneau (though her lover was only *twelve*) is what happened, I need you to stop it.

Stop it right now.

You have sadly underestimated me.

We've all heard about teachers who find a way to twist right from wrong to their own satisfaction—finding an excuse for why it's okay, telling themselves no harm will come of it, waiting until all the other students have gone home.

But I would never.

Not on your life.

No.

Once Charles left the studio and I was finally alone, rattled by emotion, flush with self-consciousness, I lost myself in my solo—tiredly at first, and then, as my energy returned after so many hours of teaching, with more oomph. At first, I wasn't sure I wanted to use "Do You Remember the Time" or whether I just didn't want anyone else to use it. By the second run through, I was convinced.

No thanks to Richard saying, "Well, since there's only been the one time."

"What do you mean, no crotch grabbing?" Richard said, one page into the script we were writing for Charles. "What about fun? Can we have any fun?"

And slowly, "Now Becomes Then" became a classic story of how the spotlight becomes too blinding for some, even if the world sees nothing but a success story. We wanted people to see how Michael's singing and dancing was an escape for him in the beginning, and how the horror of his life began with his bullying father, and too many others wanting too much from him too often—how all of that created a need for an escape that no pills or needles could give after a while, and what superstars will resort to in order to save themselves from the stardom they once craved. Mostly, we wanted everyone to see how none of us know how life will turn out in the end. "No matter how much money you make," I tapped onto the screen of my laptop, "or don't make."

"Don't write that," Richard said. "It's bad taste."

"This from someone who wanted a crotch-grab as an opener?"

I thought of every light aspect I could imagine in the otherwise sober story; but then, that was the point. I felt our enthusiasm opening like a magenta flower on a beavertail cactus.

When I looked up, Richard's face appeared just as I knew it would, happy with the story we were telling. "It's good," he said. His moist kiss stuck to my cheek.

Smooth criminal.

Richard was right about ticket sales—we had to schedule an extra matinee. "It's like we won the lottery!" I whispered to Richard peeking through the curtain on opening night, but his "ohmygodwhatarewegoingtodo" eyes flashed at me. Even the aisles were filling up, making him nervous that there wouldn't be room for tap class to make their entrance. To calm his nerves, I had to go out there and scoot everyone's legs out of the way.

The house lights went down, a hush came over the audience, the spotlight came up.

One flip of Michael's corkscrew curl and the crowd went wild!

⎯⎯⎯⎯ ⎯⎯⎯⎯

"Call the police!" a man standing in the doorway of the Tiki Lounge yelled.

From that moment on, whatever pride we had cherished from that evening was suddenly gone. There was no joy, no light—not even a trace. Even our memories of it went dark.

Charles was grabbed a block away from his home on Belmont Street.

Richard was attacked two blocks east of the Tiki Lounge.

The next morning, both were found face-up at the Salton City landfill, beaten to a pulp but still breathing. To bind their hands behind their backs, the attackers used long shreds of our since-forgotten studio banner. With one loafer stuffed deep into his mouth, Richard struggled for air. The police said they looked but couldn't find the other shoe. "Look again," Richard managed to whisper through swollen lips. "It's yellow. How hard can it be?"

The officer was studying the knots made with the banner. "Whoever did this knows exactly what they are doing," he said, making no effort to lower his voice before untying Charles' and Richard's hands and helping them to stand. Richard's hands fell downward and he started to shake like a thrashing lizard pulled from the ground by its tail. Charles' arms shot straight forward, as if he would now have to use them to defend himself. He did this twice more until the officer insisted he stop. He sat back down and started to wring the dirt out of his matted hair until the ambulance arrived.

Richard said he didn't remember much after the first blow to the back of his head. He moaned as I held his hand and sat at the edge of his hospital bed. "I kept picturing two little white crosses stuck in the dirt to mark where we'd fallen." And with the slightest lift in his tone, "and hoping someone would show up, because you know how people would rather sneak into the RV station to dump their stuff." He blew his nose hard.

I smiled weakly, thinking how, in spite of what he'd suffered, he was still trying to make me laugh.

Which made me cry even harder.

~⚬☙⚬~

We'd gone to the Tiki after recital to celebrate. We entered the bar with our arms full of bouquets. We clinked our glasses high over our heads and spilled a little champagne. We toasted ourselves, our work, our future. Over the next few days, I wondered if that's maybe what prompted it, knowing how jealous some people can be of personal success.

After my second glass, I walked back to the Star Struck alone. I was exhausted, but Richard wanted to stay. There were a few young men from out of town sitting at the bar and he was studying them intently. "Obviously I'm no longer needed here," I said, patting his back. "You should stay. Have some fun, you deserve it."

We hugged. I picked up all but one bouquet and left.

And what can still wake me from sleep in the middle of the night is what would have happened if I'd insisted Richard leave with me? With that, I feel a heaviness in my chest and I never know if it's self-blame or another try at self-forgiveness.

Or if it's ever going to let up.

~∞~

"It didn't occur to me to be afraid," I told the officer the next day, but he didn't seem to believe me. As soon as we realized who the officer was, Richard and I turned to look at each other. We could hardly believe he was the same officer, with less hair and more stomach, who'd come to the Star Struck with noise complaints way back when. I suddenly had that panicky feeling you get when too much of your past comes twirling back at you all at once. Hadn't Richard stuck his tongue out at him a dozen times at least?

Something my mother had warned came echoing back—"You never want to burn a bridge, Lucy. Not. One. Bridge." She'd gone ballistic after I'd called our neighbor a "big fat selfish idiot" for driving over our lawn to park his truck. She was forever raking grass seed into the two deep ruts his tires left behind, careful to cover them so the birds wouldn't eat them, but she never said a word to him. "Neighbors never forgive your complaining," she said. "And you don't want to live like that."

Looking me square in the eye, the officer said, "why would you walk alone at night?" as if I'd been harmed or wanted to test his authority. I'm not sure which, but it confused me. Fear of walking alone has never been strong in Yucca Springs. We take pride in our safe image. Our chamber of commerce uses a logo of a ladybug crawling over a yucca flower on its website.

All this was going on in my head, and it must have showed in my eyes because instead of saying anything else, the officer lifted his shoulders once and dropped them. Pretty much the same reaction he'd given Miss Stephanie, and then he left the room.

A few minutes later, he came back in and started re-asking Richard all the same questions. Richard explained again how he never saw the guy leaning out of the pick-up truck until it was too late. Once the two men were out of the truck, they came at him, both with stockings over their heads. One of them yelled, "Blow boy! We're gonna fuck you up!"

Later, Richard fought back tears as he told me he'd used every tactic we'd learned in self-defense class. "I yelled 'back off' at the top of my lungs. I pushed back. I tried to poke my fingers in their eyes." He was about to get away too, he said, having no doubt he could outrun them both. "But then I saw Charles gagged in the back of the truck, his head hanging to the side, and I froze. I thought he looked dead and I froze!" he wailed. His body trembled and he shook with sobbing.

I pulled another round of tissues from the box. As gently as I could, I patted the tears from under his eyes. I lied down quietly next to him and stroked his forehead lightly. Nestled together, we cried and cried. We were still crying when the nurse came in. I noticed a gentleness to her eyes that put me at ease for a moment. She said she was about to go off shift but could give Richard something stronger if he liked.

"Crying is enough," he said.

I hoped she wouldn't ask me to leave. "Well, if you change your mind," she said, scanning the room while backing out of it and giving a quick but kind flick of her chin.

Slowly, the room darkened. Outside the air was still, and I thought how, only hours before, the air had been peaceful under the stars when we left the auditorium. Now it felt like even the sky had been blown apart.

It was well past midnight when I whispered, "Are you asleep?"

Richard groaned. For the past hour, his grip on my hand would grow weaker and then, with a start, he'd squeeze it again, hard, as if the end of one panic cycle brought him right back to the beginning of another. It went on this way until finally he opened his eyes and said, "Did it really happen? Or am I dreaming?" His question was sincere.

"We'll get through this," I said.

"So it did happen." He re-closed his eyes. No tears this time. "I thought maybe I dreamed it, right after I dreamed I was back at the Tiki sharing a pitcher of margaritas with those city boys and singing old Prince songs around the bar."

⚬↬⚬

So, Miss Stephanie had been wrong about who stole the banner. "I still have my doubts," she said anyway, even after I reminded her that last we heard, Benjamin's family had moved to the East Coast so that Benjamin could attend a school that sounded really expensive.

"Good luck saving him from the prep-schoolers," Richard had said.

"So it couldn't be Benjamin's dad," I reminded her.

"Men," is all she said between tears, as if letting me know how decent and good they can be, while in the same breath, warning me how horribly bad.

As if I didn't already know.

Eight

"In my dreams I am not crippled. In my dreams I dance."
~Louise Brooks

Hope.

AS SOON AS HE WAS DISCHARGED FROM THE HOSPITAL, Charles moved with his family back to Chicago.

On the morning he was discharged, his mother screamed at the officer who said he wanted to question Charles yet another time. "Why are you standing here wanting to question him again? Why aren't you out there finding who did this to my son?"

And to Richard, I thought, but I stayed quiet. The corridor didn't feel big enough for all the fear and anger she felt, and I understood. But even so, when she spoke, I felt like she was warning us that something even worse was about to happen, and I really didn't know what to do with that. Repeatedly, I closed my eyes and tried to imagine her pain in trying to handle what they had done to her son, and to boys like him, over and over through time. Still, I would have ducked down another hallway at the sight of her if I could have. Even from a distance her eyes were forewarnings, that's what I noticed whenever I saw her, or watched her speak, and I did not have many coping skills left, or any bright ideas of how to find any more.

The officer said they were doing everything they could.

"Everything? Please. Do you even know what that means?" Her voice had been pleading, now it was cold. "Do you even *have* a full understanding of how many hate groups target boys like my son? And that Southern California has the highest number of hate groups, more than any other state, and that white supremacy groups have shot up thirty percent in just the last four years? Do you even care? My son was an initiation. An initiation into a racist cult. You know this, right? How you have to kill a black kid to get in? One darkie down, and you're in," she paused and fell quiet for a moment. "And you want to ask *my* son more questions?"

The cop furrowed his brow. Clearly, it seemed like the first time he'd ever come face to face with a force the likes of her. "We don't know all the facts yet, ma'am."

"The facts?" Then she said it again, louder. "The facts! Let me tell you the facts. The only black student and his homosexual teacher are followed, beaten, and dragged to a landfill. How many more facts do you need?"

"Ma'am, if you don't mind?" but when he tried to pass, she stepped in front of him and extended her arm, flexing her hand the way officers do when they want to stop traffic. "I do mind," she said. "The doctor said we could leave and that's exactly what we are doing. We're going home."

"I wouldn't do that, ma'am," he said. But honestly, he looked as if he didn't know what her rights were under the circumstances, or his, for that matter.

I ran up to lay a hand on her arm. "If you leave," I pleaded, "Richard will have to face this alone." I faltered for a second, "I mean he has me...but you can't just *leave*."

She yanked her arm from me like I was an irrational child. "We can and we will," she said. "And whatever do you mean by "face this"? Not one witness has come forward. I think this lily-white town would rather just wait it out until the whole thing blows over. And you! If you hadn't asked him to do such a stupid thing. Michael Jackson? Really? You might as well have asked my son to dance a jig in a minstrel show."

A hush fell over the hallway. No one spoke. Charles' father's eyes remained lowered. It looked as though he'd turned to stone.

A cell phone chimed "Don't Stop 'til You Get Enough". It was like hearing everything that had started innocently enough turn into a horrifying joke before our very eyes. Charles, who'd been watching from the doorway of his room, both hands cupping his bandaged skull, answered, then handed the phone to his father who mumbled something as he walked up to put his arm around his wife's shoulders.

Moments later, Charles, slumped forward as if not wanting to look up, was wheeled forward by a male nurse with dreadlocks stuffed under a hairnet. I heard one officer say to another under his breath that the nurse looked like a black cat in the hat, and I thought how backwards our town really was if an officer of the *law* thought it was okay to say such a thing. "I can't believe you just said that!" I cried. He shot me an irritated look, and turned his back.

I also couldn't believe that Charles would leave without saying goodbye, especially to Richard. I gave him a little wave and I waited for him to wave back. There was a slight flicker in his eyes, and for a second his glance raised up to meet mine, but a wave never came.

The next moments were devastating. I had to lean on the wall to steady myself. One officer walked me to Richard's room where, as soon as I could compose myself he,

Richard, and I walked through the entire evening again. At one point, the officer frowned when we said we did, in fact, walk into the Tiki to order a bottle of champagne for ourselves. Was he implying that this alone might have triggered something, as if Richard had no right to act so pleased with himself, as if drawing attention to himself is not the appropriate thing for someone like Richard to do in our town? I looked at Richard who shook his head at me before running his hand through his hair, forward to back. I knew what he was trying to say—"Stop talking, Lucy. Our feelings don't matter here."

But I was furious. "It's not a crime to celebrate ourselves!" I yelled, louder than I meant to.

The officer, I think because he had no idea what to say, offered Richard coffee. Richard's hand was unsteady. He couldn't hold the cup and spilled most of the dark liquid on his white leg cast. While I tried to wipe it off with a paper towel the officer passed to me—not even thinking of wiping the coffee himself—I stared at Richard's coffee-stained cast and for the first time, I let myself imagine that he might never dance again, and that I might not have the heart for it either.

But as soon as I let that thought out, I felt something rush in to whisk my worst fear away. I don't know what it was exactly, and I suppose it sounds naïve, but if I had to put what I felt into words, they'd sound something like *don't you dare believe that!* And if I were to choreograph it, I'd set a spotlight off in the wings and let it come at me gradually, and then, before fading, it would start to quiver until my worst fear had shaken off—like the sun hovers green just before it slips under Yucca Mountain. (This doesn't only happen over the ocean, people get that wrong, the flash happens here on the desert, too.) That's when I knew Richard would be okay after all the time ahead that wouldn't feel okay.

He would need time to heal, is all.

But he would heal.

I kept telling myself this, until I believed—or I chose to believe, I'm still not sure which—in the kind of hope that can and does come to us in times of high stress, even in the center of a hospital room reeking of disinfectant.

Hisssssss.

Later that evening, I told Richard, "The doctor said you can't go home alone, so that settles it. You're coming home with me."

Both of us were quiet for a while and Richard tried to appear calm, but all you had to do was look into his eyes to know how desperate he felt. Like air hissing out of a balloon, his tragedy had suddenly turned into something even worse—dependence. His expression made me shiver, the kind of trembling that rattles your limbs when you are not the least bit cold, but you start to shake anyway. I didn't know despair could chill the air cooler than the sky at night. "Oh, honey," I said.

And my newly found hopefulness? Well, I pretended otherwise, but it had sort of fizzled away, too. But I'd learned something while caring for my mother, to never come up dry in the optimism department when someone you love is sinking.

The officer asked me again if I saw anyone suspicious in the audience that night.

"It's not easy to pick out any one person under the intense light in your eyes," I said.

He started to press me about this, but the last thing I wanted was to have to give a detailed explanation on the effects of stage lighting. "You'll just have to take my word for it," I said. "The audience is nothing but a blur."

"A blur? Really? Huh."

"Sure..." I began, knowing he was more curious than pointing a finger. People who've never been on stage ask similar questions all the time once the door is opened, but Richard in a low voice said, "Lucy, forget it."

That's when the officer delivered what felt like a too-low blow, letting Richard know he was just another nine-to-five problem. "Well, let's get through the Memorial Day Weekend, shall we? And pick this up again on Tuesday?"

"Tuesday? Okay. Sure. I mean, don't let *me* keep you from your buns and wieners," Richard said, drawing out the words coolly with an edge so sharp, I knew that whatever patience was left in the officer had just been nicked away. He scoffed, as if he'd never thought of Richard as someone he'd ever let talk to him that way. He gave a little snort.

Now it was my turn to hold Richard back. I put my hand on his arm and squeezed.

Richard hunched his shoulders lower. "What? Wiener *schnitzel.* You know. Mustard, pickles, onions?" Then, as if half-expecting the officer to throw on the cuffs if he didn't say it, he added, "sir."

Ttttakatakatakatakatatttt.

The rumors started to fly.

Oh, how they started to fly.

The attack made the local news every night for two weeks. "And a brief mention on national news," Miss Stephanie said. She called about every ten minutes. "Don't worry," she said, "the rumors will die down." But they didn't die down. Online, they came at us like buckshot at the Hi-Desert Gun Club. The truth began to feel like a thin bar of soap slipping through our fingers. We couldn't hold on to it. We felt one post away from losing everything we'd worked so hard for. Everything we held dear was lied about, poked fun at, made fun of.

"Oh, God!" I cried, the next rumor snarling my stomach into a hornet's nest. "Don't they even care what the truth is?"

Richard had his earphones on, but he must have had the volume turned off. "That's not how it works," he said. "The truth is boring compared to what they can make up." He turned his face back toward the screen.

"You'd think they wouldn't be so quick to judge."

"Judging is the point."

Somewhere in the back of my mind I knew all this, but even so, the level of meanness was unbelievable. I pictured hundreds of people at desks and phones and kitchen tables all over San Bernardino County, thumbs and fingers flying over the keys. The image that came at me only made me think more about how I'd learned to identify the feeling inside of me that just *knows* when something has gone too far—when, no matter how much money it makes for some, it's just not better for everyone, especially kids. I screamed,

"It's not true!" as if I was the first person to ever be hurt by the internet.

For days, we read through tweets and posts and blabber. I went to bed every night thinking *who are all these mean people saying all these mean things,* the same thought that woke me first thing in the morning. It was awful.

One post said that I was "inappropriately involved with Charles," or Richard was, or, if you can believe it, all of us at once, insinuating we were "an interracial threesome," posted by someone calling themselves *Hubba-bubba.*

"As if it matters," I screamed, "the interracial part, I mean."

Another, eager to retweet the insinuation, read, "Ménage-a-trois at the Star Struck!" They let us know they really had no idea what they were talking about by adding, "That's what these folks are doing, I think."

Another said we "seduced young students for our own pleasure." A hot prickliness sped up my neck. I turned off my laptop.

The next morning, I thought about staying in bed all day. Eventually I got up, but I did stay inside. Richard threw pillows at the window when a reporter tried to stick his face in. "That's why they're called throw pillows, mother fucker!" he yelled.

The one time Richard let the "F bomb" drop in class, Miss Stephanie said, "I know that word is fashionable now, Richard, but from you it sounds dated." It was a button easily pushed. Richard hates to fall behind. We were maybe fifteen at the time and according to Miss Stephanie, Richard already suffered from *FOMS*—fear of missing something. The blood left his face.

My point is, Richard using the F word was not normal.

I jumped up, grabbed the broom, and started sweeping. When that was done, I descended on the dressing room to wipe every surface down, as well as on the mirrors, until every fingerprint vanished. I next marched upstairs to bake a cake, which is not normal either—not for me anyway—but I was happy to have something to do to give my nerves a breather.

Weeks before, on impulse, I'd piled all the ingredients in my cart—flour, butter, sugar, squares of baker's chocolate left over from Easter—but I never got around to baking it.

We ate the cake in one sitting, scraped the bottom crust off the pan in front of my mother's old TV where, as if to defy the dark cloud that hovered over us, we made a bond with back to back episodes of *The Golden Girls*. I think we both felt our mothers were the only family member either of us could have turned to at a time like this, and four old women living in a house full of old-fashioned furniture became their stand-ins.

"They can still *do* it?" Richard said after Blanche breezed into the kitchen bragging about her sex life. I raised my shoulders in wonder, thinking more about how much up-keep blonde hair must take for a woman her age. I think what calmed us most about the show was that there were no men to speak of. No violence. No threat.

To this day, Blanche, Rose, Dorothy, and Sophia spark a feeling of safety.

But after an entire *week* of Blanche, Rose, Dorothy, and Sophia, Richard gave himself over to the internet again, firing up his laptop. I pulled up a chair. *Ttttakatakatakatakatttt*. "Would you listen to that?" he said. "It's inhaling every lie in the world."

It was the first time I'd ever heard him knock the internet. I was pleased by it, but also a little sad. I don't think that it can ever be totally pleasing when something good happens to someone for a terrible reason.

As the days dragged by, the lies continued, worse than before. Nothing we read bore any resemblance to what really happened, but what did it matter? The lies were out there, like how I'd been seen "sneaking around the Hat Rack Motel" with one of my "many lovers."

"You wish," Richard laughed, looking over at me.

His laugh sounded forced, though, and the sound of it made me think of one of the many times I eavesdropped on Miss Stephanie when she talked on the phone with her sister—"You know what I read?" she said, "that artists tend to have strong opinions." She let out a squeal of delight and then, "I know, I know," as if her sister had made fun of what she just said and all Miss Stephanie could do was agree, "and a strong need to free themselves from the status quo, even sexually. Maybe that's why I slept with him, I don't know, but I'm not going to beat myself up over it." There was a pause. "No, I *don't* care. I get those looks from people around here no matter what. But wait, the author said something else, too. You've got to hear this," at which point she walked over to her desk to get the book and open it. "Female artists will likely have to suffer their female strength, intelligence, and self-confidence, suffer it deeply, because most of the world still prefers only its men strong and sure of themselves." After her sister replied something I couldn't hear, Miss Stephanie's laugh sounded shrill—more high-pitched and forced than if anything was actually funny.

InsiderScudNumber9 said, "that Lucy chick exposes too much skin in jazz class espesially."

"You'd think they'd use the spell check if they want to be credible!" I shouted.

"They don't want to be credible."

"What do they want?" I cried.

"Followers. Fame."

Another, obviously from someone in our one-and-only self-defense class, posted that Richard and I were "all over each other" before we had a "a heated lover's quarrel" and how one of us yelled, "before I kill you with my bare hands!"—as if those actions had anything to do with anything. The post was particularly hard on Richard. He'd taken to calling people over in Palm Springs his "tribe," and I never liked Richard feeling those men had better qualifications for being his tribe than I did. What did they know about his moods, or the way his brow wrinkles when he's thinking, or how sweat drips off the end of his nose at the barre until there's a little puddle on the floor? Secretly, I was glad when the next time Richard plonked down the word "tribe" in reference to them, he put the word "some" in front of it.

But there was one lie that really got to me, more than the others. Mr. Lawson had obviously invented another identity, quoting himself by saying that he had it on good authority from "a man of the law" who saw "them" (meaning Charles and me) "alone at the studio late one night," and how "totally inappropriate" it was for a teacher to "entertain" her students so late. He also said that "they" (meaning Richard and me) "dance wild and half naked at the studio long after business hours," and that he was sure "the other one" (meaning Charles) was there, too.

Immediately, I put two and two together. It was Lawson who'd slammed our door the night Richard and I returned from Palm Springs. True, I wore only a backless camisole and Richard had stripped down to his boxer briefs. "So sue me," Richard said.

"They'll get bored with it and gladly go back to getting toasted in front of the TV," Miss Stephanie said trying to console.

"I surely hope so."

"You *surely* hope so?" Richard said after I hung up. "Fancy language for a ho."

"Not funny, shut up!" and moments later, "I'm sorry." I walked over and tucked myself under his arm.

"Someday we'll look back at all this and laugh," he said, looking down at his cast. "In the meantime, it's not going to be easy..." He trailed off as if he couldn't find the words.

"To show our faces around town?"

"I was going to say to kick Lawson's ass."

"That man just makes me laugh," I said.

"Except you aren't."

I looked at him.

"Laughing," he said. "You aren't laughing,"

Tip of the iceberg.

Miss Stephanie had read something else from her book to her sister—"Women are generally remembered for the worst thing they've ever done, but a man for the best. Now, how biased is that?" her voice soft but serious. I could see her looking down at the page, phone to her ear.

Now that I have firsthand experience, I think the reality is much worse. I think we are remembered for the worst thing people have said about us.

I'm still not sure what word to use for what it feels like to read lies about your sex life detailed next to ads for "3D Crest White," and "Five Foods That Cause You To Bloat," and multiple ways to refinance your mortgage. Every time, it was like I had the wind knocked out of me. I had to stand, get outside, except that meant facing people. Which grocery store to subject myself to was a huge dilemma. As soon as I was out the door, I fixed my eyes on the sidewalk. I questioned every turn to take before I took it. This way? That?

But the real question remained—Was it true what Charles' mother had said about the rising number of hate groups and their initiation rites?

So Richard and I started to research, since our only personal experience regarding hate groups was one Fourth of July when a band of Skinheads rode Harley's through town so loud Miss Stephanie threw open the window and yelled, "Pipe down!" causing my mom to say, "Steph, there is no man smart enough to do what a woman tells him to do with her head stuck out the window."

When one of the men gave her the finger and started to climb off his bike, Miss Stephanie slammed the window shut and ran to lock the door. "Remember that horrible biker?" This is how my mother always began the story, with a wide smile, barely able to contain herself. She thought it was the funniest thing, but I always felt differently. I have lived that scene over and over again so many times in my head over the years that to this day, the sound of a Harley rumbling down Twentynine Palms makes me run over and lock the door.

Skinheads, we soon learned, were only the tip of the iceberg.

From: stephanielivestodance@yahoo.com

To: starstrucklucy@gmail.com

Subject: Lies & Gossip

Dear Lucy,

It's hard to think about anything else when we dance, and that's just what you need, a break, so promise me you'll keep up your daily dance practice. Richard needs a break too, though there's probably a better way I could say that just now.

But Richard would laugh, and that's what matters.

In answer to your question, no. It is not better to know what people are saying. People will say all kinds of mean and hurtful things knowing full well they aren't true, and repeat them so many times they start to believe their own lies. By calling what happened to Richard and Charles "a love triangle" and the like, they think they've put their finger on what went on, and why it did. And nothing is scarier than the great unknown, for most people.

After you read this, I beg you, turn off your laptop. Our minds are not equipped to handle so much constant input, no matter what the tech gurus say to protect their own pockets. Stop staring at your screen and reading the gossip. Think for yourself. Look up at the sky and take your sweet time to reflect. Let the authorities handle the details. They say they are working hard on the case, and I believe them.

How is our boy doing, anyway? I can't bear to think what all the sitting around is doing to our tapping tornado. Make him get up and move around more. I'm no doctor, but I know what makes people depressed. Lack of movement.

How cruel it is for a dancer to live without dancing!

I think I've just confirmed everything I know about hell in that last sentence.

Love,

Stephanie

A lot of silence passed between "Love, Stephanie" and when I finally looked up from my screen. For once there was no leaf blower noise, Jake braking, and the dogs in the neighborhood were quiet for the first time all morning.

It didn't last. But it was the best stillness for a while.

~⚬~

Like soldiers in the trench, the rumors continued to fire over our heads—piercing the air, exploding as they hit. They sat on the couch with Richard, got into bed with me. They were there in the morning when I woke, at the barre when I stretched. The only thing that brought any level of peacefulness to the air was sleeping.

And so, we slept.

At all hours of the day.

I slept until—and I could count on this happening— some sound would startle me awake and I'd lie there feeling all this humming in the air. I'd throw my legs over the side of the bed, walk to the bathroom to fish my dirty clothes out of the hamper, slam the lid of my laptop down and place it on the bottom of the hamper, then stack all the clothes in a heap on top of it again. I must have done this a dozen times during those awful weeks.

Back in bed, the hum would begin to dissipate, and not only in my head. I'm not saying the moonlight slanted in some new magical way, or that my entire relationship to technology turned into a spiritual awakening or anything. That's not what happened, but something in the air definitely felt calmer once my laptop was out of sight. And not to sound crazy, but I noticed a deeper shade of green start to rise from the wallpaper and even my bedspread felt softer.

When I said as much to Richard he said, "You're probably highly sensitive to electromagnetic wavelengths, since you're so sensitive about everything else ..." as if he meant to be helpful.

"That worries me," I said, imagining millions of tiny spears hissing through the air. The image made me understand that if I didn't take Miss Stephanie's advice and silence them from time to time, they would surely silence *me*.

"There'd be something wrong with you if you weren't worried," Richard said. "Hey, come look at this, you won't believe—"

"No, I don't want to look. I don't want to know. Miss Stephanie is right, we have to stop reading the posts."

He didn't say anything. He didn't even look up.

"Richard?"

He was having none of it.

"Richard!?"

"Jeez, okay, you're such a control-freak. Fuck!" he said, pushing away from the screen without dragging his eyes away.

Actually, he didn't say the word this time so much as he struck me with it. I stared at him. And my next thought had nothing to do with magnetic waves, or the fact that Richard was swearing again, but that we had become a living, breathing master class living under the same roof.

Patience, 101.

⌒⌒⌒

A few parents called to say they didn't believe the gossip. "Oh, please," Mrs. Prusso said, surprised I answered on the first ring. "If I believed everything spread about me in this town," and then she paused for a second. "Well, let's just say people are full of opinions about women who stand out. My mother always said, 'Nancy, it's hard to fit in when you stand out.'" I thought her telling me this was sort of sweet, even if it felt nothing like what we were going through. But no one, not even she, had called to register for summer workshop. That she hadn't registered Lisy felt deliberate, but I was too afraid to ask her why.

"Classic Nancy Prusso," Richard said.

"At least she called," I said, trying to be positive because I didn't want to jinx our only call. "When she asked how many students had signed up for Ballet II, I sort of lied when I said it all looks good."

"You *sort* of lied? No, you lied."

"It was nice of her to ask, though."

He glared at me. There was an edge to his voice, and his mouth frowned as if full of annoyance. "She's the worst gossip and you know it. She only called to find out if anyone else had called. Did she register?"

"No, but I'm sure she will." I shook my head. I wasn't sure at all.

Over the next few days, enrollment for summer classes went down to five students, and not one was Lisy. And after the first week when only one of the five showed up, I had no choice but to cancel classes altogether, but not for good. No part of me would believe it. "Only until September," I told Richard. "September is the kick off to a whole new dance year. Everyone will be excited to dance again by September!" I said, trying to sound cheerful, but Richard did not look up from his laptop and he showed no spark of enthusiasm, as if the light in his eyes had vacated, as surely it will for a dancer who can't dance.

The day wore on. The sun had nearly set. Any lingering light that filled the studio was softened by twilight. Minutes later I was in tears. "The Star Struck is my *life!*" I cried to Miss Stephanie. "And I'm wearing my worst slippers, just in case."

"Just in case of what?" she said.

"In case I can't afford to keep the Star Struck."

"Oh, Lucy. Not your grubbies?"

That was her nickname for our worst rehearsal slippers. More than once she'd made me throw away my duct-taped grubbiest when she couldn't stand them any longer. "Toss the grubbies!" she'd say. Hearing the word again broke the dam in my chest. "I have no family," I cried. "My students *are* my family."

"What you need to remember," she said to calm me, "is that dancers rarely live a conventional life, Lucy, we aren't a Norman Rockwell kind of family. We seldom, if ever, sit around a table for hours and hours. There's too much to *do*." I think she was afraid I was *this* close to throwing in the towel. She then said something that has stayed with me ever since—"What I'm trying to say is our table doesn't have four legs because it's not a table, really. It's a dance floor—that's where we bring people together. And without studio space we grow positively desperate. So, do what you have to do in order to keep the Star Struck, be resourceful. Hell, be calculating if you have to. Just don't let go of your studio. Find a way to keep it. Persevere. And remember, you will have to redefine this part of your life from time to time. It's the only way to continue doing what you love."

Her words, sincere and embracing, gripped me like a yucca vine—soft emphasis on hard truths, that was her style. I was shaking when I hung up. I tried to hold my relevé, but like a flame trying to catch, I kept falling out of it.

"Hold your core!" Richard yelled, teasingly. I hadn't known he was watching.

"We can't just lie down and give up like cows in a lightning storm, can we?" I said.

"What do you think?"

Not knowing what I thought, exactly, I watched as he dragged himself through the door with his arms. And nothing makes you more afraid for a dancer than watching him pull himself on all fours, but I think he crawled just to show me how good I had it compared to him, but not heartlessly. Still, the sight of him struggling would have done me in, except for the fact that it felt like a privilege to witness the most enduring persistence. It prompted me to say—with a confidence that surprised me, since I didn't feel all that confident—"I'm going to start renting out the studio by the hour."

"What?"

"I have to."

"Okay, you are making me a little queasy," he said, sitting up now.

"We could make this overly dramatic if you insist," I said, "but there is no putting off the rent."

"But who would you rent *to*?" he said, raising his voice.

"That's the number one question," I said. "I'm just going to have to figure it out as I go along."

~~~

The next morning, I offered the morning hours to Karen Holloway.

When Karen Holloway—middle-aged but seeming younger—first moved to town, she'd knocked on my door to ask about availability. At the time, I had none since the morning hours I used to prepare for afternoon classes that lasted until evening. "Oh, really?" she said, her mouth tightening as if pulled taut from either side, making it clear that she didn't believe me. She was also an ex-body builder, she'd boasted, and if you can imagine accomplishing so much in one lifetime, also an ex-CEO of something having to do with money—mostly making lots of it. "Just call me Kar," she said. "Everyone calls me Kar."

I could not imagine calling her Kar.

She took a step forward to look past me into the studio and said she'd moved to Yucca Springs to teach yoga and "save myself from the cutthroat hell of corporate America," which didn't surprise me. It was the first thing I noticed about her—how no matter how chirpy she tried to sound, she still blared ruthlessness. So much so that even if I had the hours, I would have flat out refused to rent to her.

"Wait, no. You're not seriously thinking of renting to that phony woman with quadriceps that defy nature?" Richard cried, pulling himself into a standing position. "No-no-*no*."

"Everyone does yoga now."

"Since when do we care what everyone is doing?" He rubbed his unshaven cheeks with both hands. "Oh? So now you are going to fill our dance studio with people who don't even want to move to music? No teacher has a right to bore her students to death like that."

"What she *has* is enough students to pay me fifty bucks an hour."

He formed a fist like he wanted to hit something. He started to thump the inside of his other hand—*punch, punch, punch*, the way pitchers do in a baseball game before they throw the ball. I knew he wasn't mad at me, but at the world. Which in my view, fully deserved it.

"I have to find a way," I said, Miss Stephanie's words still fresh in mind. I checked out my reflection in the mirror to see if I looked like a resourceful person. But that the only way to hold on to the Star Struck meant having to rent to someone I didn't like felt like handing over too *much*. I even resented Karen's ability to pay me, something I would not have resented under normal circumstances.

Later, when Miss Stephanie said she thought the experience would be good for me—that sometimes we have to sacrifice more than we want to—I wanted to think she was right, but I didn't. "I'm not sure I want my decisions to be good for me," I said. "Like eating beets. I want my decisions to *feel* right." *True as my heartbeat, sound as its rhythm.* Hadn't she taught me that? Still, I thought maybe I'd gone too far. I could hear it in her voice before we hung up. It's easy to forget about someone else's feelings when you are stressed.

Five minutes later, she called back. "I've rethought what I said and I'm sorry. Find someone else to rent to. A masseuse? Wedding receptions?"

I remember trying to talk myself out of what I suspected to be true about Karen, as though there were two of me and only one of us was allowed to worry. I knew Richard was right about her, too. I also knew we would have to wait for whatever thing that would prove it. *This must be the calculating part,* I thought.

In the meantime, I'd be able to cover the rent. Which was a good thing.

So why did it feel so bad?

The number one answer.

"It's *meeeeee*," Karen called out as soon as she opened the door.

I wanted to be the kind of professional who would treat Karen with the utmost respect, as if she were no more or less important to me than anyone else. But as soon as I heard her voice, my insides greeted her with as much enthusiasm as it welcomes the flu.

Richard was more vocal. "Her voice sets my teeth on edge," he grumbled, hobbling into the bathroom and slamming the door. From inside he yelled, "I can't stand that woman!"

Karen looked at me without turning her head to give Richard's comments any notice, which made *me* notice the lines around her eyes crinkle when she said, "Wouldn't it be great if we had a nice mat outside our door so people could wipe their feet?" she said, tossing her head casually.

Minutes later, when she pulled herself up into a handstand, I had the urge to walk right up and push her over. I gave the banister a smack on my way up the stairs, causing Karen—who, even upside down, didn't miss a thing—to wobble and nearly fall over. I smiled to myself thinking how I could have whacked her head just as hard without the slightest *tch, tch, tch* from my professional side. As soon as she left, I ran downstairs. "Can you believe she said that?" I said, trying to restrain the anger in my voice.

"I wanted to throw a roll of toilet paper at her. I had it in my hand."

"To say *we*—to call it *our* door."

Richard shook his head. "To act so cool when clearly, there are flames sizzling out of her ears."

"What I don't understand is how yoga takes credit for all the stretches we do." Even I, who considers myself receptive, was a little surprised to hear myself say this.

"At twice the speed, with our toes pointed, while keeping time to the music and remembering the choreography. I'm just saying. They look like they're taking a nap." We laughed. "But seriously, we can't trust her. She's dishonest. I can tell by the way her eyes won't look into yours when she talks to you. Which is kind of funny since she's all 'yoga is the most authentic movement,' and all."

A sliver of dread I was trying to hide even from myself poked a hole in my resolve. I fear dishonesty more than anything. "I'll be right upstairs and you'll be right outside the door. She won't be able to pull anything funny." And with that I took the stairs up two at a time, trying to put distance between myself and anything else that could possibly go wrong. Too much of my energy was working overtime already trying to pretend that everything would be okay, which sort of worked before Karen entered the picture.

But not so well anymore.

I was having a few selfish thoughts, too. At one point, I tried to convince myself that I was hurting as much as Richard was—that verbal attacks cut just as deep as physical ones. But all I had to do was watch him try to lift himself off the couch to realize that no matter how reasonable this comparison may have sounded at 3 a.m., it wasn't true by morning.

"She left cooties on the floor!" he yelled after me.

I didn't really believe she left cooties, but I made a mental note—*Lysol*.

"I think I've made a big mistake," I whined to Miss Stephanie two days later.

She took a big breath. "You know, I used to wish I could go back and delete all of my mistakes, but now I realize I am the person I am *because* of my mistakes."

I couldn't quite imagine what it was like to be looking back on my life yet. I suppose that's why I said, "But *your* mistakes are better than most people's accomplishments. You're lucky."

"Oh, that's not true," she said without pausing. "And not only because luck has nothing to do with personal success for most of us. We focus. We work hard. We keep at it even when we are exhausted and growing a little overwhelmed by it. As far as the business end, most of the time I was not quite able to pay the bills, but not quite going under either. My mistakes can make me laugh now, so I am lucky about that, at least."

I was sure she was making light of her success to make me feel better. My mother once said that Yucca

Springs enjoyed a front row seat to Miss Stephanie's accomplishments. "Oh, I don't know. She's not so great," my father piped in, waving a hand in annoyance.

My mother let it pass, but I'd come to the end of my rope with his negative comments about Miss Stephanie. "She is too!" I said quickly. "Smart people know how to live a smart life." My mother and I looked at each other, I'm sure both of us thinking what I managed to say next, "And that makes dull people jealous."

The room grew quiet, a slow dark stillness creeping through the air. I wanted to say something else to break the silence, but I heard the unsaid warning my mother spoke as strongly as I could hear the shrill, clear cry of a hawk.

Let it gooooooo.

The next morning, I snuck down the steps to watch Karen's class and Richard was right, they did look as though they might be napping—their bodies were level with the floor, their eyes were closed, their expressions blank. *Were* they sleeping? I couldn't help but compare their class to my own where there isn't a moment when we aren't moving or smiling or both.

Richard was sitting against the wall in the sun that bolted through the window, pretending to read a magazine, his leg propped up on a pillow. "I can't get that awful *om* sound out of my head," he whispered loudly. I held my finger to my lips.

"Breathe *innnnnnn*," Karen said, lungful of air. "Let it *gooooooo. Relaaaaax.*"

"How much more relaxed can they get?" Richard whispered.

Two of Karen's older students were dressed in matching red track suits. One tried to do the downward facing dog while connected to an oxygen tank, while the only man in the class struggled through without ever sitting up or turning over, his legs remaining straight out in front. Everyone else looked pretty fit and strong. One woman had on leggings with a fold of aqua blue fabric at the waist, and she was flexible. She even managed that leg thingy around her ear. I felt a pang of jealousy that she hadn't signed up for ballet. Someone's little boy stood in front of the mirror, fascinated by his own reflection, and it was all I could do to keep from yelling "step away from the mirror!" but it was too late. His hands smeared the glass.

After their last pose and what seemed like another nap, they rewarded themselves by eating frozen yogurt right out of the carton. Karen pulled white plastic spoons and napkins out of her handy cooler, right under the NO EATING IN THE STUDIO sign. I whispered sharply, "You are testing my last nerve."

"Oh sure, *now* they smile," Richard said.

But when Karen and the man started to use the spoons as swords, jokingly at first, Karen suddenly turned red in the cheeks as she dove for the last scoop of Safeway Select.

I gasped. People stepped back.

"Did you see that?" Richard sat up straight. "Her eyes bugged out! She'd gore him to a pulp rather than lose. She reminds me of... who does she remind me of?"

"Jim Jones?" I said.

Some people might grow more serious after witnessing something like this, but we started to laugh, covering our mouths at first as if we couldn't quite believe our own behavior. Richard collapsed onto the floor, laughing hysterically, maybe too. Between breaths, and with tears in our eyes, we shook with laughter. After a moment, Richard said, "I would like to choreograph this moment someday."

"Choreography as consequence," I said as soon as I came up for air, remembering what I read about choreography created as an after-effect of our own best and worst experiences.

As if on cue, Karen marched out the door without saying anything so Richard did the sexy upper-body gyrating sequence while circling his arms in front of his chest and saying, "Uh-huh, uh-huh, uh-huh."

I thought how people are always saying that nothing lasts forever, but I don't think it's true. We will have *this* funny memory between us always, thank you very much.

Ommmm.

Like Richard, a day did not go by when Karen's class didn't cause me to resent the spooky *om* sound and make me want to run back upstairs to two Bayer and a hot bath, but there was something else troubling me, something deeper. Other than my simmering jealousy that Karen had a full class to teach and I didn't, something else felt fundamentally wrong. If the latest thing is to try so hard to let *gooooooo,* won't the rest of us have to be even more proactive or nothing difficult—like finding out who hurt Richard and Charles and why—will ever get done?

And a day did not go by when I didn't throw on my sweatpants as soon as yoga was over and run downstairs to "cleanse the contradictions," as we'd taken to calling it, throwing open all of the windows and turning on both fans before moving through my routine—warm-up stretches, pliés, barre, combinations. I felt guilty passing Richard on the couch, but I had to dance and he never once made me feel bad about it. For hours, I was lost in the movement—my sense of balance returned to me, the music fading only if I thought about what Charles' mother had said about me.

Or what everyone else had said about me.

Neither did a day go by that we didn't go over to Richard's old place so I could finish packing up the rest of his belongings before driving him to physical therapy.

Fortunately for us, the therapist was Dr. Goff, father of Kayla, one of our senior students, who'd stayed with ballet right up through high school. He called Richard in the hospital as soon as he heard about the attack to say, "As soon as they discharge you, come into my office."

"Oh," Richard said, the painkillers slowing his speech, "Dr. Goff ... I ... um ... never bothered to sign up for health insurance. I guess that was a mistake."

"Don't worry about that. Just come in."

"Should I?" Richard asked me as soon as he hung up.

"Of course you should. Everyone says the rehab center is just awful. I mean, gifts like this," I said remembering what my mother said to Miss Stephanie when she stopped charging my mom once my dad was gone—"don't just fall in your lap every day." She'd meant not having to pay for my classes, but it came out sounding like she meant my dad's passing, and I saw the blood leave her face before the two of them burst into laughter.

Oh, did I mention that Dr. Goff owns the building that houses the Star Struck?

According to Miss Stephanie, in the early days of the studio, Dr. Goff had a wife but also an obvious crush on the only other dad who came to pick up his daughter, and apparently a soft spot for the studio ever since. So when the building came up for sale and there was no way Miss Stephanie could afford to buy it, he bought it and leased it back to her at "a price I could afford," she said. "I've been hoping he'd step in to help Richard. He's a good man, Lucy. The best." I wondered if she'd asked Dr. Goff to step in to help Richard, but I never asked and she never volunteered. Our lives were so upside-down, I was happy for any luck that came our way. I hardly wanted to question it.

Dr. Goff was generous, that much I already knew. On the first day of class, he was the only parent ever who offered to pay for the entire year of classes upfront, plus the recital fee and costume deposit. "In case I forget," he said. *You are not the kind of man who forgets,* I thought. He reminds us that there will always be some people who are generous by nature, who don't listen to gossip, who do the right thing—like his telling us straight away that two people had called him to offer more rent for our building—and how a small town can be extremely supportive and kind when it isn't busy being exactly the opposite—like when a certain someone who shall remain nameless (Karen Holloway) would have loved to see me go under so she could turn the Star Struck into the Skinsational Yoga Retreat & Day Spa.

Or when a certain someone who shall remain nameless (Walter Lawson) approached Dr. Goff about the Star Struck's availability and tried to convince Dr. Goff that a day spa was a better way to "utilize" his property. Obviously the librarian was out, and Karen was in. He even had the gall to say, "As a businessman, Goff, you have a responsibility to invest in our community's future."

"Like you have a responsibility to invest in your marriage's future by sneaking around town with Ms. Holloway?"

"You said that?" I said, both shocked and pleased—that wonderful combination.

"He got the response he deserved."

"Take *that*, you old cheat," I said, turning toward the window.

So the vultures were circling.

Looking back now, I wonder how it could be that not until Dr. Goff shared this news with us did we realize the greed that had been brewing as a result of our misfortune. No rumors, no gossip, not a whisper, had come flying through cyberspace to us about that.

Miss Stephanie said it was a good lesson of how sneaky pillars of the community can be when you hold the lease to good business visibility with designated parking. "Human greed can turn your stomach," she said.

Later that evening she called again to say Richard deserved whatever Dr. Goff offered. "Let us not forget that Kayla has two left feet," she said to reassure us. "And a broken watch has a better sense of timing."

Nine

*"Someone once said that dancers work just as hard
as policemen, always alert, always tense.
But see; policemen don't have to be beautiful at the
same time."*

~George Balanchine

Finally!

I picked up the phone to call Richard's family again. I punched in the next to last digit, but I couldn't press the last. Richard said his father and brother were the last people in the world he wanted to see, but I wasn't sure I believed him. I'd wait another day or so and try calling again. Still no answer on his father's line, just an answering machine with no greeting. I must have tried a dozen times to think of what to say. Not once could I find the words. On his brother's phone, a curt message, as if smug was what he was going for—"You know what to do."

I hung up. "No I don't," I said.

Richard talked a few times about his relationship with his brother. "The only thing John and I ever agreed on was that we didn't have a whole lot to say to each other." We were eating mini pizzas made on English muffins right out of the microwave—the only appliance Richard owned— set up next to the sink in the studio bathroom. "It looks like a Booth cartoon in here," he said after plugging it in, the black cord running along the wall over the sink. The "ding" was so loud it echoed through to my apartment and it took him forever to hobble from the couch to the oven, but I didn't offer to help. Dr. Goff's strict instructions to me were to let Richard move around as much as possible, and to not coddle him. Richard chewed fast, like he always did when itching to say something, swallowed and said, "Last time we talked, he said that I was like a Jewish person in that I needed to live in numbers to be safe and that I should move to San Francisco, but, and I quote, *not* to San Mateo." He went still for a moment. "He hates me."

"I'm sure he doesn't hate you," I said. "Do you really think he hates you?"

"Yeah, I do."

My insides folded. Richard's folded, too. It showed immediately. He pushed his pizza toward me and I gave him the cheese off mine. "Do you think you should at least let them know what happened to you?"

"My father still reads the Hi-Desert News. Did he contact me? No."

I changed the subject. "I never could figure out why they changed the name to Hi-Desert instead of H-I-G-H," I said, spelling out the word. He hobbled off and came back with an old newspaper, the High Desert News, and pointed at a photo of our class standing on stage. "The word 'high' was starting to make people nervous," he said. "They didn't want pot farmers moving in." I stared at the photo. Miss Stephanie's head was thrown back in a big open laugh, frozen in time.

Once, I went as far as buying a get well card and putting Richard's father's address in the corner, but just before mailing it to Richard, I tore it up. It would have been wrong for me to go that far. If my own father were alive, would he be the one to comfort me through this? Not on your life. The closest I can come to an image of my father helping me emotionally are his tail lights pulling away. I used to watch those lights the way I did the much-too-blue jeans my mother bought me at Walmart. I couldn't wait for them to fade.

When I brought up his family again, Richard said, "Look, I know you mean well, but there are some things a family can't get over. The last straw for your mom was your dad's cheating, right? And," he thought for a minute. "The last straw for a Catholic father is when his fifteen year old daughter gets pregnant. Remember the Santiago family? How Camila's dad wouldn't even look up from the sidewalk when we passed, ashamed to accept even the simplest 'hola?' Well, for my father, the last straw was me. The queer. Let it go."

So that's what I did. I let go of trying to contact Richard's family, mostly because I had none of my own left to deal with.

But once Richard admitted that he wasn't able to sleep at night, and if he did fall asleep, the nightmares were awful and he'd wake in a sweat, afraid to go back to sleep, I insisted we move the couch out of the foyer into the more private space of the studio. I could do that much for Richard, at least. When Karen objected, I held up my hand like I was the county sheriff directing Swap Meet traffic. "Don't!" I warned, stepping right up to her face where her lips, I noticed, were newly puffy and swollen. She glared at me with her hands on her hips. Forced to deal with an unfamiliar sense of herself (as in someone who didn't always get her way), she threw up her hands and said, "fine," as she looked around the room as if about to decide where the couch would be the most hidden and I held up my hand again.

"Pincushion-lips?," I said later to Richard, shifting the laundry basket I was carrying from one arm to the other. "It's sad."

He narrowed his eyes. "Desperate lips," he said and went back to photographing his cast from every angle.

Karen started bringing her own Indian-print blanket to cover the couch before her students arrived. As soon as we heard her key in the door, Richard would hobble outside and stay there until yoga was over—the furious bang of his broom handle on the floor as he made his way out the back door was a reminder of what long, hard travel it was between the lobby and the lawn chair. I could hardly bear the sound.

When I looked out the window, the glow of his laptop was like a low-lying morning star.

A week later, Richard was still asleep when the studio line rang. I ran down the stairs. The man's voice on the other end didn't belong to the officer I'd been calling every couple of hours and then, as the weeks passed, every couple of days for updates, but to a man who introduced himself as Rivers White. "The investigator assigned to the Myers case," he said.

"Oh," I caught my breath. "Let me put you on the phone to Richard, then." My heart raced.

When Richard hung up, he said he kept imagining the man's middle name as "Is-So-Very." We laughed but we never, not for an instant, believed, naïvely, that we could get through the next phase without solid, mature direction. We were too ignorant about the law to not be at the mercy of a guiding professional to help us through the maze of rules and rulings, if only one would step forward and apparently, one just had. The man called it an investigation, but it felt like more to us. It was as if we could finally hand a part of the nightmare over. So, to me, he appeared less like an investigator and more like a guardian angel dropped from the sky to offer protection. *Richard*, I had thought a hundred times, *I am your best friend and I love you, but we, together, are not enough to handle this. Not by ourselves. Not this time.*

That night, just before falling asleep, I felt a charlie-horse come on strong in my calf. I hopped on one foot to the fridge to swallow a gulp of apple cider vinegar—"high in potassium!" Miss Stephanie had preached—and in the middle of the night I woke from another spasm, even sharper. I rubbed and massaged until the muscle relaxed. Desperate for a sign, any sign, I thought that with any luck, the tension in our lives might begin to ease up, too. I know how crazy this sounds, but at the time, I honestly believed my cramp was an insight.

But the next few days were anything but easing.

As the days passed without another word from Rivers, Richard became hysterical from the smallest things—the tingling under his cast sent him into a tizzy. He went to pieces when the kids passed by the window on skateboards, their youthful cries made him nosedive onto the couch.

All I could do is let patience play its part and try not to say anything. There are times when words, even well-intended ones, do more harm than good, I knew this. I also knew Richard just needed an excuse to let off steam, and for a few moments he'd found one. Afterwards, he'd cross his arms in victory and fall back down again, dropping onto the couch with a self-possessed plop.

And then our guardian angel knocked on the door.

He was tall and well-mannered, except he wouldn't remove his hat when I offered to take it. In a black suit and tie, though it was nearly a hundred degrees outside, Rivers White looked intently at Richard's cast. "I can't tell as much while it's still on," he said shaking his head.

"Wait," Richard said, and as if he'd been planning it all along, pulled a small hand-saw out from under the couch cushion and started to saw at his cast. Little pieces of white plaster littered the floor. I noticed the fine groove already cut, as if he'd been working on it a little at a time like a prison mate digging for escape. I ran upstairs to call Dr. Goff.

"I wondered what happened to my panel saw," he said. "I'll be right over."

Rivers bent down on his right knee and glued his eyes on Richard's bruises. It didn't take long for him to conclude that Richard had been hit with something metal "like a pipe," but not a wooden baseball bat like Richard thought he remembered. He also said that the attack was "in all likelihood" targeted, a hate crime. "But there's no proof of that," he said. "Not yet."

"But look at his leg. What other proof do we need?" I said. "It doesn't make sense."

"Nothing about assault ever makes sense until we fit all the pieces together, maybe not even then. The only given," he said, pulling on disposable gloves before picking up the removed cast and putting it in a large clear plastic bag, "is that on the evening of the attack, two men drove to Yucca Springs."

"But we already know that," Richard said.

"My job is to prove they did so with the sole intent of harming you and your friend."

Fear passed over Richard's face. "Charles," he said, "was my *student.*"

Rivers looked at Richard. The sticking point for Richard, I think, was that Rivers didn't say anything back. Richard must have convinced himself that it was an act of aggression to turn a blind eye to what he said, so he pulled on his ear and said it again. "Charles was my student. Not my friend." And looking back on it, I can see that touchiness might not have been the right response to someone offering to help us, but for Richard—I guess the simplest way to put it is that he felt he had so little left but the truth.

"No worries," Rivers said with no trace of caring one way or the other, and that helped Richard relax, even though we learned that it's nearly impossible to prosecute without courtroom-solid evidence, nearly impossible to prosecute without a witness, nearly impossible to prosecute without security camera footage, and that the cameras at the garbage dump hadn't worked in over a year. "But I have a few leads," Rivers said.

"You do?" Richard and I said at once.

"I'll be in touch," he said, and with that, he tipped his hat and was off.

Seconds later, Dr. Goff stuck his head through the window. Obviously, he'd waited for Rivers to leave before barging in, but it looked more comical than that. He reminded me of one of those old Jack-in-the-Boxes where the head pops up out of nowhere. "You know it's wrong to steal, right?" he said to Richard teasingly as soon as he was inside.

"Um-hmmm," Richard said coyly.

I expected River's visit to relieve us, but it only made us more anxious, just like I expected Richard to feel calmed once he was free of his cast. But instead, our worry doubled by the look of his leg underneath—part of his calf was shrunken in on itself. The other part was as swollen as a balloon, right down to his foot where the space between his toes were mere slits. His toenails were yellowed and long and I'm sorry to say this, but I let out a disgusted noise. Hard as I tried to keep my voice steady when I apologized, it wavered. I kept my eyes on his toes and I wanted to smooth lotion on them and trim the toenails, but I knew it would be too much an invasion on Richard's pride, so I let Dr. Goff do the clean-up work.

"Toe fangs," Richard said, wiggling his toes.

"Now the real work begins," Dr. Goff said. He rinsed a towel under the sink and ran it over Richard's legs.

"Ooo, cold," Richard said in a tone that sailed through the air, making a beeline from Richard to Dr. Goff. *Smitten,* I thought. Whenever my mother saw romance in the works, she'd say, "They're smitten," in a way that made me see that it was something she could have used more of herself.

"It's a good sign you can feel that," Dr. Goff said.

Richard shrugged. "Maybe I'll run in the Palm Desert Marathon tomorrow."

"It's only a half-marathon," Dr. Goff said, amused. "Shouldn't be a problem."

My face felt hot suddenly, flushed. I turned my back and ran upstairs to call Miss Stephanie. "I can't believe how fast they fell for each other," I said, nearly breathless.

"Actually, I think he's had eyes for Richard for some time."

"Really?" I said, surprised. I knew if she wasn't sure, she wouldn't have said it—blurting out something she'd regret.

"Though I could be wrong... " she said, leaving the only reply that didn't escape either of us hanging in the air— *Except we both know better.*

Dr. Goff worked Richard's legs until Richard was nearly in tears.

I'd turned the volume of the phone down when Rivers pulled up, so it was only after Dr. Goff left (as in jogged off with a great big smile on his face), that we listened to the new message from Miss Stephanie: "Stephanie here. Listen, Lucy. After we hung up, I was contacted by the investigator, Rivers White? We talked and he got me to thinking about that boy Joey again. Remember Joey? I know, who could forget him? Anyway, I never told you this but the drawing on the bathroom stall wasn't the only one. There were others. I fished one out of the trash and I found another in his shoe cubby. I tore the first one up. I just didn't want to think about it, which I know is wrong, but I think I begrudged that boy even though I know a mistreated child isn't to blame in any way. But I know I saved the second drawing. I stuck it somewhere, in a book I think, I can't remember. My instincts just told me to hold on to it. So when Rivers asked me if there was ever a student who made me nervous or uncomfortable in any way, or did anything out of the ordinary that made the act difficult to overlook, well, Joey came straight to mind."

My ears pricked. There was a change of tone in her voice when she said the name Rivers, as if they were old friends. Richard heard it too, I could see it in his eyes.

She went on. "And his father was just awful, bad-tempered and vulgar. The only time he picked Joey up, he dragged him out of the waiting room by his ear. By his ear! I wanted to call the police. I should have. I don't know why I didn't. Anyway, Rivers is coming to San Diego to talk to me, did he tell you that? He wants to see the drawing, so that's what my sister and I are doing tonight. We're going through every book of mine until I find it. I told him I could just mail it to him, but he said he could use the drive, which I found a little odd, don't you? But he sounded very... nice. Just know that I carry you both in my heart every day." After a pause, "I'm sure I saved the drawing. It's just a little matter of finding it."

Her sister's voice followed in the background. "And that's a *big* little."

We played the message back a second time.

"She's right, you know. Miss Steph has a *lot* of books," Richard said, turning his head away from the phone to look out the window.

She *was* right. The first time I laid eyes on Miss Stephanie's apartment there were books every which way—on her bed, in piles on the floor, four even stacks made up legs for a coffee table where more books were scattered on top.

My hair was pulled back and suddenly I couldn't stand the tightness another second. I pulled out my rubberband and let my hair fall free. Richard sighed, as if releasing my hair gave him permission to stop staring out the window, and say something he'd been afraid to. But when he opened his mouth, nothing came out. I could tell by his reaction that he was glad things were finally moving along, but he and I were just so far in over our heads, that I think the feeling stalled in his throat. He looked down at his leg. "Disgusting or what?"

"Hideous," I said.

Ten

"Dancing is the world's favorite metaphor."
~Kristy Nilsson

Highly lasagna-able.

TOGETHER, RICHARD AND I DECIDED TO DELAY REOPENING the Star Struck until the case was settled, whatever that meant—we really had no idea. I cringed at the thought of September rolling around. I told myself the year off would not only give Richard more time to heal, but me time to work on choreography.

"No way we're giving this more than a year," Richard said looking away. Since we were kids, we met each other's eyes and held them for a few seconds when we were dead serious, but I knew he wasn't any more sure of what he meant by "this" than I was. Closing the studio? Is that what he meant? Or the legal process we felt helpless within?

"Definitely not," I said stepping back, almost tripping over the catalogue he'd left on the floor. I think that was the worst of it for both of us, how much uncertainty seemed to penetrate everything around us, even the air. It made me think of when I spread my mother's ashes. I had thought they'd blow away light as pollen, but they didn't. I had no idea how heavy and sticky they'd be. I had no choice but to keep shaking them out, but I did not expect the effort to be so graceless and clumsy, and I had never been so upset.

The memory is still so upsetting, I had to throw a skirt over my tights and take a walk to Star Market to fill my basket with three kinds of grated cheese, two jars of Ragu, a box of noodles, and a mound of red peppers to roast under the broiler, all the makings of my mother's lasagna. "To lift my spirits," I told the checker, Colleen, who smiled in her easy way I've known my whole life. "Your mom made me a lasagna once and I thought I'd died and gone to Eye-talian heaven." I flinched at the mispronunciation, but I loved hearing stories about my mother around town. The grateful stories, I mean.

I stood in the aisle feeling for the firmest pepper skins, remembering what my mother had said—how I should pick out the peppers because I had touchy sensitivity in my fingertips. "Actually, you can be touchy about *every*thing, so you pick out the peppers," is what she said, and her saying so hurt my feelings. My heart started beating higher up in my chest and I just wanted to get away from her. She knew what she said bothered me because she said it *to* bother me. She was just like that sometimes, despite the fact that neither of us really knew why or what to do about it. When she tried to cover it with her best apology smile, her lips grew too tight to really mean it and we both knew that, too. (I'm learning to stop and let in memories like this, even the ones I'd rather not remember. When I can recall exactly what she said and how she said it, I don't even try to leave out the sting, as much as I might like to.) After that, I kept my eyes down and avoided eye contact. When we got to checkout, she told Colleen that I'd selected every one of the peppers myself so she knew they were perfect, still trying to make up with me. As soon as we were in the sunlight, she put her arm around my shoulders to give me a little squeeze and I let her. I could never stay mad at her for long.

That's what I remember now whenever I see peppers— red, green, yellow, it doesn't matter. I walk right up and let the weight of them fall on me. And then I squeeze one of each.

"No," I tell Colleen when she asks if I'm having a special friend over to dinner, but not in a nosey way, just making conversation. "Just Richard."

"Give that boy my love, will you?"

"I will."

"You take care now, " she said handing me my receipt.

How little it takes to cheer someone up, I thought. *A smile. A few kind words.* I headed out of the store, arms in a bear hug around my bag.

"What's this?" Richard said eyeing the bag.

"No big deal," though it was. "It's just," I had to think about it. "I was remembering something my mother said," I said, holding up the bag and starting for the stairs, "so I bought all this."

"I get it," Richard said. "I love my yellow loafers," he caught himself. "My yellow loa*fer*, mostly because yellow was my mother's favorite color. She and I bought them together at a shop in El Paseo."

"You never told me that," I said, feeling even worse about asking him to tone himself down the one time. "I didn't know she bought them for you."

"I'm telling you now. And she didn't. She was with me, but I paid. She thought they were crazy. She thought *I* was crazy, but they made her laugh."

It had taken him such a long time, years, to tell me this story.

"But it's weird, because if I look in the mirror now and see her face, I start stretching my cheeks and straightening the skin around my eyes." All during this exchange he is forced to basically crawl up the stairs using only his arms. Half way up, he took a break. When he finally jimmied himself up the last step, I could see his chest muscles expanding and contracting under his T-shirt. I brought my wooden spoon to my forehead in salute.

"It's not exactly bungee jumping, " he said eyeing the table settings. "Lucy, why are there three plates?"

"I thought we'd invite Dr. Goff."

"Obviously, you did more than think about it."

"Because we're celebrating."

"What are we celebrating again?"

"Your cast coming off. Highly lasagna-able. Even if you hacked it off before you should have." I continued to stack the layers: noodles, cheese, sauce, noodles, cheese, sauce. "I was thinking, how will the drawing, if Miss Stephanie ever finds it, help us exactly? Since Joey knows he drew it and we know he drew it, how will it help convict him, if he was, in fact, one of the men who hurt you?" Just asking the question made me step up the pace of my layering.

"DNA? A fingerprint? A microscopic hair? I don't know. I don't want to think about it. I'd rather think about. . ."

"Dr. Goff?"

"Lenny? No. Well. Yes." Deflecting the question, he said, "Did you say you were making tiramisu for dessert?"

"No. I did not."

He exaggerated a pout with his lips. All this time, he was sitting on the floor with his back propped up to the wall—

slender-hipped, broad-shouldered, strong arms (he'd been pumping iron like crazy), and legs white as chalk where they weren't blue, yellow, or some awful shade of purple so troubling, I dropped the last half-full jar of sauce to the floor where it splattered open. I put the lasagna in the oven and shut the door, wiped up the mess, and began slicing peppers. He watched and for the next half hour we didn't say much. I think we'd just learned to appreciate the quiet more.

"It smells great in here!" Dr. Goff said soon as he reached the top stair.

"Thank you, Dr. Goff," I said.

"Please, it's Lenny. And another thing," he said, looking back down the stairs, "don't make a habit of leaving your front door open, okay?" It wasn't the first time he'd brought up my not locking the door. To Richard, clearly happier now, he said, "So? How are we today?"

We. I wondered how it was, what it felt like, to be *we.* I don't think the feeling of jealousy can ever be ignored, and it's easy to make too much of it, but I'm afraid that's what I did. I walked over to the refrigerator, opened the door, and pretended to look inside, all while thinking how Richard's life had expanded to the starry-eyed size of two. I suddenly longed to have someone else to talk to, a boyfriend or a close girlfriend my age, but there was no one other than Richard. And now that he had someone else, I didn't know how to feel about it. I tried to brush it off. I took a deep breath and went back to stirring the sauce. Suddenly, the peppers started to blister and I ran around the kitchen like a headless chicken. "I don't really know what I'm doing here," I said. I managed to save them, wondering what my mother would have thought of my not letting them marinate overnight. "Actually, this is an abbreviated version of my mother's roasted peppers." I said.

"Who can resist abbreviated roasted peppers?" Lenny smiled, pulling at a pepper skin. I thought how he could have said the opposite, but there was something about him that would have made it a comfort anyway. I was happy for Richard.

After we sat at the table, I stood up to pour more sauce over Lenny's lasagna, and when I sat back down, I looked down to see Richard's swollen toes resting on Lenny's foot under the table. I looked up to see something deep in his face had relaxed, which should have made me even happier for him, and it did. But even so, I quickly excused myself.

What followed was a little pity-party. I sat on the toilet with my head in my hands and thought how Richard finding Lenny made me realize that his life was moving forward in spite of what happened to him. But was mine? I don't remember what I said when I finally came out of the bathroom, but it was one of those moments when you have to decide to do the right thing, because any other decision would be completely selfish and wrong. The right thing was to sit back down and be elated for Richard.

Later, I would tell Richard that I was just reacting.

"To what?" he said.

"To yearnings," I said, raising my eyebrows in a way that left no room for questions.

As soon as I was seated again, Richard shifted his weight, turned to Lenny, and said, "Lasagna costs a fortune. The cheese alone."

"Richard!" I narrowed my eyes at him.

"Actually, I've been thinking about your lease, Lucy."

"Wait, no. Richard what did you say?" I turned back to Lenny. "I did not invite you here to talk about my lease, I promise you."

"I know that. I also know that the Star Struck has done huge things for my self-confidence over the years." Richard and I looked at each other. "As well as for Kayla's. And it goes without saying how much this community has benefited. So here's what I propose. Why don't you work for me in the mornings until you are fully up and running again. We can call it even on the rent and you can keep whatever class fee you collect."

"I... I..." I didn't quite get what he was proposing. "But what would I *do*?"

"What you're best at. I'll refer my most sedentary clients to you and you'll get them moving again. A lot of people come to me who just need help. They need a routine. Not everyone can motivate themselves. Show them how to stretch, get their knees and hips functioning again. Most of them have been sedentary or deskbound their entire adult life. Dancers have perfected the best form of physical therapy, daily stretching. You'll be my dance consultant. Most insurance plans are covering Movement Therapy now."

I must have had a stunned look on my face, trying to process what he was offering.

"There's no finer dancer in the valley than you, Lucy."

"Excuse me?" Richard said.

Lenny reached over and ran his finger down Richard's cheek.

"I don't know what to say," I said.

"Say yes. Though I know it's a lot to ask," he said, as if he needed to make up for something hesitant inside of me.

"Are you kidding? If you send me students, I'll actually have students again."

I thought of the year my father died and Miss Stephanie told me that someone had donated the money for my recital costumes. When I said what I suspected, that no one had donated it and that the kindness was hers alone, she stuck the end of her pencil into her ponytail. "Graciously receiving is as generous as giving," she said sternly.

I looked Lenny straight in the eye and said, "Thank you."

Richard's hands were folded behind his neck and he had a grin on his face that let me know he was in on the whole idea from the beginning. "Now, will you kindly tell Karen to find another place to delude herself into thinking she's a calm and gentle person? If I hear her say one more time that *ommmm* is the sound of creation, as if she knows, I might do something I regret. I'm not getting my beauty sleep. I'm sleep-deprived. I'm an open nerve."

I slammed down my hand on the table so hard it hurt a little. "Done," I said.

As if to test my sincerity, Richard handed me his phone. He'd already tapped in Karen's number. I left a message that she had two weeks—to which Richard dramatically mouthed "two?"—to find another space because I had morning classes of my own to schedule again, and quickly hung up. I have to admit, I was eager for some way to get even ever since we learned she was sneaking around behind our backs. I immediately felt more at ease. "That was fun!" I said which led to a hug, which led to Richard tucking his head against Lenny's shoulder.

"Brava!" Lenny said, spoon in his hand. "I think I'll have another slice of lasagna to celebrate."

"Since no one made tiramisu," Richard said.

"Men," I thought, feeling Miss Stephanie's presence like an elbow.

After Lenny helped clear the dishes, he suggested we go dessert shopping. "We need to get out," he said. The three of us piled into his car.

Normally, Richard didn't want to go anywhere except over to Lenny's. He thought people would pity him, but Lenny wouldn't give in. "You need to tackle this head-on," he said, encouraging Richard to use a shopping cart to steady himself. He put a case of bottled water in the bottom to make it more stable and then, slowly, we walked into Vons.

"I don't think those men have moved since the last time I was here." Richard said, nearly in a whisper, about the three old men who like to sit just inside the doors on the only bench.

"I like to think they remind us of what old age was like before nursing homes," Lenny said. When one of the men tipped his straw hat at Richard as we passed, I felt like running over and giving him a great big hug.

Other people smiled in our direction and when a few came up and patted Richard on the back—it was clear he loved the attention. We gladly met people's eyes with a sense of relief you wouldn't recognize in yourself unless you'd been through a time when the compassion hadn't been there.

Or had we imagined it wasn't there? Was it over then, the gossip? Had people stopped believing the lies? *Telling* them?

My questions were answered soon as I noticed one woman look quickly away, and then a few seconds later, squint in our direction again, scowl, and shake her head. I kept her rudeness to myself. Richard was taking considerable more time talking to people than he needed to and I didn't want to spoil things.

The smells of the bakery swirled around us. Lenny and I walked on either side of Richard as he surveyed the bakery case. "I know there are people who can eat cake every day and not gain weight," I said letting go of the cart to walk closer to the frosted cakes. But Richard, comfortable in familiar surroundings again, pushed on with Lenny without waiting for me to finish my sentence. I watched them walk away. "I only wish I was one of them," I said, meaning nothing about cake. I watched the two of them laughing sweetly each time Richard stumbled so that Lenny made him hang on with both hands again. Lenny dressed so smartly, making me think of the phrase my mother used to say while applying her lipstick or pulling the curlers from her hair before leaving the house—*fare una bella figura*, "to make a good showing." I thought about how the greatest gift Lenny gave to Richard and me that day was showing us that self-pity and isolation were unacceptable.

I lifted the largest tiramisu from the cooler and shut the door.

Back at the Star Struck.

The phone was blinking again. *Blink. Blink. Blink. Blink. Blink.*

"I can't find it!" Miss Stephanie's voice cried from the speaker. "We looked in every book, searched every box, every folder, every envelope. I know I saved it, I'm sure I did."

There was a short silence and from the sound of it, I could tell there was something else she wanted to say. "But you know what I did find? A photo of Richard catching your stag-leap midair. It was the year we sprung for Curtain Call dresses and Richard matched the color of your dress with his glittery eyeshadow that went right up to his brow. Your whole body is suspended in air, perfectly arched. But it's the look on your face I treasure most, like you had just returned to us from somewhere far away."

I stared at the phone.

"Anyway, Mr. White, *Rivers*, and I talked about something I wanted to share with you." We heard her take a breath and exhale, as if nervous to continue. "I never knew this, but apparently a social worker had suggested Joey come to our studio. She's retired now, but she told Rivers that she'd suggested tap dancing to Joey's mother as a physical activity that wasn't aggressive, after, in front of the other kids at school, he'd pulled the feathers out of a quail during recess and God knows what else. So, what the legal issue is here, Rivers explained, is that Joey was already in trouble when he came to us, see, and no one thought to tell us. Rivers said I should have been informed, I should have had the opportunity to object to a seriously troubled child being around my other students. But I told him I wasn't about to complicate things, it was water under the bridge, what good could come from me objecting now? By the time he drove off, I was confident he'd get to the bottom of everything." After a pause, she went on. "Have you ever met a man named Rivers before? I haven't. It's beautiful to be named after a waterway, don't you think?"

Richard and I looked at each other. "I only wish he didn't wear his hat indoors. I'm hopelessly old-fashioned," to which Richard mouthed *oh my god*. "It was such a long way for him to come only to leave empty handed, and I do feel bad about that. But he's the right man for this job, I'm sure of it. I believe him. He won't give up. And I'll keep looking for the drawing, I'll find it, don't you worry. Love to you both. Bye b..." *Beeeeeep.*

Now we both stared at the phone. We should have been more upset about the missing drawing, but what really got to us had nothing to do with that. Her message brought back the moment the house lights go down just before the stage lights come up, when we finally get to stop over thinking every step and just dance. I wasn't sure I wanted to remember that feeling quite so specifically. Her words bothered me more than any photo could have done and they reminded us what our work had been like which made losing it feel twice as devastating. Work we were forced to give it up for... what? For feeling cut down by two men without one-zillionth of Richard's goodness? For sitting around waiting for the police to find out who did this?

It was too much.

I knew it was too much for Richard too, but he didn't want to say so and neither did I. Our eyes met. As one, we looked down at the phone. In silent agreement, we decided not to play the message back a second time. I deleted it. *Click.*

"There," I said.

"There," he said. And after a moment, "God, I loved those dresses."

Pure joy.

That night I dreamt Richard and I drove to Vons again. "Richard!" I called from the driver's seat as he struggled to get out of the car, scanning the lot for an empty cart. "You don't need a cart, leave it!" As soon as my feet hit the pavement, energy reared up. I grabbed Richard's hand and we sashayed to the door in matching yellow tap shoes. Strength tore through our legs. We danced through the aisles, every muscle on alert, the tension pushing us to new heights. We executed moves we thought beyond our capabilities before. We spun to the left, leapt to the right. Our pace was fast, flowing, synchronized.

When reality plunked itself down again, it landed softly, like coming to the end of a piece of choreography, when the lights dim and we are left to find our way backstage in the dark. But in the first few seconds of daylight, the dream felt so real that if I'd had wings, I'd be flying over the bakery case for a third pass. I keep wondering now, as I think back on this dream, what other insights I would have gained, if I hadn't been startled awake by my own joy?

"It's like I had to have a little talk with myself in my sleep, to remind myself of what I'm passionate about when I'm awake," I told Miss Stephanie, describing my dream.

"I never thought I'd hear myself say this, but maybe this break has been good for you, Lucy. You've stepped back enough to gain perspective." This didn't surprise me. In class she'd told us, "Choreography is a like an oil painting, you have to step back to take in its fullness." But after Kayla grumbled that the steps were too hard, Miss Stephanie looked at her for a second before saying, "Confidence works the same way. Now step back, close your eyes, give it a little time. . ." With her own eyes closed, she waited a few seconds before asking Kayla, "Now, can you *feel* it all coming together?"

Kayla opened her eyes, blinked, and it was like you could see the wheels inside her head turning as her eyes grew ready again.

Knowing what I know now, I think Miss Stephanie was talking more about herself than about Kayla learning the choreography. Still, it was the perfect thing to say. Things weren't going well at dress rehearsal for Kayla, and the minute this happens, the wings of confidence fly off.

And it's the director's job to stitch them back on.

Holding on.

An adagio is more difficult than fast-paced choreography. The slow movement, the balance it takes to sustain an extension—each fluid step seamlessly linked to the next. I knew this, but it came as a shock to remember just *how* much more difficult it is to move slowly. Beginning students fear speed more than anything, and *adult* beginners panic easily. They have difficulty relaxing. If they don't get a step right away, their confidence can grind to a halt. "Plus the mirrors embarrass them," Richard said. "Which is understandable."

So, whenever I begin a new class, I watch how my students see themselves. Do they automatically go to the back of the room or demand the front row? Do they mingle or keep to themselves? I did all this, but I was used to eager, young, flexible bodies. Inflexible older adults were all new territory for me—hip replacements, knee surgeries (before, after, or trying to head off), back injuries, each carrying fifty or sixty extra pounds ("at *least*," Richard chimed in). Weight was the most obvious hindrance—no agility, no give, no grace.

"Stiffness is all, positively all, it takes for the body's energy to go dormant," Miss Stephanie said on the phone as sympathetically as she could.

And yet, and *yet*, as soon as class was over and my last red-faced student trudged out the door, my heart overflowed with pride. I only hoped they'd return the next morning. I went to the window to watch them walk to their cars. "I don't even mind if I have to slow everything down to the pace of. . ." I was searching for the word.

"Yoga?" Richard said.

I flinched. But the next morning, when after I said, "breathe in slowly through your nose and out through your mouth, now, let your breath *gooooo*," while everyone let out their breath in much the same way they let out their aches and pains, in deep sighs, my wall of judgement tumbled down. I realized it wasn't yoga that I found insufferable—it was Karen I found insufferable.

The only man who showed up had shy eyes that kept looking down and a flushed complexion that grew even more so as soon as we started to move. He had an obese person's gait—heavy, cumbersome steps, the most heartbreaking wobble for a man his age, and he seemed resigned to fail in a way I didn't see in the women. In a shaky voice he said, "I haven't exercised since high school."

"How old are you, if you don't mind my asking? Forty, forty-five?"

"Twenty-nine."

It was like an egg cracked and fell. All eyes went to the floor and, so help me, I could have lost each and every one of them right then and there. "Oh!" I said gently and smiled. I longed to put my hot cheeks against the cool mirror.

"Doctor's orders," he said with a shrug.

Next, we tried walking in a circle while matching our inhale/exhales to the pace of our steps. "Press *through* your feet," I demonstrated. "Oh, that's good!" I roared like a mother lion. To exhibit flexibility, I grabbed my ankle and brought my leg up to my ear. Someone whispered, "my *God,*" so I tightened my grip and pulled my leg even higher.

Richard says I was clearly showing off, and maybe I was. A little.

In dance, extreme flexibility is the golden ring. The eye is naturally drawn to the endpoints of a movement, and in ballet that often translates to the highest extension. But now that I'm a teacher, I realize Richard is right—extreme flexibility can be seen as boasting to someone who can't move a muscle without moaning.

Next, we tried walking our circle backwards. "Or we can play dress-up," Richard said popping his head in, excited by having people around again. Around his neck was a fluffy-pink boa. Everyone laughed, everyone but the only other man in the room, who stormed out. Only it was more like he plodded out. "Like watching a bull walk from behind," Richard said once everyone was gone. "Which proves we really *are* what we eat." When I didn't laugh, he hobbled closer. "I'm sorry. I'm bored. I'm jealous. Forgive me?"

"Don't worry," I said. "He'd already made up his mind that he wasn't coming back before you said anything. Men have a harder time doing things they aren't good at, especially in a room full of women. I think he was glad you showed up, actually. It gave him an excuse." I was organizing my music with my head down and suddenly I heard his makeshift cane drop to the floor. He walked all the way to the mirror and back. Then, with twice as much will but only half the oomph, to the door and back. That's how I left him, counting out his steps, one, two, three, three and a half, and so on, all the way up to a ten because Lenny encouraged him to increase his routine in the morning, again in the afternoon, and again in the evening, after completing his series of weight-bearing exercises.

Lenny confided in me that it was going to be a long, hard climb for Richard. "There was soft tissue injury, muscle damage, bone fractures, awful pain. Healing is going to take time, especially because he won't even wrap it."

"He thinks the air will help it heal faster," I said, "but I'm not so sure."

"Well, what you can be sure of is that the emotional healing will take even longer. He'll be short-tempered at times, testy, impatient, frustrated, even mean. It's likely to come at you in little digs as things set him on edge."

"I'm pretty much used to that already," I said, smiling.

"I just want you to be prepared that it could take a while, Lucy, and that maybe you should consider reopening the studio when *you* are ready."

"But I have reopened, thanks to you."

He nodded. "And the comments I've heard are great. They like that you aren't too easy on them."

"I don't even know how to be easy on myself," I said.

"Kayla always said learning from you was like breathing fresh air."

I was taken aback. There are times when you wonder if you'll ever receive the one compliment you've been waiting your whole life to hear. Then, when you finally do hear it, it comes as a surprise. It convinced me that it's not wrong to want to hear a sincere compliment now and again, not at all, especially when you work so hard at what you do. I made a silent pledge to give more of them, not to hold back.

Lenny's generosity had created a whole new level of intimacy between us, which was only natural now that he'd become part of the household—coming and going during the day in various states of animation, telling us lively stories about his side of Route 62, trying to cheer Richard up until Richard laughed along.

If Richard was having a hard day—say, the sky was overcast, which made the studio feel twice as deserted, and him twice as miserable—it could take only a few minutes after Lenny left for Richard to slide back down again. "I'll never dance again, those days are over," he'd say, or something like it.

Lenny's words played over in my head: *impatient, frustrated.*

"That's not true," I said.

"You don't know." *Testy.*

"I don't know that the sun is going to shine tomorrow, either. But I've lived on the desert my whole life. I can *tell*."

He looked at me, but didn't counter.

The next morning the sun blazed. As soon as I was down the stairs, I smiled at Richard, but I held my tongue. With lines from the quilted bedspread on his face, he said, "Easy call," dismissively. *Mean.*

I turned on my heels and ran back upstairs, supposedly to get dressed.

To be honest, I might not have described Richard's first attempts to walk in true detail. It's fairer to say it was more of a gawky kick of one leg and then a stiff drag of his other as he leaned onto the grocery cart or his broom handle. Some mornings it was such a heartbreaking struggle that it stole away any sense of cheerfulness either of us had woken with. At that point, I'd escape to the barre and while stretching, I'd repeat a few sayings I knew by heart: TAKE THE PEBBLE OUT OF YOUR SLIPPER *BEFORE* IT BLISTERS. THERE WON'T ALWAYS BE MORE TIME TO PRACTICE, BUT THERE *WILL* ALWAYS BE LESS. Things like that to make me feel better.

And by day, I noticed, it was easier to feel better.

But by nightfall, things got trickier. My dreams left me wondering about one thing or another, and not always in a positive way—which is the point of dreaming, I know, but one morning I woke up and the first thing I felt for was my mother's hand.

"You had a nightmare last night," Richard said.

"I did?" I said, trying to sound blasé.

"I heard you say, 'it's okay, you can let go now.' What were you dreaming about?" he said. Then he said it again, only differently, "What were you letting go *of*?"

"I don't know." I lied. "I can't remember."

My mother's last drawn-out day had come back to haunt me. I was wiping beads of sweat off her forehead, trying to help but even so, I could see how dying is long, slow, difficult work. "I had no idea how hard I'd have to work at this," she managed to whisper. "And it's getting really boring."

It was such a big surprise to us both how much will and concentration it takes to let go.

Everything ends up in the junk drawer at least once.

My own library consists of every book Miss Stephanie left behind. I was looking for one in particular, *The ABC of Ballet*—a small book, more of a pamphlet, written to help teach young children the fundamentals of technique. I'd been searching for it ever since beginning my adult class, which struck me as funny.

That morning, Richard tried fitting into his tap shoes again but his feet were still too swollen. He insisted the exercises were a waste of time and spent the rest of the day watching movies on his laptop in coffee-stained boxers, until Lenny came over to move Richard's leg forward and back *for* him while Richard whimpered like a baby. I raced upstairs. A few minutes later, I walked back down with a cold quart of beer and three mugs.

After a few sips, Richard stopped sulking as much, but his disappointment was still obvious. So was his affection. I couldn't help but see how each of us felt something entirely personal just then. Richard was feeling defeated, but under Lenny's soft touch, his willingness returned. He just needed Lenny's good push in the right direction. Lenny kissed Richard's forehead so gently that love is clearly what he felt. And I felt that I'd been wrong about dancing being the only way to be happy. Possibly not being able to dance wasn't the worst thing in the world for Richard, or for me, but not finding someone to love as tenderly *was*.

This is the thought that kept me awake that night, so I got up and tried looking for the pamphlet again. Anything was better than tossing and turning. I tried the kitchen junk drawer again, this time sending my hand all the way in to the very back edge. I grabbed hold of a stack of paper and pulled it forward, thinking it couldn't hurt to do a little housecleaning while I was at it. I switched on the overhead light and that's when my eyes found the drawing. I stared at it closer, taking in the larger ballet slipper unmistakably shaped like a penis and wrapped in four soft ribbons that belonged to two smaller "slippers" floating off to the side as if dangling innocently, almost like butterfly wings fluttering off the page.

I stood for a few seconds listening to the sound of my own breathing. "Richard!" I grabbed the picture and ran downstairs.

Eleven

"Dancing is just discovery, discovery, discovery."
~Martha Graham

Last Kiss

Two weeks passed before Rivers returned to the
Star Struck, and another week before we were to hear the
facts of what finding the drawing meant officially, as well
as what it implied psychologically about its creator.

It was a sweltering day, one of the hottest of the summer.
It made me think of something the visiting nurse, Marjorie,
said, in a hoarse voice that brought a smile to my mother's
face. "When I got out of my car, honey," she said, pausing
to inhale her cigarette. "I think I left a patch of my rear-
end behind," exhale of cigarette. The stub hung out of her
mouth, low on her lip like a fang, and I got the feeling that
as soon as I left the room, she passed it from her lips to my
mother's. When I asked my mother if my suspicion was
true, she said, "What does it matter now?"

"It does matter!" My voice was louder than I'd meant
it to me.

"I don't have the energy for this," she said and closed
her eyes. When Marjorie came back into the room, I
stared at the floor, refusing to look at her. But once she
and I were alone in the kitchen, I asserted myself. "Second

hand smoke," I said, feeling a little disloyal to my mother's wishes but not enough to stop myself, "isn't good for my mother *or* for me." The sun was low in the sky by then and it spread a soft glow over the countertops. It was so much less lonely sitting there with Marjorie that I almost wished her smoking didn't bother me as much.

"You think so? Nah, I don't think so," she said, shaking her head and reaching across the counter to run her lit cigarette under the faucet anyway, and far as I know, she never smoked in the house again.

Until the day I asked her to.

When my mother couldn't keep anything down, I put my hand on Marjorie's hand. When I felt that it was trembling, I whispered, "Have a cigarette, please. It's okay." In two seconds flat, she was sucking on a Newport. And when I heard my mother murmur, "my turn," her desire visible as the puff of smoke billowing out of Marjorie's mouth, it broke my heart.

I took the cigarette and held it to my mother's lips.

Two warm stones.

Rivers arrived at the exact time we expected him. We took that as a good sign. Despite the heat, he wore a suit jacket, dress shirt, jeans, black shoes, and socks, as well as a different hat this time, like the caps you see in old photos of newspaper boys in knee socks and shorts. When I asked if he wanted to take it off, he declined.

"Are you sure?" I said. "We don't have air."

He threw back his arms to remove his jacket, but his eyes were intent. He'd be keeping the hat on.

As soon as he'd gone, I called Miss Stephanie. "It covers his bald spot, that's all."

"Oh!" she said. "Why didn't I think of that? I never saw my father without his hat on either,' not even when he napped on the couch." I could hear how much she enjoyed comparing Rivers to her father. "And did you notice how he talks about his work with such conviction, but he doesn't try to impress you with it, he doesn't boast?"

Right away I remembered the leg-to-ear stretch I just *had* to do in front of my class. (The upside of such an embarrassing lesson is that it made me begin to understand the real difference between doing and teaching.) I thought how Rivers reminded me of Charlie Brown, the way the corners of his mouth curve downward while his eyes light up, but I hadn't given any thought to his conviction. I figured he had to have that or he wouldn't be working as an investigator for the state of California. When I didn't answer, she said, "And he doesn't talk only about himself, he's..." she took a breath, "interested in what *you* have to say?"

I took note of the pause and thought, *If there's a way to tell if someone has a crush by hearing them take in a breath, I just heard it.* "Well, he," I thought about it, "seems serious enough to know what he's doing, and humble enough to feel trustworthy."

"That's it, that's exactly it, Lucy! You've always been intuitive. But listen to me rambling on like this. Tell me everything he said about the drawing."

"He didn't get to say all that much, really. The woman he brought with him did most of the talking. Teresa? I can't remember her last name. Richard says it sounded like too many consonants fighting for space."

Silence from her end of the phone. But the question on her mind thundered through. "Teresa? Who is this Teresa, exactly? "

"She's an art therapist," I said. "Apparently that's a thing now, like dance therapy." And I thought about describing—but didn't—Teresa's black-framed glasses, tailored grey skirt, white blouse, black heels, and the awkward moment when Rivers introduced us to each other and she extended her hand. Because while I admire stylish, professional women, just not when they appear at my door without warning and I'm caught in sweatpants, no bra, and there are still crusties in the corners of my eyes, since I hadn't washed my face yet.

This was all on the tip of my tongue, but I kept it to myself, because I didn't know how to communicate to Miss Stephanie delicately enough how reassuring Teresa's appearance was. She looked like the kind of woman who wouldn't fall to pieces in a tragedy—who just might be thinking twice as fast as the men. And that's exactly what Richard and I needed, whether we liked her or not.

"But she was sort of," I searched for a word, "harsh."

"I see," Miss Stephanie half-sighed in the way people do when they want you to go on without wanting to ask.

"Anyway, it was pretty clear from the beginning that she would do most of the talking."

"I've always admired women like that..." Her voice trailed off like she wanted to say something more, but it sort of petered out before it gained any momentum.

I described how Teresa studied the picture and wrote things in a notebook, while Richard picked at his leg scabs and I tried to make small talk with Rivers. "Who mostly wanted to talk about you," I said. I told her how his voice kept falling to a whisper, as he struggled to sound like his interest in her was no big deal. "I had to fight not to laugh because I could tell what a big deal it was," I said. I shared how Teresa tapped on the picture with the end of her fingernail, as if running through a mental list—how she seemed less puzzled by the drawing as the minutes passed. I described how she looked up and said, "I can assure you that we have a very confused boy here." Finally I said how, though I admired Teresa and the work she does, I just couldn't warm to her, hoping Miss Stephanie would take it as a good indication that Rivers wouldn't warm to her either.

It was clear Miss Stephanie barely heard a word after I mentioned River's interest, if she'd heard me at all. I could sense her brow raising. "He asked about me? What did he say?" Before I could answer, she said, "Don't answer that. I'm sorry, I'm being ridiculous. What else did the therapist say?"

I told her how complicated everything Teresa said was, but I knew she was only half listening after she repeated, "I see," one too many times, trying to make it sound like she was paying attention while clearly blind sighted by the one thing she was dying to ask. "Is Teresa pretty?"

I was just trying to make Miss Stephanie feel better when I said the first thing that popped into my head, "And it's weird, but her ponytail doesn't swing when she walks, it stays *put*." But the truth is, if you take away Teresa's stare that can chop you in two, she is lovely. I knew it best to step around this fact, though, like when you eye a fallen bobby pin on stage, and you either have to kick it to the side or leap over it, but you don't want to draw attention to it. I smiled to myself, remembering how I'd struggled to keep Miss Stephanie's loveliness from my mother in much the same way.

"I'm sorry," she said. "Go on, before I embarrass myself any further."

"When Richard asked Teresa what she meant by 'confused,' she said 'sexually' and gave him a quick nod, as if she'd already started to grow impatient."

"A quick nod? Oh no. Richard doesn't react well to quick nods."

To hear the word "sexually" spoken so coldly made my knees go weak, but for Richard, it was much worse. Rivers stepped forward to look closer while Teresa shared her thoughts. "See here," she said, "how the ribbon pulls tight? How incomplete the penis is under all the heavy shading?" This caused Richard to cringe, me to catch my breath, and Rivers to say a soft, "geez." She then collected her things from my desk, stood, and said, "come, sit," like she was directing a couple of school kids. "Let me explain."

What she meant by "explain" was that ninety percent of communication is by non-verbal information through facial expressions, posture, all types of body language like handwriting and other physical habits. "Color preferences tell us more about a person's state of mind than speaking does," she said. "This is why drawing is a language of its own. It gives us quite a lot of insight into character."

"Character?" Richard said. "Is this a joke?"

She stared at him for a second. "I can assure you, it's not a joke."

Richard put his head back and studied the ceiling for a moment, biting the corner of his lower lip. I was getting that sinking feeling in my stomach that comes along when everything seems too complicated to take in.

"We pay special attention to color choice," Teresa went on. "It says a lot about a person. The boy who drew this used a lead pencil on white note-paper. The choice of a color, or lack of it, reflects not only psychological traits, but emotional health—a person's struggles, say, with confidence."

Richard's right hand flew to the side, knocking over the plastic water pitcher I'd set out. I reached over to pick it up. Rivers ran to get paper towels.

To someone who doesn't know Richard, it might have seemed like he was getting angry at Teresa, but I knew what was happening. Some of us can only cope with one difficult challenge at a time. I wanted to put her on hold, until Richard had time to take in all the details at his own speed. It's asking for trouble to rush Richard through to the next frame while his attention is still fixed on the last. He doesn't whoosh through and spin out.

I'm sure Teresa had no idea that there was so much about the things she was telling us that did not relate to the world we live in—or thought we lived in. As she talked, I watched Richard try to come to terms with how it feels to be caught between two entirely different worlds. It was like asking him to join the army, when all he ever wanted was to protect himself against violence. Teresa just didn't seem to understand that people need more time when they are presented with facts that make them feel defenseless. I didn't want her rushing through any more of them in the same detached way she gave a nod.

"And yet," I said to Miss Stephanie, "it's not her job to console us, only to inform. I know that."

"I suppose by the time she's called into a case, the shoe has already dropped, and her job is to make sure people understand just how hard," she said, trying to see both sides. "You know how it is. We can't get emotionally involved with everyone we work with. But," she went quiet for a bit, catching herself because she never talks badly about anyone pointlessly.

"I know, but still. I would have thought that an art therapist would be more, I don't know, understanding about people's differences, more sensitive to them."

"I think a young, smart, competent woman can easily annoy people, in one way or another, no matter what they do," she said with a quick laugh. Once I got what she was laughing at, I laughed too, but with a tighter stomach once I applied what we were laughing at… to myself.

Rivers soaked the water up and Teresa turned toward Richard and continued. "Color has symbolic overtones," and I saw Richard's eyes spark a little, as if he wanted to add something but thought better of it. The word "overtones" did not escape the artist in Richard, and it really touched me how hard he worked to control himself, to stay quiet, to listen and not interrupt until Teresa was finished. His own expertise hadn't been tapped for too long and I could see it bubbling up. He'd been live-tweeting his healing process, but our frustration with the anonymous world of followers had spotlighted just how lonely you can feel, even when thousands of people call you their so-called friend.

Teresa went on. "Dark blue can mean intense concentration—self-study—while red is often a sign of strength, eccentricity, uniqueness, but it can also be a warning of aggression and hyperactivity. Yellow is generally a positive choice, showing optimism and curiosity, but in some, it can trigger a sudden sense of immediacy."

Richard's eyes widened. I put my hand over his. The thought of hearing many more troubling facts about the colors of a rainbow was disheartening. My heart was pounding. I wanted to stop her, I really did. There was no emotion—her approach was all wrong, but that was about all I could come up with, so I sat tight.

"A lot of children prefer violet over blue. It's the color we refer to as intuitive, but too much of it can bring actual physical discomfort to the picture." She dug through a folder, as if looking for one thing. "And see here," she held up a color chart. "There's a lot of tendency to internalize in grey, and destructive tendencies where too much black is used. But the most fascinating part in this instance, using only black can express a strong desire for change. Like right here," she pointed at the drawing again, at how harsh the shape of the penis was, but also how delicate under the shading, causing her to say, "obviously here there are two distinctly conflicting thoughts on the issue of sexuality."

Just when we thought we'd absorbed all we could, she added that the number of colors used is very important. "Five to six colors can mean that the level of emotional development is balanced. The wider the use of color, the greater the range of emotions. And you see," she tapped on the photo with her nail again. "Black. Only black."

"What if he only had the one pencil?" Richard asked.

"Stephanie told us she kept a box of colored pencils and crayons in the same basket with the scrap paper," Rivers said.

"Oh, yeah. But we stopped all that years ago," Richard said, as if he couldn't think of anything else to say, so why not that. He looked to me for support.

"That's right," I said, sitting upright. "We believe it encourages parents to think of us as babysitters."

"*Any*way," Rivers said, dismissively. A little too, I thought—the way men do without even realizing they are doing it because men have ignored women's opinions for so long, it's a natural reaction for them. I wouldn't bring it up as a red-flag to Miss Stephanie or anything, but I knew if things were to get serious, she'd either set him straight or send him packing.

"If you look at the explicitness of the drawing," Teresa immediately returned our focus, "the structure of the picture, what and who the child has depicted by drawing it—it's generally what he or she is most attached to, or repulsed or confused by, especially if the child has put himself or herself in the picture. And I think he has. I think both the penis and the slippers are his."

Richard narrowed his eyes on the picture. "If I click my heels together, can I go back to Yucca Springs now?" he said, trying to cope by being funny, but I heard the crack in his voice. I put my hand higher on his arm.

Teresa glanced up, but only for a second. "We also pay close attention to how the picture is drawn. Do you see how many times he erased the same lines? Overly anxious children often don't finish pictures. Constant correction can point to excessive anxiety. Or that the child is looking to be noticed."

Richard crossed his arms in front of his chest, let them slide free, then crossed them again. There was something heartbreaking about this, but also heartwarming.

"That's it, really," she said. She could have said "class dismissed" by the way she spoke. She handed the photo back to Rivers, reached out to shake both our hands, and said, "Excuse me a moment, will you?" smiling at me to ask if she might use the ladies room.

"The overhead light is out, I'm embarrassed to say. Richard used to fix these things." I, too, tried to sound cool and professional, like someone who could walk into a boardroom and crack the whip, but things you pretend never sound true. "But there's a nightlight with a motion sensor," I said, for the first time feeling self-conscious that it was shaped like a ballerina. I stopped myself, just short of telling her I got it at Walmart on sale.

Even then, she acted like nothing as trivial as a light source could phase her. Was she always this way? Did she think she needed to be so stern in order to be taken seriously? I wondered.

Seconds later, a little scream came from the bathroom, not of horror, but of female-disbelief-of-repeated-male-inconsiderateness. Miss Stephanie was right—Richard would never learn. I looked at Richard. His eyes met mine. "Oops," he said scraping his chair back, reminding me again how a single word can seem light and harmless, and at the same time, ring mean-spirited to your ears. Rivers snuck a sideways glance at Richard and chuckled to himself. Oh, good, I thought. Humor is the best sign that a man can be trained—*or the news won't be good.*

After giving Teresa's shriek the silence it deserved, we sat quietly until she breezed back into the room and said to Rivers, "Shall we?"

Rivers insisted on carrying the pitcher to the sink first. When he was through, he said to Richard, "I'm sorry to have to tell you this, but I was counting on the tire tracks from the dump. Unfortunately, they graded it the day after. We told them to leave the site alone but they said it was scheduled for drainage reasons, and no one thought to tell the truck operator not to comply. Sloppy work, if you ask me," he said and lowered his head. "But I think we have enough to go on."

He said this last statement as if he was talking to both of us but he looked directly into Richard's eyes, as if trying to apologize for Teresa, who'd already turned her back to walk out the door. Rivers tipped his hat and said he'd call soon.

So, yes, we were definitely more informed, but even more confused. Exactly *how* the drawing would help move things along, what we could expect next, and even what Rivers had to go on was still unexplained. I suppose I could have called Rivers to ask the questions, as he'd given me his cell number, but I decided not to. The hope he'd left us with felt like two pebbles hot from the sun, one in each of our pockets. I think we just needed to hold on to their promising warmth a while longer, cracks and all.

Before turning them over again.

Highly important things.

That evening I was standing on a step ladder in the bathroom. Richard was holding the ladder's legs, lost in his own thoughts. He handed me the lightbulb. Exhaling deeply, he said something that sounded like it had not just come to him, plain as day, but that'd he'd actually been thinking about it for some time. "If you think about the rotten home life Joey had, there's actually a lot of beauty in his drawings."

Swinging around to look at him, almost falling off, I said, "You think so?" I paused. "Really?"

He looked up at me, but didn't answer.

In choreography, you can have this total confusion for a while, but eventually a pattern comes to light. When it does, you sense it like an animal can sense a storm brewing. I think this is what happened to Richard—he began to see something beautiful take shape in the drawing, in its depiction of boyhood, neither his nor Joey's alone, but belonging to every child who suffers cruelty from parents who are supposed to protect them, but don't. It took me a while to figure this out, but once I did, I turned from thinking Richard and Joey had nothing in common to seeing, especially from Richard's point of view, how much they did.

I climbed down the ladder and went about my chores. Slowly, steadily, I felt Richard's compassion creep into a wound of my own. The one that has always wondered if it's possible to forgive someone who has really hurt you. No matter how complicated everything was, and more so by the day, Richard had somehow managed to turn to compassion, the way other people turn to religion or alcohol or drugs to get by. I thought that if I could be half as compassionate, I might try to forgive my father... *finally*.

I thought of Richard's father too, how he didn't even know what Richard was going through, and would he care if he did? And I felt like what I'd heard, between the lines of Richard's newly-found compassion toward Joey, was how desperately he needed his own father's love and respect. And the fact that he, and so many kids like him, had probably *never* had the love and respect they needed, from the person they most needed it from. Hurts can shape us forever if we let them. I was just beginning to understand this, but Richard didn't want to let them define him, not anymore.

The most recent news he'd shared with me about his family was that his mother hadn't gotten around to stating her desires in a will. About a month after her funeral, John informed Richard that everything was automatically left to their father, which was code for "everything will go to me", because his father, Richard said, would never leave anything to "the Powder Puff." He went on to say how he waited for John to say, "Don't worry, I'll split everything with you when he dies," but he hadn't said it. This led to fewer and fewer emails, less and less contact, and eventually a total parting of the ways. "It's what my father wanted. He never wanted John getting too close to me, as if I'm a communicable disease."

"I'm so sorry, Richard. I'm so, so—," I extended my arms to pull him into a hug.

"But the part that really gets me is that there was no fight. We were just *over*." He pulled away. "I mean, you have to fight for someone you love, but neither of us bothered. I still wonder how we could have been brothers all those years growing up, but not be speaking now. In the beginning, he was nice to me—my big brother and all— but as the rumors spread, and they were way worse than what they say about me now, he started to fear my being gay would affect *his* reputation, so he turned his back on me. He turned his back on all of us… " he thought for moment. "Like how he treated all the boys who weren't good at sports. We didn't count, we didn't exist. Sports has always been my brother's scale. It's how he weighs everything. I feel sorry for him."

"Do you think Charles had to prove himself to the jocks?"

"I didn't think so at first, but probably on some level. People are expected to live a certain way around here. But lately I've been thinking how it might be even worse in the suburbs. People are expected to dress alike, paint their houses the same shade of appropriate, drive a new SUV.

They can't say what they really think to the neighbors, if they even know their neighbors. My brother fits right in to all that because he doesn't have the guts not to, he never did. He might have grown a healthy set of pecks playing all that football, but he grew an even bigger set of blinders." At this point, he dropped his cane, and started to walk pretty quickly without it. I was impressed, and I said so.

"And when my parents were sitting in the bleachers cheering him on, *I* grew a healthy set of wings, and flew the coop." He waved his arms up and down, gracefully as a swan.

Considering my own arrival at the Star Struck, I said, "I think Miss Stephanie was my first example of how to not let it get the best of you, that people make fun of you sometimes." I marched upstairs, and decided that our studio would come back stronger than ever because of what had happened to Richard and Charles—or in spite of it. I still didn't know which. But everything about my excitement made me happy just then, and everything about it scared me to death. And I'm sorry to bring this up again, but anyone who has ever watched someone leave this world, knows what it looks like when half of you is caught in place, while the other half has already let go.

You have to surrender. There is no other choice.

The more I thought about this, the more I understood what Richard saw, or wanted to see—not only in Joey's drawing, but in Joey himself.

⁓⟳⟳⟳⟳⟳⟳⟳⟳~

The next morning I asked Richard, "Do you really think you can forgive the men who did this to you?"

He glanced at the floor. Then he looked up at me. I think he'd given as much thought to our conversation as I had. "I think so. I want to."

I've thought so many times—*so* many times—about how he looked at me with such willingness in his eyes. Richard showed me that there is another way to look at things once you've been hurt. You don't *have* to blame someone to death.

As for the source of Richard's willingness? Once again, I think it began by reading one of Miss Stephanie's boldest signs: "ANGER STIFLES CREATIVITY, FORGIVENESS ASSERTS IT!" I believe its meaning had seeped into Richard between his every tendu and arabesque.

She hung the sign high over the mirrors at a very low point in her life, just weeks after one of the marines from the combat training center north of town asked her out on a date. Gorgeously handsome, he showed up at the Star Struck in uniform, wearing a blue jacket with a wide white belt. His hat was white too, which surprised and delighted us no end, but not as much as the red stripes running down the side of his pants. "Jazzy pants," Richard whispered and everyone giggled. The man must have heard us because he started to rub at the stripes.

One look from Miss Stephanie, in full command of the peripheral, is all it took for us to put a lid on it.

His black shoes were polished so bright that the sunlight bounced off them. For the life of me, I couldn't understand how anyone could march off to war while looking so smooth and polite. The next day, every class was streamlined so Miss Stephanie could have time to get ready for their second date.

After their third, I heard her tell my mom that he'd shipped out. "Only he never bothered to tell me that part until last night," she said.

The very next day, the sign told the story. It was direct. It beamed out over our heads.

After class, I heard her on the phone with her sister again. They talked all the time. It's why I liked to stay late to Windex the mirrors. "I was up all night just hating that men can't think of a better way to solve the world's problems than with terrible, petty wars," but she was half way up the stairs and kept walking so I couldn't hear the rest.

A few weeks later, out of nowhere, Miss Stephanie cancelled class for two days. She left a message on our phone. As soon as we listened to it, my mother dropped her shoulder bag on the floor and called Miss Stephanie. "Steph," she cried, "you had yourself a genuine hero. How many of us can say that?"

When we returned to class, the sign had disappeared, replaced by a clear glass vase shaped like a test tube. It held a single Angelita daisy.

Unfortunately, it crashed to the floor as Richard tried to perfect his three beat shuffle.

A few more days went by before a battery-powered clock went up in its place. "Now we can tell time even when the power goes out," Miss Stephanie said chirpily without further explanation or sentiment. Her chirp was strained, though, as if trying to convince us of something and nearly succeeding. But not quite.

The clock didn't seem all that out of place, really, since promptness is very important to Miss Stephanie, but her red and puffy eyes did. Her voice faltered as she called out, "Shall we go over the golden rule of dance class again?" turning to face us after fidgeting with the clock's levelness, immediately asking the question that always came next. "If you are fifteen minutes early, you are on time. If you are on time, you are..."

"Late!" we cried. There was only the one answer, and she had worked steadily since day one to make sure we knew what it was.

My point is, her signs still work like cushions. No matter what cliff any one of us is about to topple over, they position themselves to break the fall.

That night, I pulled the covers up tight under my chin. I realized that dance had not only saved Richard and me from a few sadnesses too painful to bear, but Miss Stephanie as well. I wondered if her signs and posters ever come to her late in the night, the way they do to me, to remind her of highly important things like: "DISCIPLINE AND DEVOTION WILL PULL YOU THROUGH!"

Because they do. They pull me through all the time.

Twelve

"Dance first. Think later. It's the natural order."
~Samuel Beckett

Heat.

AS SOON AS HE BLEW INTO THE STUDIO, I WAS STRUCK speechless—by his smile, such a smile; by his scent drifting in my direction; by his hair, wavy and falling over a pair of Ray Bans fixed in the middle with a band of duct tape. Richard said you can tell a lot about someone by their sunglasses, and I thought the tape came off as relaxed. By the way he rubbed his stomach and said he was getting fat—by the way I never expected a man with a belly to catch my eye.

And it was weird because I'd woken that morning with a sense that something was about to happen, for the better or for the worse. Either way, for good. I lied there wondering if I even believed in premonitions.

My insides didn't cave when he spun a circle with his arms up and said, "Imagine a lug like me taking ballet." That happened when he said, "and you must be the lovely Lucy I've heard so much about."

Goosebumps ran up my arms. "From who?" I said, which sounded like I was fishing. I was fishing. He wouldn't meet my eyes. And he seemed overly put off by my question, evasive even, which should have been a red flag, especially after he said "can't remember" with a shrug. I have never liked it when a person shrugs instead of answering, I think only someone with something to hide does that. I thought maybe he was protecting a private conversation between Dr. Goff and himself, so I dropped it.

No, that's a lie. I didn't think that at all. I told myself that so that I *would* drop it.

"So, " he said pointing to a poster of Baryshnikov— shirtless, tights rolled down at the waist. "Can you make me look more like him?"

It took me a few seconds to answer. "Yes. And no. Yes, my name is Lucy." I stuck out my hand, half expecting him to kiss it. "And no, I can't *make* you do anything. But I can help." He shook my hand loosely. "And you are?"

"Billy," he said, and that was all. No last name, which should have been another red flag, but I wasn't paying attention to flags at the time. I may have snuck a peek at one, but I brushed it aside.

"Nice to meet you, Billy. We'll get started soon." And with that, I turned my back, picked up a CD, and pretended to read the back cover, thinking how easy it is to forget that Miss Stephanie lives in San Diego when I count all the times she shows up beside me. It was something I wouldn't have thought about just then if I hadn't felt that it was her hand choosing the CD instead of my own. I remember thinking that I might even name a child after her someday.

If I ever had a child.

Which I couldn't believe I was thinking exactly one whole *minute* after meeting handsome potential.

Class had steadily grown in size. One new student came to me after knee surgery, another after hip, one after a spinal fusion a year back, others after Dr. Goff's suggestion that they could avoid surgery if they set their minds to it. They filed in, claimed a place on the floor. The sun sliced across the wood to illuminate the beads of sweat already sparkling on most foreheads, and I watched them intently out of the corner of my eye. Before they all sort of fell away.

Why? Because I couldn't get ahold of myself. I couldn't get hold of my yearnings!

Ever since, I've been thinking that, probably what happened is ever since my Natural Gas Disaster (a.k.a. my broken heart), I'd been protecting myself. Which had been sort of easy because there'd not been one man I passed on the sidewalk who made me think: *Oh! There you are.* Add that to the list of firm rules—no married men (no-brainer), no transient hikers on their way to Joshua Tree, no natural gas scouts, no fleeting windmill engineers, no parents of students, and definitely no students.

Who did this leave me exactly?

My choices were few.

Less than few.

There was no one, really.

Until Billy showed up.

Let me make this clear: this would be like hiking for hours without hydrating and then finding a full bottle of water at the end of the trail with your name on it. He made (something in) me come alive.

In my patient teaching voice, I said, "Stand with your feet slightly apart and your toes pointed forward. Drop your head and slowly begin rolling down your spine, one vertebrae at a time."

"What if once I'm down," the youngest woman of the group said—fingers extended toward the floor, black tights strained against her legs—"I can't get back up?" A few people chuckled.

I walked around the room, correcting people with a soft touch to the small of their back. Everyone but Billy that is. I snuck a glance at him and was pleased to see that his fingertips were nearly to the floor. Standing a foot away from him at least, I said, "Go softly now. Don't push. That will come later."

"Hmm, I hope so," he mumbled under his breath.

Now, I have a whole childhood behind me of listening to a man mumble under his breath, my ears are antennas. Yet somehow I managed to convince myself that it wasn't as inappropriate as it sounded.

Why, *why* do we do this?

He tried to hold my eyes. "So what happens next?" he said.

I brushed the question off by answering to everyone. "There isn't a magic number of days it takes to become more flexible, but once you begin to stretch on a daily basis you'll start to feel more supple and strong, I promise."

Leslie in the baggy cargo pants said, "My spine must have shrunk over the years. My ass, on the other hand…" This time, everyone laughed.

"Stretching doesn't just lengthen your spine, but your whole," I couldn't think of words to express what I wanted to say. "Mindset." *Did I just say that?* I thought. Honestly, every teacher has to feel their way through class—there's no clear way to go.

"So you're saying it's all in our heads?" Lynette asked looking at her toes skeptically.

Feeling a little chagrined, I say, "a little, maybe," except Lynette is nothing but kind. She doesn't ask a question to make herself feel important. She is also, and there is no nice way to say this, fat. She isn't chubby or chunky or big-boned, or any of the other things people say when they don't want to sound like the kind of person who would say *fat*.

Even so, when I think of her, I don't think of her like that. I think of her as *blue*.

Not because she wears the same navy tights and light blue sweatshirt to every class, that's not it. She has a pale face with skin so translucent you can count the veins in her forehead, but that's not it either. I think of her as blue because of her eyes. There is just something in them that looks sad all the time, even when she smiles, like she could cry at the drop of a penny.

Now that I know her better, I realize it's even more than that. She is always trying to please, insisting on it, and so it's hard to know what her needs are. I've come to see how this is because she doesn't really know what her needs are. And the hole this leaves behind can be deep. So deep, that if she were to let me in close enough to peer below the surface into the center of her, I think what I would see is all this endlessness—like sky, but even bluer.

"Well, good," she said. "Because I doubt all the thinking in the world would get me down to one chin." Everyone looked up with sympathetic smiles. I worried that I couldn't promise her any less of a chin. Even if she lost a hundred pounds, one chin was a stretch. I took in a breath and smiled as supportively as I could.

"Let's form a circle and place your right leg forward into a lunge that faces me," I instructed from the center of the circle. I noticed Billy kept trying to tuck in his T-shirt. "Now, can you lift your hands off your thighs and reach into the center of the circle a little further?" I said. But I don't think I said that exactly, because what Richard says he heard me say is, "Can you reach into *me* a little further?"

To which Billy responded, "I'd sure like to try."

This time, loud as a bullhorn, the warning voice inside me went off.

Except, wait. It wasn't my voice. It was Richard's. He was standing in the doorway with that look that says, *Wait! Are you kidding me?*

As if to release the tension, someone passed a little gas. It happens. Head to toe, we are nerve endings. When things start to give, the river starts to flow. It's perfectly normal.

It's also embarrassing. So the best thing to do is to ignore it, but that's really hard to do. It only makes it worse. We tried not to laugh. We pretended to concentrate, until Lynette gave a little snort confirming who'd done it, and everyone collapsed into giggling. This happens a lot with children. First they start to twerk, because as long as things are so funny, why not jiggle your butt shamelessly. Then they totally lose it.

Then another sound broke out. *Blip. Blip. Blip. Buzz.*

"What's that?" I said.

It felt like just yesterday—*just* yesterday—when Miss Stephanie asked the same question with her back to us, her arm springing up. Like a bomb-sniffing dog, she pointed at our backpacks. "Please tell me there isn't a phone ringing over there." We all froze and looked at the heap of packs by the door. "Because that would mean that someone left their phone on, and no one leaves their phone on during class."

Richard was famous for looking up blankly when you talked to him, then right back to his phone without blinking. Miss Stephanie knew how to strike the perfect tone with him so that he knew there'd be a penalty to pay if he didn't remember to turn his phone off, yet he didn't have to live in fear of his forgetfulness, either. "It's a tricky balance," she confided years later. "Especially for a woman. How to reprimand but not humiliate. But even if we find the perfect balance, we're bound to be called the 'B' word anyway."

"That's my beeper!" Lisa said. "I'm so sorry. Wait, there's one text I need to answer first."

"Oh?" I said quickly. I tried to, but I couldn't think of a way to strike the balance.

"Ugh, I can't do this!" Betty cried, saving me the trouble.

Betty.

First class, before she would come out of the bathroom in her purple leisure suit ("I drove all the way to Sam's Club to get this for you, honey," she said, smoothing down the front of her jacket), she yelled out, "Now close your eyes!" So, of course, everyone craned their necks to get a better look. "I said *close* them!" Everyone obeyed this time. "There's a whole lot of purple coming out of this dressing room and I've got to see it for myself first."

I wanted Betty to feel comfortable in front of the mirror, but it's a really big mirror, especially if you've been avoiding one for a while, and by the way she lowered her eyes in front of it, I suspected she had been. "Okay, you better not laugh," she said, in full view now. The clincher was a big purple headband stretched around her forehead, which is quite a lot of purple for anyone to pull off. It was enough to make it easy to laugh without thinking, but no one did. Her courage humbled us.

Jesus, it's a mess under here," she said lifting her jacket up and looking down, one eye squinting. I walked up and gave her a great big hug. A hug can help people through all kinds of things they don't think they're capable of, there are few things I know as clearly. It's a great feeling when you can give one to someone who really deserves it. She pretty much collapsed in my arms, nearly pushing me over.

Betty came to me after two back surgeries and a year of physical therapy. "I was about to jump into our swimming pool but I landed face up on a concrete slab. I went down around noon and stayed like that until my Fred got home after six. And the good Lord must have thought it time to teach me a lesson, because I'd been meaning to put down grip-strips for years." She looked down, "I've been meaning to get myself back into some kind of shape ever since the kids left, too, but I never did anything about that either. I'm just hoping I can do this," she said.

"You can do this," I said.

A little breeze came out of nowhere to give us all a little letup from the heat and my eyes rested on the album cover left behind by Miss Stephanie—Aretha Franklin's greatest hits. "We tend to outgrow our earlier tastes in music, but some songs touch us for life," she wrote in red ink on the white paper sleeve.

Happy I'd saved her old turntable, I put on I Say a Little Prayer for You. The tune smoothed over us like cool water. I tried not to look in Billy's direction. I didn't want his presence to throw me off again. I wanted Betty's first class to go well.

It did.

Blinded.

Richard didn't need me to drive him over to Lenny's once my class was over since Lenny had already picked him up so they could breakfast together—something they did with more and more frequency.

Other mornings, once my last student had trudged out the door, I'd take clips of Richard's healing challenges—he was back to being thorough about documenting his recovery. Then I'd drive his car (that had slowly become "the" car, then "our" car) to Lenny's office, then drive myself home, happy to be alone in the studio.

But that morning, left alone with my racing adrenaline, I gazed out the window at the San Bernardino mountains gleaming with sunlight. When I looked down, I noticed Lisa still sitting on the front step. I went over and opened the door. I thought maybe her ride hadn't showed up and I was about to offer her one when she said, "You don't recognize me do you?"

I looked at her more closely, studied her eyes. I shook my head. But after starring a few more seconds, it came to me. "Oh my god, you're *that* Lisa, I can't believe it!"

"I went to see Dr. Goff about the pain I've been having in my knee. He told me I could talk about losing weight all I wanted, but the only way to get back into shape was to actually do something about it."

"He doesn't mince words, does he?" I sat down on the step beside her. "I've thought about you so many times over the years, ever since…" I paused.

"Ever since I couldn't stop bawling? You don't know the worst of it. I crapped my pants before we even got outside."

"I wondered what happened to you."

"We moved to the valley. My mother wanted me to go to Marywood Palms."

"Private school must have nice."

"It's about as private as living in Yucca Springs." We laughed. "After I tore a ligament in my knee a few years back, I stopped exercising altogether. And now, well, look at me."

I could tell how much she was battling with her weight.

"But you look amazing. And you're teaching…"

She let the sentence drop. I was glad she did. I said, "I remember thinking you were really missing out because this," I looked back at the Star Struck, "seemed like a much better place than anywhere I'd ever been."

"I remember thinking you were brave."

"Brave? I was scared to death, just like you."

"But you looked so poised. You still do. Even when you walk, it's like you're floating. You're the quintessential ballet dancer, with a body to match. I hate you."

That's when I knew we'd be friends. "No one has ever called me a quintessential anything before," I said, thinking that I must be doing a pretty good job at hiding all of my inadequacies. "I was afraid, too, especially of what such a strange, tall, beautiful teacher expected of me, but I think I was drawn to this kind of fear." I thought for a minute and then I knew what to say. "My frame of reference for different kinds of fear was more limited back then, but somehow I knew the fear I felt of Miss Stephanie was good for me."

"I love that you still call her *Miss* Stephanie."

"It's silly, I know," I said, taking in a sidelong glance of her body that took on a different form in my teacherly view. Something I hadn't seen before came into focus—from her feet to her neck and all the curvy places in between, a solid dancer's body. Rusty maybe, but there, hibernating under a layer of Lycra. I imagined her gathering concentration before executing— absolutely killing—a pirouette. I wanted to say as much, but I decided to wait.

No! Remember? You've crossed this bridge. Your parents were skimpy with praise, and it always bothered you. My heart still caves whenever I remember the way, if someone complimented me, my mother would say something like "that talk will swell her head to the size of a watermelon." (I don't like putting my mother in a negative light again, but as you well know by now, along with all of the wonderful memories, the other things you start to remember after someone you love dies are the hurtful things they said or did, too, because they are only forgivable with time.) Without further hesitation, I said, "Lisa, do you mind if I ask you something?"

"No." She looked a little unsure.

"Did you study ballet at Marywood? I know they have a dance program."

"You can tell? I mean, by the looks of me now?" She scooted in a little closer, sat on her hands. "I took class from fourth grade through my senior year. And it's weird, because I came back here thinking I just wanted to get back into shape. But after only one class, I remember how much I love to dance. I want to stay with it this time." She didn't say anything more for a moment. "Except I've gained, like, a hundred pounds."

I waved my hand, as if at the nonsense of that.

"Oh, before I forget. I actually stayed to apologize about my phone. It's just that I'm on call. I'm a vet."

"Iraq? Afghanistan?" I suddenly feared too-huge a gap between us, and that because of it we'd quickly run through everything there was to say to someone you haven't seen for so long, and I didn't want that.

She burst out laughing. "No, a veterinarian."

"Oh," I nodded slowly. "And medical school didn't scare you, but ballet class did?"

"I've always loved being with animals—studying them, helping them. Veterinary care is natural for me." She looked down at her thighs, "You know what? I don't think wearing black hides the pounds as much as people think."

"Veter…" I paused so as not to pronounce it incorrectly, "…in-ary. Geez, I can't even pronounce it naturally." I didn't feel the least bit embarrassed, though. I've thought about this, because it's something you can't really figure out until you've known someone longer, but Lisa has this way of making me feel comfortable enough to be truthful about myself, so only my truest self comes out.

"I guess I'll see you Monday," she said standing to walk toward her car, sidestepping the mound of tumbleweed that blew past her legs.

"I guess you will," I said hugging both knees to my chest, the heat of the sun drenching my arms and legs. "You know what does feel natural?" I whispered to myself. "That she's come back."

Alone again, the day stretched out ahead of me. For the first time in a long while, I felt like I could just sit on my stoop and let time pass without feeling like I had to make something happen. So I let my thoughts wander back until I figured out who Lisa reminded me of—the triage nurse I'd met during the long days at the hospital with Richard. "Triage is pretty straightforward," she'd said, "and not all that difficult once you know a surface wound from one that bleeds internally." I loved how even while talking about blood, her voice had a twang to it—high pitched one minute, back to normal the next, soothing yet serious, making it clear no one could afford to *not* listen to her. She wore wispy feather earrings that seemed too dainty to belong to a woman in charge of grading the seriousness of a one truck vs. two car pileup, but maybe it's why she wore them—to stay in touch with the lighter side.

While wandering around the hospital to pass the time, I stumbled on a horrific scene—EMT's flying through the door, pushing one stretcher after another—and I wanted to turn away, but I couldn't take my eyes off of *her*. I was just beginning to understand how much you need to know about something to be truly effective—to be able to make tough decisions quickly and stand by them. Remembering how fast she'd prioritized the stretchers, without second-guessing herself, made me feel like I had every right in the world to make Lisa my number one priority, dance-wise.

I know, I know, hardly a life-saving decision. But I'm always curious about what it is about someone that makes me feel inspired by them from day one.

"I won't give her extra attention in class, only in private," I said to Richard after picking him up and telling him all about Lisa. "But don't say anything to her, not yet."

"You can water board me, I won't crack." In every way, he seemed livelier. Staying with Lenny was good for him.

"Your hair looks great, by the way."

"There was a hairdresser in Lenny's office who felt a burning need to go at me with scissors. I've been so busy feeling sorry for myself, I've let my beauty regimen go. She's new in town. She thought maybe I'd been in a car crash."

"Lisa didn't bring it up, either. Not everyone gossips."

"Everyone gossips."

I sighed. "I don't want my other students to think I'm playing favorites."

"Oh, come on. The point of teaching is to teach, so what's the big deal? Lisa still has time. The others will think it's sweet." He paused. "Or they should. But the point is, you need to dance with someone who can actually *dance*, or you'll go nuts. That's what *I* know."

"Because I can't stop talking about it?"

"Because you can't stop smiling," he said, quietly waiting a moment. "Unless you're smiling about something else. Your Freudian slip, maybe?" He lowered his chin.

I jutted my head forward toward the windshield.

The full moon was up, a perfectly round disc that reminded me of a necklace my mother admired once. "I think the big white bead makes a bold statement," she said holding it up at the jewelry counter. I was sixteen. I stared at the cheesy necklace, but made no real effort to explain why I totally disagreed. Just like I made no real effort to explain to Richard what I was feeling about Billy, because I was about to go where my heart led.

And I needed to go there. Alone.

As in, without Richard.

And I know it's not really true to call what was leading me my "heart," but it sounds better than "desire," which means "strong physical urge to have sex with somebody, usually without associated feelings of love." (I sat with my laptop on my lap, studying the exact definition, and when I finally looked up, I felt flushed.) I've since realized it takes only the slightest shift in the moon's cycle to cause a woman's clear judgement to blur. And that you can learn a lot from the things you refuse to believe about our connection to nature at first.

Once inside the door, I saw two messages blinking this time. "Do you remember when we'd have at least twenty messages to deal with in a day?" I said to Richard, walking toward the studio line. I played the first message back.

"Hey, it's me. Billy. I don't want to wait until Monday to see you again, " I punched my finger into the machine. I tried to smile at Richard but my lips wouldn't budge. He was staring at me, hard.

"What?"

"The thing is, he's a student."

"What are you talking about? You just said yourself there's a difference between teaching kids and adults. Oh, I know. We can only date our physical therapists, is that it?"

"Not the same thing at all. You know very well what people will say."

With a lump in my throat, I said, "Richard, we can't go on defining our lives by what people are going to say about us. People will think what they want. I'm sure you read the rumor that Lenny, you, and me are a threesome?"

"When we reopen, I'd like a clean slate. That's all."

"We *have* reopened," I said. But Richard's assumption that my new class didn't count was written all over his face. "Besides, what on earth is a clean slate anyway? This doesn't sound like you. You can't smudge away what happened like chalk off a board."

He limped up close to me and put his face up to mine. "You're right, but there's just something about him. Aren't you going to listen to the rest of his message?"

"Not until you go into the bathroom, turn on the overhead fan, and shut the door."

Our studio is a big open space, but you don't quite realize how big, until you mentally record how long it takes someone to repeatedly smack a broom handle against the floor the whole length of it. Knowing how much I like mirrors free of fingerprints, he purposely dragged his fingers along the glass.

"Nice!" I yelled. I turned down the volume, and leaned in to the speaker to hear Billy's voice. "So let's meet up? Go for a picnic. That's romantic, right? Up by the stone church? Anyway, here's my number." He spoke slowly, one digit at a time, each number feeling like a tease. I definitely remember that.

The next message was from Rivers. As soon as I heard his voice, I shouted for Richard who was already hobbling toward me.

Rivers said he wanted to come over tomorrow to talk. "With more time and evidence, I think we can build a strong enough case to file a hate crime," he said.

We stared at the phone, neither of us wanting to dwell on the words *I think*.

A really ugly place.

Rivers cautioned that playing online detective would raise our fears, but we couldn't help ourselves. I ran upstairs to dig my laptop out of hiding. Richard followed on all fours, but fast, stronger all of a sudden.

I took a deep breath. The first website clarified the definition for us. "It's easy to think you know what a hate crime is until you actually have to explain it," I said. "Did you know it's a federal offense?"

Richard raised his left arm high, then let it fall back to his lap. His right hand never left the mouse. Seconds later, his expression went from hopeful to struck, as literally thousands of hate crimes came up like seed bugs, swarming, each as horrifying as the last. We scrolled through names like: Berdoo Skinheads; the Confederation of Racialist Working Class Skinheads; Revolution Aryan Warriors or RAW ("they have their own acronym?" Richard scoffed); Comrades of Our Race's Struggle; Deadline Skinheads, not to be confused with Deadline Family Skins; Insane White

Boys; Golden State Skinheads; Nazi Low Riders; Riverside Skins; Sacto Skins; San Fernando Valley Skins; Skinhead Dogs; White Heat Productions ("They have their own record label, too, apparently," I said, thinking how many racist lyrics that would be); Western Hammerskins; United Society of Aryan Skinheads; Orange County Skins, and the North*west* Orange County Skins ("Orange County is a really competitive place," Richard said); Public Enemy Number 1; Superior Minded Aryan Skinheads (setting me off to say, "Oh, see. They even hate each other."), and Small Town Peckerwoods. "These groups are known to target Blacks, Mexicans, Gays, Asians, Indians," Richard read aloud, his voice coming out in more of a whisper. "Any race that, according to their ideology, stands in defiance of the proud white race." He paused. "And all we ever hear about is how afraid we're supposed to be of terrorists from the Middle East."

The article went on. *"Authorities suspect that the attacks have increased, and have become more and more violent, possibly as a reaction to the current president. The organizations are based on racist ideology but are also driven by criminal profit from narcotics and human trafficking, extortion, and armed robbery. They are active in recruiting new members. Recent attacks include Ronald Lee Bray, from Huntington Beach, pleading guilty to a felony hate crime. He pushed an African American man in a wheelchair into a light pole after spitting on him and using racial slurs. He then raised his arm in a Nazi salute. Edward Topper, a self-proclaimed skinhead from Canyon County, was arrested for threatening to kill three Hispanic children."*

I turned to look at Richard. He looked at me, then followed my eyes back to the screen.

"Robert Coffman received a life sentence for beating and kicking a homeless man to death in Ventura County. Brian Tobias, received a sixteen-year sentence for attempting to kill an African American man in Lancaster in a drive-by shooting. One police officer testified that drive-by shooting a non-white person is often part of an initiation rite into a Skinhead group. Two Small Town Peckerwoods allegedly murdered nineteen-year old Rose Ann Johnston by setting her car on fire where she burned to death. She was a possible informant in the murder trial of another member. Two Skinheads allegedly beat a young Hispanic man at a mobile home park in the San Jacinto Valley. They knocked the victim unconscious and then stomped and kicked him in the head. He now resides in a long-term care facility with permanent brain damage. Local authorities suspect that the gang may have been involved with four other racially-motivated attacks which were committed in the area around the same time."

Another site stated that *"many hate groups are active in gay-bashing, Paki-bashing, and hippie-bashing."*

"Uh oh." Richard tried to kid. "Some of your clothes would definitely qualify as hippie."

The sun's heat bore down but I was chilled to the bone. I told Richard that the closest I'd ever come to anything like this was a Law & Order episode where one tattooed bald guy was in jail after climbing in through a window to kill another tattooed bald guy, only the dead one had a swastika around his neck. "And I thought, well, this is TV, isn't it? These things don't happen in Yucca Springs. But I got up, threw on my robe, and ran downstairs to make sure all the doors and windows were locked."

It got worse.

A scarier site instructed (instructed!) how to "simply and effectively abduct the enemy." I knew what followed was more in depth information than was a good idea for either of us to read, but we continued to read anyway, every word. To my heartache, tears slid from the corners of Richard's eyes. I said we'd read enough, but he reached over, turned the screen in his direction, and read aloud. "*You will need a vehicle with a deep enough trunk for a body, chloroform, rope, duct tape to use as a gag, disposable latex gloves, and a tarp or large plastic bag to protect the vehicle from any DNA remains.*" Shocked, I turned the screen back to read the all-cap warning: "*DNA TESTING HAS BECOME VERY SOPHISTICATED. TAKE EXTRA CARE TO COVER YOUR TRACKS. REMEMBER TO TAKE ADDED BAGS FOR THE VICTIM'S CLOTHES AND SHOES.*"

I gasped and thought about Richard and Charles ending up in such a bag. "How can it even be legal to have a website like this?" It felt like all the hatred in the world was spreading like a virus worming its way in to our homes to make us all sick. I snapped the lid shut.

How still the quiet was.

Rivers had warned that Charles' and Richard's attacker had been clever, leaving no obvious or traceable DNA. They'd worn gloves and hats and refrained from spitting, peeing, defecating, or wiping their nose near the scene. Richard asked if there was DNA in snot, and I detested how we'd come to a place where such a question was even necessary. "The cells lining the nose," Rivers said, sensibly. "They slough off. The same is true when we eliminate waste."

I think it was those words, spoken so matter-of-factly, that drove Richard over the edge. I looked at him. He was studying the end of the broom handle that had cracked down the middle. "This goddamn thing is under too much pressure!" he said before throwing it across the room.

An even more startling fact was that the prosecuting attorney's office indicated that without any witnesses, DNA samples, or suspects in custody, they weren't certain they'd be pursuing the case. I squinted my eyes at the phone, Richard looked away. We'd been out back when the second call came from Rivers, looking up at the sky where, waving his hand at the billowing cloud forming overhead, Richard had said, "Remember when drought was the only thing we had to worry about?"

"What I can't understand is that I thought Joey *was* a suspect?" I said, after we were back inside and I played the message again.

"So what happens next?"

It was the second time I'd been asked the same question that day, though it didn't seem like a good time to share this fact with Richard. "I have no idea," I said on my way up the stairs to take another shower. After we'd both read all we could stomach—more, actually—I took a shower and then Richard took one. I let the water beat down on my face. I think we both hoped the water would help restore us to the people we'd been before learning of so much organized hatred in the world, much of it only miles away. Some of it even closer, possibly right next door. When I came back down I said, "I'm going to find you something more sturdy than a broom handle to lean on."

Richard stood to reach in to his back pocket for his wallet. "My treat," I said. He sat back down, putting his arms behind him and lowering his weight down slowly. "Lenny was tough on me today. Hack squats, who knew?" And then out of the blue, "I'm just worried about you, that's all. You need to be careful." I turned to go. My silence implied I wasn't going to ask him what I was supposed to be careful about. He said, "I'd like to be able to trust... things again."

My curiosity got the best of me. "Things?"

He tapped his cane on the floor, trying to pretend he meant the broom handle, but I knew he didn't.

"I hear you have a date?" Lenny said over the top of my head, grabbing the door just as I was leaving.

Can't a girl have a secret for two seconds? I thought, walking away into the fresh air without answering.

In the beginning, I called Lenny "Dr. Goff." I also like to call him Richard's "knight in shining armor." He is both these things, but if someone were to ask me what I'd call him right then, in what felt like our own little self-contained cocoon that bordered on suffocating sometimes, I'd have to say "family."

And sometimes you just need a break from family.

A clue and a suspicion.

Richard's first question for Rivers the next morning was whether or not we needed to hire a lawyer. I knew he'd been up half the night worrying about it, and I didn't sleep well either. I cleaned everything that night, even the appliances. Fatigue mixed with fear is how we both met Rivers at the door.

From the look in River's eyes, I knew it would be a long, drawn out morning. He sat down slowly as he explained the difference between a lawyer who takes on a personal injury lawsuit and the state's prosecuting attorney. Embarrassingly, we hadn't researched the difference. We'd left every legal implication up to him. At least, I know I did.

"I didn't even know how much I don't know about everything you just said," Richard said, putting his hand up slowly like a student afraid to ask a question.

"You're lucky," Rivers said. "Okay, let's say you are injured in a car accident. You may have a personal injury claim against the party who caused it. A personal injury claim is when someone's negligent or unlawful conduct caused your accident or contributed to it, and as a result of that person's behavior, you suffered financial, physical, or emotional damages. But what happened to you and Charles was no accident. It was deliberate. Which is why it becomes a criminal offense against a person or property motivated by the offender's prejudice against a race, religion, cultural background, or sexual orientation. A hate crime, essentially."

I can remember choreography in a heartbeat, but I could not repeat one word of what Rivers had just said. Like rain on Sunnyslope Drive, his words ran off. I looked over to see how Richard was doing, and I could see he was straining to process the details too, harder once it sounded too complicated, which was pretty much from the beginning. "Uh-huh, uh-huh," he kept saying. "We read that last night online."

"Right," Rivers said. "I'd wash my hands of the internet if I were you. Ask me your questions." It was the way he said it that made me think *this man is going to help us.*

"But if the prosecutor won't take on the case, do we even have a case?" Richard asked. A good question, I thought.

"Typically, personal injury claims include things like car accidents, slip and falls, medical malpractice, product liability, even wrongful death. But the point is, they were caused by negligence or carelessness. Generally, they aren't premeditated. In a personal injury case, you can claim damages for your injury, including past and future medical bills, lost work time, and pain and suffering, but again this is not the kind of case we have. Your attackers didn't hurt you by *accident*."

I wondered if Rivers had any idea just how little grasp of the sleazy, seedy underworld it takes to make certain people really nervous—certain people like *us*. I looked at Richard. He squeezed his cane. His knuckles were so red they looked like two flames flickering on top of his hand. If I could have, I would have fallen to my knees and begged Rivers to please, please, take this complication from our lives, and resolve it one way or another. I would have kissed his feet if he would just tell us what to do, or, better still, do it *for* us. I had to hold back, for fear of sounding too useless to help Richard through all that would come next.

Whatever that was.

"What happened to you becomes a criminal prosecution, where the legal standard is guilt beyond a reasonable doubt," Rivers said sitting down in front of Richard. "In a personal injury case, the legal standard is a preponderance of evidence. This means all you have to prove is that the defendant is more than fifty percent likely to be responsible for your injury. These different standards explain why defendants who are acquitted in criminal cases often lose personal injury lawsuits based on the same evidence."

As though daring himself to understand, Richard said, "We have a personal injury case, then?" his voice rising.

"Say we find a suspect we can bring to trial, and say we lose the trial. Then yes, you would likely be able to file a personal injury case."

Richard made a noise with his lips that sounded like a horse, when you step up to the fence with a big red apple in your hand.

"Then how will the drawing help *any*thing?" I said reaching for a straw, any straw. It would have been easier to run naked through Yucca Springs than have to live with the thought of another dead-end—nothing resolved, nothing better happening soon. (This is where Billy comes in, I see it now.)

"At this point we have a clue and we have a suspicion. But..." he took a deep breath and looked out the window.

Richard leaned in closer but was silent. He looked drained, worn-out.

"But what?" I said.

"Well, this Joey kid. He doesn't know what we have or what we don't have, or how much we know, as opposed to how much we suspect."

Richard and I look at each other as Rivers, before our very eyes, becomes a larger-than-life TV detective who lives by his own shrewd set of instincts—who is going to find out who did the crime and why, ready to sniff out, outsmart, and outmaneuver the offender. "I've gone on a lot less," he said, addressing the window again.

I couldn't wait to hear the thrill in Miss Stephanie's voice when I told her that if there was ever a more clever and generous man, I hadn't met him.

"I've got enough to warrant my driving to Cottle County, Texas," Rivers came by to say the next day instead of calling to tell us, which I found touching. He'd not only found Joey's home address, date of birth, height, weight, eye color, but also his criminal record that winds through several states. "There's an incident of inappropriately groping a girl at school when he was a minor, loads of outdated parking tickets," he said. "One from Yucca Springs on the night of the attack."

Richard fell back against the couch. "That's the evidence we need, right?"

"It proves he was in Yucca Springs the night of the attack. There's also a report of attempted rape at a party in Narcisso, but the charge was dropped. I'm figuring the girl didn't want to get dragged through the mud in a town the size of a church choir."

"And you want to go there, why exactly?" I said.

"I want to talk to these girls," he said sounding all business, but his eyes showed a lighter expression. "And I was thinking..." he let the sentence drop for a second, looking down, as if not wanting to meet our eyes, "that I might take another little side trip to San Diego on the way."

"San Diego isn't on the way to Texas," Richard said, unsuspecting.

I brought my finger to my lips to shush him. *I see,* I thought to myself. *On one hand, our hard case. With nothing but softness in the other.* I followed him out to the parking lot behind the Star Struck where his car was parked. Out of the corner of my eye, I saw Karen sneak inside Mr. Lawson's office. A second later, his shade came down in one swift pull.

Rivers leaned against the hood of his car. He stood very still for a minute. He stretched his arms in front of his chest, and linked his hands before dropping them into a fold. I could tell he wanted to talk about Miss Stephanie, and I waited quietly until he got his courage up. Funny, isn't it? How a man can take on the cruel, cold, violence of the world, but have so much trouble conquering his fears of women. I felt for him. After a few more minutes of his kicking up the dust, I couldn't take the silence any longer. "I'm sure she would enjoy a road trip. But only," his eyes lit up, "if she can find a sub for her class. How long does it take to get there?"

"Two hours to San Diego depending on traffic. Texas will take at least," he cleared his throat, "a couple of days." His cheeks blushed.

"I want you to know how much this means to Richard."

"We have all the pieces. We just need to fit them together." He turned to open the car door, then quickly turned back to say, "She's something special, isn't she?"

"She is."

I half expected him to say more, but he climbed in the front seat without speaking, and the car filled with the rumbling sound of someone bound and determined to get things rolling.

On all fronts.

∼⚬⚬∽

Late the next afternoon, I stood on the back step surveying the town. It was Saturday—no class, no pressing concerns, other than what to wear, before hiking up to the entrance of Desert Christ Park and the stone church where Billy would be waiting with a picnic basket. Technically, the stone church is the Rock Chapel. And it's set in the middle of Desert Christ Park, high up over town, created by a man who sculptured Twelve Apostles, the Virgin Mary, lots of angels, and a fifteen foot, three ton statue of Jesus, all in hopes of inspiring world peace. It's like walking through someone's vision of holy. I nearly gasped when Billy suggested the park, but I couldn't find my voice to object. I ran upstairs to fix myself up.

As soon as I hit the bottom stair, Richard took off his headphones, lowered them to his shoulders, shook his head at what I was wearing and said, "*That* looks like something you'd wear only if everything else you own burned up in a fire."

I looked down at myself, unable to know with any faith if he was wrong. I'm not nearly as good at casually-feminine as Richard is. "There are too many colors going on," he said limping closer, zig-zagging his finger over me, his eyes darted everywhere at once.

"You're saying that to be mean."

"I'm saying it because you look like a buckeye butterfly."

I sank onto the bottom step.

"And what's going on with your eyes?"

"What's wrong with my eyes? I followed your instructions to a T."

I had. At the last minute, I'd layered on my "theater eyes," patting my lids with a base, tapping aqua shadow to the lid from my lash line to the crease, and using the same shade below my lower lashes, carefully smudging. "Too much?"

"Not if you're going for drag queen," he made another zig-zag with his finger.

"Is the lip gloss okay?"

"Did I say anything about lip gloss? Double up on the lip gloss."

I ran upstairs to try again.

While trying to tone down my color scheme, my phone rang. I put Miss Stephanie on speaker while I redressed and she talked—oh, how she talked. Her voice came quickly, almost breathlessly, like a little girl at her own birthday party just before she blows out the candles. "Listen, he said, 'why don't you come with me to Texas and I said *me?*' And he said we could leave tomorrow and be back in a few days and I didn't know what to say at first. My sister said I should go, no question. I'm not getting any younger. But the thing is, he wants me to talk to Joey and I'm not so keen on that. So then he said, 'tell me something, Stephanie, do you trust me?' And I said yes, 'of course,' I didn't even have to think about it. And he said, 'well, Stephanie, that's good to know.' I have to admit, I like the way he says my name, but is that enough to take a three day trip with a man? I guess I know the answer to that, because I already asked my studio director, Maria, if she would cover my classes."

Of all the things I could have responded to, I couldn't get over how strange it sounded to hear Miss Stephanie refer to *her* studio director. I imagined a younger brunette version of ballet authority. I felt my heart beat faster. I was imagining *me*. (I have these moments sometimes when I feel my heartbeat speed up like this, like bat wings at dusk, as if to remind me how fast time is flying by. And I have this overwhelming sense of how silly it is to worry about anything at all.)

There was a pause, as though she was shifting herself at the barre. A few seconds later she said, "So it looks like I'm off to Texas." With only the slightest hint of insincerity, she added, "Richard and you are the most important reasons why."

"I think we just might get somewhere now that *you* are in charge," I said.

When I came back down, Richard was sound asleep. His face appeared childlike, beyond boyish. Sleep had returned him to innocence.

I tiptoed past and slipped out the door.

Going to the chapel.

If you grow up in Yucca Springs, the Rock Chapel is likely where you experience your first kiss.

And likely more.

I hadn't been up there in years. Ever since my mother told me that the chapel was where she and my dad used to go in their "necking days," I felt like I'd worked too hard to point my mind in the opposite direction to want to go anywhere near it. I didn't want to be like my mother making out in the church. I didn't want to be like any of the girls in high school making out in the church, who dated non-stop—and were looking for someone to marry ten minutes after graduation or before, if things got tricky. Which they did. On a regular basis.

Every time I heard about the vandalism happening up there—like when someone stole an ear off one of the statues—I'd wonder if I'd been conceived right under the eyes of forty life-size statues of Christ's disciples. It would be just like my dad to thumb his nose at all their cold-eyed disapproval by unhooking my mother's bra in plain sight, then stealing one of their ears as a souvenir.

When Miss Stephanie said the chapel was the perfect metaphor for a small town, I asked her what she meant by that. She said, "well, it's both charming *and* claustrophobic."

I can honestly say that before she said that, I'd felt like someone on the outside looking in at everyone else necking in the chapel, feeling all smug about the fact that you didn't have to be a genius to know you shouldn't smooch in a house of God. But after she said it, I felt shaken, as if I was just another girl from Yucca Springs. And if someone asked me where I was headed looking all dressed up, I'd have to say, "to the Rock Chapel, where else?"

Next, when I told her my first date with Billy was going to be in the chapel, "where my mother used to make out, can you believe it?" hoping she'd find it funny, and she said, "Well," lowering her voice in that way that always makes what she's about to say next sound really important, "you *are* both from Yucca Springs, so I imagine there will be a few similarities to your dating lives," I froze for a second and there was all this pressure behind my eyes. "Billy suggested it," I said quickly, as if it mattered. Then I made some excuse and hung up.

But even before all that, I knew the chapel didn't feel like the right place to go. But I'd persuaded myself it was high-time to let go of the past.

Looking back, I'm pretty sure I didn't believe it. Not for a second.

Now, whenever I think about what went on in the chapel in my family alone, all I can think is that I hope to *God* the statues are as blind as they look. For weeks leading up to Yucca Spring's annual potluck at the park, I won't go to any cashier who knew my mother. I won't talk to the lady at the library who says she adored my mother (but slept with my dad anyway). I especially wouldn't go to the Post Office where the Postmistress went to school with my mom and is still the biggest gossip. The first time I'd stepped up to her counter alone, she said, "You look more and more like Peggy every day." I do look like my mother, but I think what she really wanted to say was "*tsk, tsk.*" How many times had she embarrassed my mother by remembering, out loud, the awful day my mom had to leave high school sobbing after she was told she wouldn't be able to attend graduation. "You poor thing," she kept saying to my mom, just to rub it in.

I'm just really glad they sell stamps at Walmart now.

Brava!

It was a bright afternoon with a hint of moisture in it. I was nervous walking up to the gate. Tingles ran up my legs at the sight of the only vehicle parked in the lot—standing out against the parched hills, a red Jeep.

I felt the color like a warning. And when I decided to pay it no mind, I felt that too. Well, I thought, if it is a warning, I'll know soon enough. I opened the gate and walked through, like a jackrabbit goes on hopping with its forelegs, even after a car mashes its hind-end flat.

A few quail raced by. The skies were just beginning to darken with the promise of rain, and the wind had come up slightly, tickling the hair on my arms. I bent over to flick a few sticky willies from the hem of my skirt. When I looked up, Billy was walking toward me, his smile as wide as I remembered, his right hand over his eyes to block the sun. In natural light, I could see that his hair had a sprinkling of grey and, given my years, it felt a little scary. It might have been a turn off yet, oddly, it only made him more attractive to me.

Not to be depressing, but—okay, it *is* depressing when a young woman falls for older men (the natural gas man was, I think, *forty*) because she's missed out on any kind of real love from her father. If that is what you are thinking.

Since it's what I am thinking. Right now, that is. But it wasn't clear to me then. There were too many stars in my eyes.

Meanwhile, on another level (a more pathetic-but-common-to-young-women level), I went to the chapel mostly because Billy took an interest in me. Even if he only pretended to take an interest, sometimes we feel what we *want* to feel and sort of make up the rest. When Billy whistled and said, "You're a sight for sore eyes," I thought how they were just words, corny even, yet I let the air spin around them soft and sweet as cotton candy.

Out of nowhere, the Robert Frost poem I memorized years before in Creative Movement came back to me: "*Oh, come forth into the storm and be my love in the rain.*" Miss Stephanie added the class to help us get in touch with our "inner uniqueness," she said. But not wanting even our uniqueness to look sloppy, she decided that anyone signing up had to have at least two years of ballet first, which some of the more-hippie moms felt was unfair.

I've heard people say there is a calm before the storm, but anyone who's been through a monsoon knows that there's a lot of built-up tension in the air. "One photo behind stage shows more truth than a hundred I take in front," is how Richard compares it.

And tension is what I felt as Billy and I walked past the statues and into the chapel where he'd set food out on one of the wooden pews. He made tuna sandwiches with crunchy bacon. "I haven't had bacon since my mother used to make it," I said.

"There's no smell as good as bacon frying," he said.

I didn't agree, not at the moment, anyway. I was getting whiffs of his soap again, but it was the aftershave that was affecting me. I felt no other smell could be half as good. It made me feel afraid. It made me feel brave. Both at once, surprisingly. "Never underestimate the power of a woman's perfume," my mother said about her own once. But I'm here to say a man's cologne is even more effective.

I can do this, we whisper to ourselves backstage. And then, we *do*. Fear and then conquering it is what the stage had taught me. As soon as you leave the safety of the wings, fear rushes out of you like a burst in a pipeline. I think I missed performing so much that I needed to know if I was still capable of facing my fears—if I still had what it takes.

There it is, the sad truth.

I can do this, I thought. *I can lift his shirt out from under his belt.*

Done. One quick flick, faster than I deal with a mosquito.

I even thought of licking the beads of sweat off his brow, from the fold where his stomach spilled over the top of his thigh, and from every pudgy finger on his hand.

As if to mock my thoughts, in one hard pull he popped open a bottle of champagne and passed the bottle to me. "I thought champagne would be good," he said.

"Maybe too," I said. But I grabbed the bottle and took a sip. Then another. Then a swig, one after the other. *Dangerous.* Was it the almighty stares of the statues with their beady little eyes and stone cold faces?

As if to break the spell, a girl pulled up to the open door of the chapel on her scooter, talking so loud on her phone that I thought of something Lenny said about a new patient he was seeing who'd suffered a fractured pelvis after a serious bike accident where the oncoming driver had been talking on his cell. I repeated the story to Billy, just to say something. "My friend Lenny thinks millions more people would be on dialysis if they had to choose between giving up a kidney or their phones." Billy laughed and said something about back in the day when spam was still pork in a can, which made me wonder just *how* old he was. As the girl sped away, the smell of gas vapors spread through the chapel. Lost for words, I was about to mention the odor, but he put his finger on my lips to silence them just before leaning over to kiss me.

I pulled away.

I wanted to kiss him, but something stopped me. I even began to feel a little sorry for myself because my body couldn't (or wouldn't?) give in to the seizing arousal it felt. I even remember thinking what an unreasonable thing it felt like to let guilt get in the way like that. And that's when I saw the statue of Jesus pointing his finger. At me! Or at the part of me below my waist and above my thighs. As if to say, "Young lady, *there* is not a good place to give in to right now. How'd that work for your mama?" Stunned, I put my hand on Billy's shoulder to push him back.

Except my balance was a little off.

Then, well, I don't quite know what all came over me, but the guilt, the reluctance, the trying to control myself—I still don't know what it was—dared me to dare myself. Even though, and this is the least sexy part, I also have this clear memory of hearing my own voice say, *I have this sneaky feeling that you are about to repeat history.*

I still wonder what strange and powerful urge took over my body. Was it fate? Destiny? Voodoo? Or just plain old lust, allowing myself to be capable of what I was biologically capable of? Or some other sad cliché like "the apple doesn't fall far from the tree." Was it some crazy uncontrollable impulse to hang on to my mother, her memory?

Or was it that I missed performing so much?

Or sex so much?

Or both?

I'm afraid I'll never know for sure.

I do know this: It was empowering! I'll never forget that. Billy was putty in my hands.

I was rapt. *Rapt!*

The first time I heard Miss Stephanie use the word, she was so proud after recital she put both hands over her heart and said how *rapt* she was by our performance. All I could think was "in what?" I remember asking Richard what he thought Miss Stephanie was wrapped in. Young Richard didn't know what the word meant either, but he leaned both elbows on the vanity, narrowed his eyes as if he did, and said, "Us, silly."

Billy's nostrils flared open like a bull when you walk by with a handful of hay. I stuffed any veto way back in my head. I knew the danger of letting my thoughts pull me in one direction while muscle memory needs to pull in another. So that's all the thinking I allowed myself. "Don't move," he said, lifting me up with the muscles in his forearms to remove my panties. Sparks rushed up my thighs. Real live sparks! I swear. He straddled me. I felt like I couldn't breathe, like I might be squashed.

But I wanted to be squashed, a little, didn't I?

The rain started to fall. I said, "I should lock the door," and hoisted myself up from the pew and ran to the doors to lock them tight. Then the feeling came over me again, the spell. I decided to walk back like a model on a runway, executing a pivot turn into a double Chaîné turn: right, left, right, left, *right*. Like a butterfly landing on a large pink petal, wings open in wide second position, I sat on Billy's lap, wrapped my legs around his back until my calf muscles bulged, and clung to him like a baby possum.

Let me leap from the wings and slide myself onto you so willing, so smooth, so strong.

Rain splashed onto the roof. The chapel grew darker. I cried out "ahh." *This*, I remember thinking, *is the purest music of the body.* I could not tell you if Billy was making any sounds. I could not remember the first thing about Billy. He disappeared, along with the rest of the world. That's what always happens when you are working really,

really hard for something you want. Like in Pointe class, you raise your torso up, work at finding the perfect balance, and wait for the magic.

When we finally rolled onto the floor facing each other, our breaths slowing, he said, "I told you."

"What did you tell me?" I said, startled.

"That you *can* make me do anything."

Make you? I waited for him to explain, but he didn't. It took me a minute, then I remembered what he'd said earlier and all I could think was *that is so not the point*.

Or maybe it was the point.

It prompted the other side of my brain to kick in. Miss Stephanie once said that most people are followers— monkey see, monkey do. "But as an artist, it's your job to question everything." And that was all, positively all she had to say. I've questioned copycat behavior ever since. It used to drive my mother crazy. "Can't you just do it, Lucy, like everyone else?" she'd yell. Prompting me to yell back, "No. Mom. I. Cannot."

I lay there questioning if it is really such a terrible thing to behave like a Cholla bud, latching out on the first passerby? I mean, buds need to bloom. A bud can only wait so long. Especially after too many nights of wondering if the natural gas man was *it*.

Of course, I was thinking all this *before* Billy's tongue licked the inside of my thigh again, which immediately made me spend less time thinking and more time feeling. Which is good because I didn't want to expose my private *thoughts*, since I didn't know this Billy all that well, now did I?

I sat up, drew my legs apart with my hands on my knees (my turn out has always been exceptional), exposing, of course, so much more.

Brava! Lucy, you are so brave!
Brava! Lucy, you are so bold! Unflinching!
Brava! Lucy, you are the most self-willed woman ever!
Oh, and Lucy?
Yes?
There's just one little thing you forgot.

~~~

I think Billy was relieved when I said I wanted to walk home, staring at me like he couldn't believe what I'd just said—or his good luck, I'm not quite sure which. "You sure? " he said. But he didn't insist on driving me, which is the surest way of saying he didn't want to. His taillights grew dimmer until he became a tiny red dot on the horizon.

History repeating itself, indeed.

I couldn't even decide in what direction to walk home in. I literally had to will my feet to walk me down the hill. I could make a promise to myself, though, so that's what I did. I promised that I would not feel ashamed. And since shame is drilled into Catholic girls pretty much from day one, I said it with every ounce of conviction I could muster, just to be sure it stuck.

So this is the way the whole afternoon evolved, the best and the worst of it.

The best is that it's not every young woman who can say she was in complete command of her sexuality—*not* taken advantage of, but the other way around. Not lead on, but deliberately leading, with conviction.

And *deliberately* is key, Rivers had said it.

The worst is that the more I thought about it, the more I realized that the courage I had found—that rose up from deep inside like a root reaching through earth—is *the* feminine power that so many supposedly holy men throughout time have tried, with just as much conviction, to keep under wraps. (Rapts!)

And while I didn't know the whole of my premonition yet, I did feel that no matter what happened, the next phase of my life had begun courageously.

And that meant a lot to me.

Despite Billy.

Despite everything.

And so, as soon as I was inside the door of the Star Struck, I ran upstairs and had myself a good, long, congratulatory cry.

Thirteen

"The truest expression of a people is in its dance.
Bodies never lie."
~Agnes de Mille

Light and warm.

No matter what stage you act out on, a Saturday performance is generally followed by a Sunday of rest.

It was nearly noon when I rolled out of bed with a pounding hangover. I took a shower, letting the water beat down. After toweling off, I stood staring at myself in the mirror.

I took a good long look.

More of an inspection, really.

I didn't care what my butt looked like, or whether my small breasts had been appealing to Billy or not. My inspection didn't have anything to do with that.

After a few moments I took a step closer, wiped the steam away with my hand, and I don't know what I was expecting to see—or was afraid to see—and I haven't told a soul what I did see because it's really hard to describe without sounding crazy. It's just impossible to explain something you don't quite believe yourself.

But I will try.

Not only was there something odd about the flush spreading over my cheeks, but from deep behind my belly button (and here's the part that makes me sound like a lunatic) I felt a little prickle. Not a poke, but something pricked me, like a stiff tag you have to cut off the inside of a new shirt.

The desert is full of all kinds of things that prick and stick and sting, that's what people would say. So I didn't try to explain it to anyone—much less myself—how I knew, but I did. I knew my future at once, just like all those years ago in pre-ballet when fate was a welcome relief in the stifling air. People say it's not possible to know so early on, but I'm here to tell you again, *oh yes it is.*

You could have knocked me over with a goldfinch feather.

I stared pretty hard at the floor, fear the root inside me now. I closed my eyes briefly. And who knows why my thoughts went racing backward—to grade school— instead of ahead. More precisely, to Norita Jeanne.

Norita Jeanne was a girl from school I didn't much like, but I guess I've always struggled with the idea that if someone liked me well enough to invite me to my first overnight, how could I refuse? I first learned this clumsy, compromising truth about myself through Norita Jeanne.

At one point, after we'd changed into our pajamas, she crawled into bed and shone a flashlight up from under the tent of sheets. The orangey-red light looked like a heart beating, spookier than I liked, and she kept poking at the sheet with the flashlight—poke, poke, poke. When she came out from under the sheets, the heart disappeared, but my memory of it held on. Every time I closed my eyes, there it was again, pumping with life.

I turned away from the mirror and told myself that it was the effect of too much champagne. But the truth is, you can't know what you know and have all that much luck denying it. It's too late for that. Had I been able to talk to my mother, I think she probably would have said something like "oh, no." Then she would have gone into the kitchen and lit up a cigarette, before coming back to put her arm around me so we could both cry on the sleeves of each other's bathrobes.

I turned back to the mirror and, after the earth gave way under my feet for a second, I knew that what I was about to say needed to be said. For the first time. By me. "You're pregnant."

There. You said it. And though there are some words you never get used to saying, no matter how many times you say them aloud, you have to say them anyway, until the dark sky overhead gives way to the first blink of dawn.

And so it was true. I laid back down. *You'll manage, Lucy. Managing is what a life of discipline has taught you... I'm almost sure of it.*

Hoop dee do.

I sat down on the back step with my laptop on my knees, ready to read an email Richard said was waiting. "They're on their way to Texas," he said, but he didn't ask about my date with Billy. He wanted to, I could hear it in his voice when he said, "you look like you could use this," and handed me a large glass of orange juice.

From: stephanielivestodance@yahoo.com

To: starstrucklucy@gmail.com
richardbdancin@yahoo.com

Subject: We're off!

Dear Lucy & Richard,

We left San Diego in River's convertible with James Taylor playing in the CD player. Fortunately, I brought a few tunes of my own.

The rest of the drive made me want to stick my head out the window. The freedom! It wasn't long after the coast disappeared behind us that we began to pass through field after field of yellow clover until we came to a small town outside of Eloy where dogs really do loll around in the middle of the street.

We'll spend the night in Tucson, River says. I feel about sixteen, I'm so nervous. Except, everyone is beautiful at sixteen. I'm afraid my tummy's grown a little soft.

In any event, we'll cross into Texas tomorrow. "Not to worry," Rivers says, "we have this one in the bag." He's fond of saying things like that.

And the rest, well, I'll have to rely on muscle memory—.

Love, Stephanie.

I hit reply: "*You ARE beautiful. Inside and out. And I'm not just saying that.*"

I was glad I liked Rivers. It's hard when you don't like somebody someone you love falls for. I closed the lid and without meaning to—I choked up. Hopefully the admission we needed from Joey was only hours away, but that's not what was affecting me. It was the tension I imagined in River's car, the flirty front seat. Miss Stephanie finding someone to love is what I'd wanted for her since as far back as I could remember, so it should not have made me cry.

But it did. It made me cry so hard. Miss Stephanie would say that we should all give more credit to our subconscious.

The screen door smacked behind Richard. Not able to contain himself any longer, he said, "What did he do?"

"Billy's not why I'm crying." And before I could even wipe away my tears, he came out with what he'd been holding in since, if I know Richard (and I do), mere minutes after I'd left to meet Billy, and he'd fished around until he caught something. "He's married."

I couldn't speak. It took too much effort to speak.

"He has a wife and son in Seattle."

In the distance, I could see all the rooftops of our little desert town and I remember a sense of feeling trapped all of a sudden, as stranded by my choices as my mother must have felt by hers.

The rest of the day passed in a daze except for a few chosen words that came at me in a continuous loop—all the names my mother had flung at my dad: *Fool. Fraud. Cheat. Con. Double-crosser.* And the worst, "You're an asshole!" she had screamed. "And when you've been an asshole your whole life, you really start to stink!" She'd laughed after she said it, but it was too much to take in about someone I thought I should love. I was nine. I didn't have the tools.

Then suddenly, it was his voice I heard—my father's: "Now *there's* the biggest hoop dee do out the left side of the car, I tell ya, the Star Struck Dance Studio, la de da de dum, dream a little dream of me" as if he'd come back just to mock all my big dreams. "Gotcha!" he taunted. "Gotcha good." Then he disappeared, tail lights glowing red.

I look back now and I get it, how my refusal to wear the sparkly red tutu in my first Nutcracker was really no mystery. I've had a mistrust of the color red ever since I can remember, so I wanted to wear the white tutu. I insisted on it. And I did wear it, after I cried and cried about wearing the red one.

My dance life and my emotions had become one.

Another thing that's no mystery is what my mother meant when she said, "Mind your p's and q's, Lucy. Especially your yes's and no's." She wanted me to understand that even if we had no idea how our actions would affect our future, we should always behave as if they would make some kind of difference down the road.

When I think of the way I rolled my eyes at her, I could just die.

"I guess what our moms try to teach us comes in one ear and out the other when we are kids, right?" I said staring at my tummy. It was the first question I asked of the life growing inside of me.

No mystery here, either.

My solo had become a duet.

Three hard knocks.

In the days after finding out about my "situation" (the word people would use, I was sure of it), I started running the numbers again in my head again. Money was all I could think about. I started to obsess, adding up what was coming in and comparing it to what was going out, over and over. My fears of business failure loomed larger, more pointed and more upsetting. I wanted not to tell anyone how worried I was, but I always wound up telling Richard.

He, of course, told Lenny, who, of course, was even more determined to help. "I've got an idea," he said turning on his heels. The next day he sent a mass email to every past client and to his colleagues' clients. By the next week, I had to add two more classes.

Lynette, Leslie, and Lisa were still coming, but there were so many others now, including a neatly-dressed fifty-ish man who insisted on keeping his shirt and tie on. As soon as he bent over, a couple paperclips fell from his breast pocket. "You're a mobile Office Max," Leslie said, though I'd never seen her remotely interested in teasing anyone before. I wanted to tell him to peel off his tie but I knew to let these things happen on their own time.

Another man came out of the bathroom and scanned us all with a squint. I couldn't place where I knew him from, but then it came to me. Mr. Mike! I would have needed to see him in eyeglasses, khaki pants, and a *Food 4 Less* name tag over his shirt pocket in order to recognize him. But Mr. Mike in swimming trunks and gym socks? My pride turned somersaults.

Mr. Mike had saved the freshest loaves of bread for my mother and she loved to flirt with him. "Now, Mike, you did *not* save this loaf just for us, did you?" she'd say in a sing-songy voice she never used at home. There were still people around town who weren't willing to meet my eyes, or Richard's—how they'd almost see us but not quite— but Mr. Mike never stopped saving my dignity by smiling and handing me a warm loaf of bread when I shopped. By coming to class, I felt like he'd saved the day.

By far the most fascinating new student was Hu. "Still suffering from the lifelong pain of early foot binding," Lenny emailed. "My husband drive me all the way from Beaumont to take your class," Hu said as soon as she was inside the door. Her gray hair was pulled back in a tight bun so that her scalp showed through the silvery strands. She was tiny, less than five feet tall, with Kleenex tucked into her sweater sleeve. Atop her head sat a pair of purple-rimmed eyeglasses that, unbelievably, stayed put whenever she bent over. She wobbled in with a blue yoga mat under her arm, moving her tiny pale feet over the floor like soft paws tapping the wood. It took Lynette saying, "Oh, Sweet Jesus, you're the smallest person I've ever met," to make Hu smile. I am in awe of Lynette. So much heart in all that blue.

"They bound her feet when she was four years old, can you believe it?" I said later to Richard. I was eating a bakery cupcake. He dabbed a little frosting from my lips. Mr. Mike brought a box to class but I think people were too embarrassed to eat them in front of us. So, as soon as they'd gone, we ate them.

"History is ruthless," he said grabbing a cupcake. Then, as if thinking better of his words, "Of course, there's always the present."

And I didn't mean to tear up when Hu told us that when she was a girl, foot binding was a way to display wealth and beauty in China. But as you know, I've always been a crier and pregnancy makes me even more of one.

Trying to cheer me up, Lisa said, "Don't worry, honey. They don't bind feet for status anymore, they carry Louis Vuitton." I could tell she was sorry as soon as she said it, but it didn't insult Hu. She laughed, so I laughed too, or I tried to. But a lot of stress had formed between my ears since the weekend, and laughter didn't exactly echo the mood of everything I was thinking like—how on earth I would concentrate if Billy showed up.

He didn't show up. Ten minutes after the hour, I locked the door and began class with the easy-to-count beats of Sade. "For everyone who is new today," I said over the music. "I promise to take it slowly. And for everyone else, there isn't one of us who can't benefit from going over the basics again."

"You got that right," Leslie said. Lisa nodded, a little afraid to speak again, I think.

I reached up, slowly with one arm, then with both arms.

Then, three hard knocks on the glass.

I turned to see Billy. Like an old house, I stood upright, but my frame started to buckle. I thought I was stronger, tougher, and that seeing him again wouldn't mean all that much since it was only the one time... or the two. Still, how could I have known that I'd crumble at the sight of him? Saint Valentine himself wouldn't have known.

Lisa must have noticed the panicked look on my face. I watched, helpless, as she lowered her arms and walked over to the open curtain that hung between the waiting room and the studio and, in one swift motion, pulled it shut. I thought, *she is so in tune with animal natures, she can sense my fear like the cats and dogs she tends.* I remember her quick reflex, how everything about her was so coolly in charge and I think: *triage.* I closed my eyes and listened to the knocks taper off and then to the sound of Billy's engine starting up. Before speeding away, he stepped on the gas hard as if to say, *Jesus, what's the big deal? You wanted it as much as I did.*

And he is right about that. I did.

Except he couldn't be as casually-consensual about it now, could he? Not with a wife and kid at home. Sometimes I wish I could go back to that moment so I could run out there and say... what?

The fact that I still can't think of anything useful tells me I probably did the right thing to ignore him.

I opened my eyes, relieved to see Lisa standing confidently in my periphery again, as if she hadn't just lost her concentration to be super supportive like that.

To this day, whenever I think of Lisa, I think about the way she totally had my back that day. How naturally she'd been able to recognize what I wouldn't let myself see when I first met Billy, and what my mother had refused to see about my dad until it was too late—that the man on the other side of the curtain was not worthy of me.

Two strong wings.

I didn't grieve over Billy.

I cried, but I didn't grieve.

Because I know what grief is. Grief is emotionally and physically exhausting, dragging down everything you say and do. But after the truth about Billy sank in, I actually had more energy.

Anyway, all of my emotions surrounding Billy felt much more complicated than they do today. Today, it's pretty simple. The second I saw him, the biological clock people talk about started to tick. Short sharp sounds, one for every second of time that passes really is a good metaphor. Because truthfully, I think I actually wanted a baby.

Or part of me did. The part that longed for family.

Also, thanks to Billy, I realize how close I had come to being a twenty-six year old woman who'd slept with only one man... and because of him, there's been exactly two.

And I'm fine with that.

For the time being.

But can I tell you a little secret? There are nights I let myself revise the choreography in the chapel. I stand in fifth position, feet set for the slow, sustained adagio, my leg slowly rising into passe and with control and ease, développé. All of which may sound technically innocent, but here's the clincher: my suitor is stretched out on the floor directly beneath me, head back, staring up with a huge smile on his face. The whole scene is like a little gift waiting for me under all the layers of stress. And nothing the naysayers, worrywarts, or fusspots say is true. When the flesh of your thighs come to life under your own direction, it does feel as good as it does with a man. The body wants what it wants and hardly cares who comes along for the ride.

For those few breathtaking seconds anyway.

Still, I hope to find someone who really matters to me one day.

I was stretching on the barre thinking all this—not for the first time, mind you—when the curtain, hung so children can play on one side while their siblings dance on the other, came into focus. And every time I stare at it, I can still see Lisa flying into action, and how sliding it shut was not only the most literal way to close a curtain on Billy, but the most effective.

And I'm always reminded what two strong feminine wings look like, and what they can do, when they pull together.

A couple of days passed. Days of wondering. Days of waiting.

When Rivers and Miss Stephanie finally drove up, they sat in the driveway discussing something before climbing out of the car. I felt pretty sure they were about to tell us something bad—we were half expecting it. When they walked up to the door, Rivers looked down at his feet. As soon as he was inside he said, "Stephanie has something for you." Then he tipped his hat and moved backwards out of the room.

Moments later, a handwritten note from Joey was in Richard's hands. He said he needed to work up the nerve to read it, but instead, he called Lenny. Seconds later, Lenny spoke so loud I could hear him, "Hold off until I get there, love, okay? I'm on my way."

But Richard couldn't wait. He took a breath, clamped down on his cane, pushed it forward and back a few times like a gearshift, and began to read the note aloud. His voice was so shrill it could have belonged to a cactus wren. "Yeah, it was me. Me and my dad." Then he stopped reading, pulled himself up, shifted his legs, and started again. "We beat those two fags up, sure as shit we did. There are too many fags, too many kikes, too many coons, too many wetbacks and ragheads, someone's got to do something. The government ain't doing shit."

And then the signature: Joey Gordon.

What on earth did homosexuality have to do with African Americans, or immigrants for that matter? And what, pray tell, is a raghead?

As soon as I thought about the nice man who works at Joshua's Café, who likes to match the color of his tie to his turban, I knew. But it was the words "me and my *dad*" that stunned us the most. Richard wheeled around to look at Miss Stephanie who sat next to us on a folding chair. She'd sent Rivers out for takeout and a bottle of wine. "I'll make that two," he said as he backed out the door.

I glanced out the window to see Lenny pull up just as Mr. Lawson was closing up for the day. Lenny got out of his car and gave a quick flick of a wave to Mr. Lawson, but there was nothing rude about it. Mr. Lawson not only ignored the courtesy, he lowered his brows and narrowed his eyes. What struck me as sad—I mean, really sad, but I kept it to myself—was that on Richard's lap was this horrible confession of hatred and ignorance and bigotry, while another example of it stood right outside our door, claiming to be a pillar of the community.

Lenny moved quickly to come inside. Richard took one look at him and started to sob. Lenny dropped down next to him. "Oh, love," he said hugging Richard tight, "this is good news." Then, with even more affection, he repeated himself. "This is *good* news."

Richard passed him the note. His eyes grew wide as he read. When he set it down, I picked it up and that's when I noticed the words were in black ink, but the commas were blue. Did he use two pens? I wondered. I think all of our minds raced ahead with questions.

"If you told me in the beginning that he'd confess as soon as you showed him his own drawing," Lenny said to Miss Stephanie, "I would've said you were crazy. How did you get him to write this?"

"It's like Rivers said, guilt is a like a powder keg. And we were the match."

Right after she said that, Rivers came in with a sack of groceries, set them on the floor, and pulled up a chair next to Stephanie. I noticed the way he looked at her, like everything about her was remarkable. Out of the bag he drew a bunch of daisies I assumed were for her, but he walked over to give the flowers to Richard. Something told me it was Miss Stephanie's idea, but still, it was the sweetest thing. They did seem made for each other.

The pizza slices were passed around, the wine was opened, which I refused but no one seemed to notice, except Miss Stephanie who notices everything. She tilted her head and looked at me with a quizzical look in her eye that made me remember how, when I was sixteen, I was about to pop a Tic Tac stored up my sleeve, and she said in her "I have eyes in the back of my head" voice, "no eating in class," as if to show me what she knew, and would always know, even with her back to me. She might as well have looked me dead in the eyes. I padded softly across the studio to throw my mint into the trash.

Stuffing ourselves with warm, soft dough while talking about cold, hard people seemed to help a little. Richard piled the pepperoni from my slice higher on top his own. Rivers said that sometimes it's the men who suspect that they are gay themselves who sometimes perform the most violent acts against homosexuals. "If they hear things about themselves that opposes the hateful rhetoric they hear at home, or learn something about themselves when a certain teacher shows them respect, they may think, 'wait I don't understand my feelings, this goes against my father's teachings, so I need to hate you.'"

I felt a little sick to my stomach. I put my napkin over the rest of my pizza. *I see*, Miss Stephanie's eyes said. *I see what's going on here.*

"So wait, you're saying Joey is gay?" Lenny said.

"Or the old man is," Rivers said. "Or both."

"I told you," Richard said to Lenny, shifting in his seat to face the rest of us. "It's the only thing that makes any sense. I don't mean that it makes it right, just that it makes its own kind of twisted sense."

Then, because she clearly heard compassion in Richard's voice and was likely feeling a great deal of her own, Miss Stephanie described how they'd waited for hours before Joey finally drove up. How before arriving at Joey's house, they'd knocked on the door of the girl's house from the party, and reluctantly, her mother opened the door and quickly called her daughter on the phone. "She wouldn't talk to Rivers, though. Plus she'd moved to Montana with her boyfriend, which," she looked at Rivers, "is a long way from Texas."

"There was a neighbor who said he saw Joey and his father come and go late at night a lot," Rivers said, lifting his plastic cup to his lips. "Though he couldn't give specific dates." He took a sip. "Unfortunately, even if he could recount that on the night of June twenty-fifth Joey's truck never returned home, any drunk," he corrected himself, "any witness intoxicated at 11 a.m. is basically useless. The prosecuting attorney would never see him as reliable."

"What did you say to Joey, exactly?" Lenny asked, bringing the conversation around again. By now, Richard had curled into a ball under Lenny's arm. Looking at the two of them made me see how far in this they were together and how Lenny had not once tried to pull away. I put my hand on my belly and held it there. I've been thinking a lot about this question of attraction between people lately, and so far, I've learned the best I know from the two of them.

"I'll let Stephanie tell you," Rivers said turning to her and taking her hand. "It was all her doing. Joey was putty in her hands."

Miss Stephanie regarded him for a moment, took a deep breath and said, "You set the stage, I just played my part." Then looking at Richard, she said, "He was getting out of his truck when we approached him. After Rivers told him why we were there, I said, 'look, Joey, I saved this picture you drew, remember this?' As soon as he saw it, this look came over him and there was all this confusion in his eyes. After that, he seemed eager to tell us everything, as if so much ill will had been fermenting inside of him and it was ready to pop. I told him I believed Rivers had said something to me about a match, which technically wasn't a lie because, as Rivers instructed, I didn't say what specific match I was referring to, only that Rivers had mentioned one. I didn't bring up DNA. I could have been talking about a relationship or even a light. But I really didn't need to say anything else, you see? "

We all nodded as if we did.

"And since he's such a dumb fuck, he panicked," Richard said, his eyes shifting from a vague expression to sounding angry at Miss Stephanie and Rivers, as if he'd been listening to his favorite music under headphones and someone just yanked them off his head. "He's been beaten down his whole life. What's one more time? Don't you get it?"

His words were like a gavel coming down. No one said anything, but I think we all tried to take his questions to heart. I knew Richard's emotional recovery depended on him tying this circle together. Once he found a motive he could believe in—where the evil began, and why—I suspected he would finally be able, after turning himself inside and out, to accept what happened. Possibly, even forgive.

We sat for a few minutes not wanting to speak.

Finally, Rivers said, "When people are essentially victims themselves, it's typically easier to get them to talk. That's the sorry truth of it. Honestly, I think he caved as soon as he saw Stephanie. Vulnerability is pretty easy to take advantage of no matter what side of the law you are on."

"And so you do," Richard said, his voice softer now.

"And so I do, yes." He bowed his head. "It doesn't make me the finest person in the world, but it does make me a good detective."

Miss Stephanie looked at Rivers and tilted her head at him, this time as if trying to absorb all of what he'd just said before speaking. After standing to walk over to Richard and kiss the top of his head, she said, "I told Joey that all we wanted was to see this thing settled, so I thought he should speak to us just to indicate that he was taking things seriously. And when he asked if he was going to jail, I told him he was one of the people who we had not eliminated as a suspect, though I could hardly believe I'd found the nerve to say *we*."

Rivers looked down at the floor and smiled.

"Rivers assured me that I'd instinctively know just what to do when the time came," she said sitting back down, "and he was right." In spite of the seriousness of the conversation, her words were terrifically-truthful to those of us who knew the whole story. It was Rivers who laughed first.

With her cheeks still glowing red after burying her face in her hands for a minute, Miss Stephanie took a deep breath. "What I mean is, as soon as I saw Joey, I didn't feel any of the things I was worried about when we got to Cottle County, mostly that I'd lose my nerve. Rivers was convinced I'd have some kind of maternal power over Joey's conscience and he was right about that."

I couldn't help but think how the confession was a harsh reminder of something Richard and I already knew about fathers—just because a man is one doesn't mean he knows how to be one. What we found most disturbing was not only that the other attacker involved was Joey's father, but that Joey didn't think twice about giving him up. Lenny was the one who brought this up, and after we talked about it—coming to it from different viewpoints, sharing personal stories—Lenny reached for Miss Stephanie's hand after she shared how living with her own father had been like living in a dugout. "You can live that way, but it's suffocating." Finally, she told us how Rivers had clinched it. "He told Joey what it would be like for a jury to see a video of Richard dancing, the sound of his tap shoes filling the air, and Charles playing football. Then, cut to pictures of their bodies after the beatings. Joey barely blinked before he started talking. Rivers handed him a piece of paper and he wrote out his confession on the hood of his truck."

"That's not all of it," Rivers said slapping his own knee. "Stephanie said, and I quote, 'Joey, do you mind if I put in a few commas to make the paragraphs easier to read?' And he said, 'no ma'am,' like he was back in grade school and afraid to disobey."

"No one is supposed to tamper with evidence in any way, but I didn't know that," Miss Stephanie said, shaking her head.

"It'll be fine," Rivers said affectionately. "So I walked down the road a ways to make the appropriate phone calls to the authorities. And to Charles' family."

"What did they say?" I said it lightly, but it was no indication of how heavy it felt to hear Charles' name. From the look on Richard's face, his feelings were the same.

"I'm afraid I had to leave a message. They haven't called back."

"The three of us just sat on the grass and waited for his father to come home," Miss Stephanie said.

"And that is pretty much it," Rivers said.

That wasn't true. I could tell right away that it wasn't. For one thing, there was something off about the way he said it, as if he was trying to bring the conversation to a too-quick finish. And Miss Stephanie started to look a little funny, and then she, the person with the most impeccable manners, got up and moved toward the bathroom without saying "excuse me" first. Richard picked up on it too. "Hey, what's going on?" he said squinting an eye.

Rivers walked over to the window.

"Tell them," Miss Stephanie said, stopping at the door of the bathroom but not going in. "It's going to come out and Richard should hear it from us."

"What is?" Richard said trying to stand. His leg bumped the table. A few white pedals from the bouquet went flying.

"When…" Rivers paused. We stared at him. Sweat beaded up on his forehead. "When the old man drove up, there was," he wiped his brow with the back of his hand. I could feel him tensing. He walked toward Stephanie. She made a *shh* sound and put her hand gently to his cheek. He walked back to us, looked directly at Richard and said, "Your other loafer was hanging from his rear-view mirror."

I put my hand over my mouth. I felt that I was being pulled into quicksand, deeper and deeper under.

Lenny clamped his hands down on his knees. I watched the knuckles turn white, the blood draining away. Richard cocked his head as if maybe he hadn't heard right. The light left his eyes and the color left his cheeks. When he lowered his gaze, I saw that it was really his soft yellow loafer he was trying to picture. It tore a hole right through me.

Rivers walked over to open the window wider. Cooler air rushed in. Richard started to shiver. Lenny wrapped his arms around him and whispered, "I've got you."

Pas de Deux. A dance for two. Both partners hold on to each other where they can't sustain the position on their own.

Dusk descended. And so did we. Like leaves after a windstorm, we sat limp and silent. I thought how, up until now, Richard had come through, determined to forgive.

But now? After hearing this? I thought that being forced to see his beloved shoe hanging like a trophy would be a scar too deep, worse than the ones that run crosswise down his calf, branching in all directions from his kneecap down—that forgiveness was out of the question.

But I was wrong.

~⚬⚬⚬~

That night I had the most ruthless dream. Richard's loafer was enormous and made of rubber, which right off the bat caused the dream to be even more ridiculous. Richard would never wear rubber shoes. There is nothing *Crocs* about Richard.

Anyway, I was running for my life away from this giant, banana-yellow loafer down Twentynine Palms and suddenly all these familiar faces were yelling things at me from the sidewalk: mothers who had kids in my classes over the years, mothers who had *been* in class ages ago, people who'd moved to the coast and I hadn't seen forever, kids from town with skateboards under their arms. Mr. Mike was there too, with a loaf of whole wheat in one hand while (wait, what is this?) holding hands with Wade with the other, so only Wade was able to wave. And he did, he waved so hard his tie flapped up and down. They seemed so relaxed and happy.

My mother was there too, big bag slung over her shoulder. A comforting feeling washed over me. I nearly stopped to rush into her arms. "No, Lucy, run!" she shouted, slapping my outstretched hand with such enthusiasm it gave *me* enthusiasm. Next to her, my grandmother sat fanning herself in front of Roy's Tires in a black muumuu, black flats, a Patent leather pocketbook dangling from her forearm. It was mean of me, but when she shook the back of her curled up hand in that exaggerated way of hers and said *"Una signora non dormire con sconosciuti,"* I stuck out my tongue. She'd always put too much importance on what others thought, and that had been a big part of my mother's insecurity, I think.

Colleen from Star Market was carrying a huge handwritten sign that said, "Run like you just stole a filet mignon!" She was standing alongside Marjorie who naturally dangled a cigarette from her bottom lip, a real hazard if you are also dragging an oxygen tank behind you. I cringed. But Lenny, already unrolling a garden hose from a big red reel, had snuck up behind her, just in case. Teresa was there, too, dressed in a way that meant she definitely had not just come from work. She cheered and yelled, "You know how wonderful mom jeans can feel when you've been too professional to wear them your whole life? Now run!"

But not everyone was cheering, a few cast their eyes down. The woman from Sassy Nails never lifted her head from buffing her nails just to let me know she still believed the gossip. And Karen stood in a tree pose, shoulder blades hiked up around her ears—her eyes full of reproach. She didn't cheer. A sneer maybe, but not a cheer.

But most people from town were waving their arms and shouting things like, "You can do it, Lucy! We're rooting for you!" Their excitement made me happy, or happier than seeing some of them in person would have. And my entire class showed up! I wanted to run over and hug them with my whole body. This is another prenatal change that's come over my nature. When I want something, my longing doesn't seem to come from a single sure spot inside of me, but from every muscle, bone, and nerve ending. I wanted to squeeze my students with such a strong intensity that when I couldn't, I ran past them feeling deprived.

My dad didn't show up, big surprise. But Billy did, sitting on the huge white planter box in front of city hall with my first 'natural disaster' who'd swept me off my feet. And that's when I knew how and *why* he'd found my class. I should have known. The way energy-men come to town and think they can pass around unsuspecting local women is just unbelievable. They were arm-in-arm, bonded, and the sight of them together smacked of harem mentality, like medieval men who pull women around by their hair. My skin crawled. Then, for whatever reasons that make smart women do really stupid things, I slowed down and called out, "Billy!" which I hoped would not happen. But it just came out. Without looking up, he yawned and said, "Not now, I'm watching this," meaning the football game on his phone. I doubted he even remembered my name.

The shoe was gaining on me fast. I feared I'd be eaten alive when suddenly I was aware of another voice, Miss Stephanie's. Forever determined to lift me up, she shouted, "Fly!" and like that, my legs mastered a stag-leap so high I flew up and over Home Depot. And then another leap even higher. I could barely catch my breath between leaps.

We were neck and neck but the shoe kept gaining, dripping slobber all over the place. And right at the point where it was either going to swoop down and swallow me whole, or I'd leap over Black Rock Canyon just in time to get away, I woke up to the ear-piercing sound of cicadas.

I got up and tip-toed downstairs where Richard was sleeping next to Lenny who was snoring softly, embracing Richard with one arm, burying his face in the pillow. They'd polished off the second bottle of wine apparently, and must have decided to stay put, snug as bugs on a single inflatable mattress.

I noticed Richard was also having a dream, not a nightmare, at least it didn't seem like it from my end. He let out a peep, like a bird chirping after the rains. I sat down on the floor. I can't remember if I covered my mouth when I heard him laugh. What matters is that he laughed, making all these lovely little *ohh* sounds in between, as if absolutely delighted with himself. His legs jerked. From one second to the next, his left leg would kick up, then his right leg kicked before settling down on the sheet. I imagined him soaring over the clouds. I didn't want the laughing to stop, he sounded so happy. But after a few more seconds, it did stop.

I never asked him about the dream. I decided to go with how it sounded because I think people create all kinds of sounds and images to keep themselves going. On the desert, when hikers run out of water up at Joshua Tree, they talk about the trickling pools they not only can see wavering in the distance, but *hear*. We call them mirages, but I think what's really going on is that when faced with the worst, our senses get this supernatural ability to detect nothing ahead but every little thing that could possibly help.

And by every little thing I mean *hope*.

Just picture such faint, thirsty people able to overcome their fear simply by trusting the promising sound of a trickle. What I like to think is that in both our dreams that fitful night, Richard and I were finally able to outrun our fear, too.

The worst of it, anyway.

Fourteen

"Stifling an urge to dance is bad for your health. It rusts your spirit and your hips."

~Terri Guillemots

The whole set.

THE (MOSTLY) GOOD PEOPLE OF YUCCA SPRINGS HAVE traditionally turned a blind eye to two-timing men, but not so much to the women they two-time *with*. "I'm afraid this is one of the greatest unfairnesses we still share with the rest of the world," Miss Stephanie said.

As a result, Lucy Maglietta, *moi*—three months pregnant and beginning to show—was hardly most people's idea of a suitable ballet mistress. "I can see it in their eyes," I said.

"I discovered midway through my thirties that we just might not want to give *too* much thought to what other people think," Miss Stephanie said.

So most days I tried to care less. I gave it my best shot, and slowly, I gained new confidence. Right along with a few extra pounds. I even found the guts to look straight into Lawson's disapproval and say, "This," pointing at the bulge through my sweatpants, "what you are staring at, is the kind of good that puts all the petty people like you into perspective." I held up my forefinger above my thumb with the smallest space in between. I walked toward the back door of the Star Struck, and without looking back, slammed it shut.

On less sure-of-myself days, and there were a lot of them, I'd duck behind a cactus rather than face anyone.

Miss Stephanie assured me that it's never in the cards to be liked by everyone. "It's simply not possible," she said.

"I just wish people would remember to wait until they pass me on the sidewalk before they start to whisper." I patted my stomach. "But I'm actually doing a lot better than I thought I would."

"I don't think any of us are entitled to more," she said.

Three months before this conversation, and five long minutes after I'd stared at a test stick, I came running downstairs to tell Richard. "I'm having a baby," I said.

"Like, no kidding," he said. I knew he knew. We just hadn't officially talked about it yet. He flopped down on the couch in the way he does when he's pretending things he's about to say are all spontaneous, but they aren't, he's actually given them a lot of thought. "Sit," he said patting the couch. "So this little devil you're having..." he paused, his voice quivering suddenly like he was about to tear up, which he probably was. Just like me. "Well, what I think is..." he took a long swig from his new stainless water bottle with the words "NO PLACE FOR HATE" printed over a globe (a gift from Lenny) and finally said, "I think it's a sign."

"Of what?"

"That everything that happens from now on," I stared at him, waiting, "is what's supposed to happen because we've done our best to get through this. Okay, maybe you," he said waving his hand over my stomach, "in a less discreet way."

"Why, thank you," I said rubbing my stomach. I'd come out of the bathroom fearing that, without needing to say the words, Richard would find a way to say *told you so*, because my dread got the best of me. I think single pregnant women are always half-afraid of what people will say, especially the ones they love most. "At least I don't have any relatives in town to embarrass," I said, the only time I could remember admitting to Richard how scary it felt sometimes to not have family to lean on now that I was about to *become* a family. Mostly because he *was* my family, in its chosen state, handpicked.

But something in me was rattled after dropping by the *Funky & Darn Near New* store to buy a few baby things, because the first thing I saw was this dainty floral tea cup sitting on the counter. It wasn't expensive, Vons used to give them away to regular customers. And one December when things were really tight, my mother set up a rummage sale in our driveway. She sold her entire china and crystal collection that were handed down from her mother, as well as some of our everyday dishes, and a lot of other things she said we didn't need. At the time, I never thought either set of dishes would mean anything to me down the road—they were too "old fashioned," I told her. But seeing the cup again, the homesickness I felt was not for our dishware, but for being part of a family again, my heart either melting or freezing depending on which memory I let swirl around in my head.

I shop at rummage sales on a regular basis now supposedly for baby stuff, but I'm always on the lookout for more of my mom's dishes, especially the heirloom pieces. Even though my own child will probably eye them one day and say, "Mom, those dishes are so old fashioned. It's embarrassing!"

And twenty-six years later, feel exactly the opposite.

Bless them.

BLESS MY CLASS. BLESS THEM. BLESS THEM. BLESS THEM.

I decided to tell everyone since I suspected they, too, already knew. Everyone clapped like crazy, as if pregnancy was my finest accomplishment yet. I found that a little disturbing but, even so, you should have seen the smile on my face.

And they are always forgiving when I'm a bit slow or clumsy, like when I drop my CD twice in a row because my fingers are swollen or I can't find my iPod, or when I finally do find it, I can't find the song I want, or decide what song I want. Or when I confuse my right leg with my left because I'm distracted by how swollen my feet look. Or when my heart is racing and I have to hold on for dear life to the barre. Or when I'm too short of breath to demonstrate another time. Or when I stop to eat half a chicken leg in the middle of class like a bobcat chomping on prey.

Most days, as soon as class is over, I tackle the simpler tasks. Needless to say, the Star Struck is spotless. Everything shines from the mirrors to the inside of the waste baskets. It drives Richard crazy so many nights he stays at Lenny's. I guess you could say we continue to deal with the future in different ways. Richard needs to get stronger and he is doing that. Day by day he is closer to his old physical-self. And I clean, organize, and reorganize my nest.

"I read that we have a really strong nesting instinct when we're pregnant," I told Hu after she was quick to cluck her tongue when I rushed in to scoop up the tissue that dropped from her cuff before she had time to retrieve it herself. She looked at me and said, "No worry. It's what women do in your situation." She said it in a nice way, though.

And I do my best to remember—when I try to execute a pirouette and the room begins to spin and my stomach turns a cartwheel so that I start to panic, thinking I'll never be able to dance the way I used to—that nine months isn't really so long. "Actually, I'm a little relieved not to be planning a recital this year," I told Miss Stephanie. "Recitals have a way of diminishing some of the simpler joys in life."

"Like what?" she said.

"Like wiping down the mirrors," I say spraying the Windex, "for the third time today." We laughed. Miss Stephanie can always be counted on to have a sense of humor about my obsessions, mostly because she has a few of her own, and my pregnancy continues to present us with openings to tease each other about them. And to talk about other deeply personal things too, like the women we thought we were versus the women we've become, and how she very much approves of me having this baby. Neither of us have said as much, but I think we'd both been lonelier before. It still amazes me that what had once sounded like the most tragic outcome, the worst thing that could ever happen to a young ballet dancer, could suddenly feel so different now. "Even the heartburn doesn't bother me half as much as I thought it would," I confided, "or my belly button that is popping out like a prickly pear."

And when the morning queasiness finally eases but my lower back starts to burn like crazy, Lisa was sweet to notice how I bring my hand up to support it. She got the whole class to chip in to buy me my first professional massage. Hu was dying to let me know that she had given the most money. I know this because she gave a quick nod to the envelope and said, "I give the most."

I pretty much melted onto the table as soon as the masseuse marched his fingers down my spine. At one point, the pressure was so intense that I cried out and he jumped back, causing my sheet to move a little far south, but he tucked it back in so quick, *tuck, tuck, tuck* that I knew it must happen a lot.

I guess what I'm trying to say is that I think most people view single motherhood as, well, single, lonely, alone, and there are days it's easy to feel absolutely alone, I'm not going to lie. But I'm growing really tired of the word *single*. Because the truth is, I'm beginning to feel like I have more of a family around me than ever before. And I've saved many of their numbers to my favorites list because the day is coming when I'm going to need one of them really fast. Fast as I need a saltine to keep from hurling.

And when Richard makes fun of me to entertain himself, like when he said no playpen is going to sit in the middle of our waiting room ever, I decide it's a pretty sweet thing to say, all in all. But when I was eating my lunch and he said, "You aren't going to wear that getup outside are you?" I raised my spoon and shook it at him. "This is the only thing that doesn't dig into my armpits (an old ballet dress slit up both sides)!" I was adamant.

Good old Fred and Ginger, I thought.

But there was something more on the tip of his tongue, I could tell, like how I probably *thought* I was rocking my homegrown maternity clothes, but he kept it to himself, knowing I am super sensitive about my weight gain. I still have months of eating for two ahead of me, and to be perfectly honest, I'm having major trouble controlling my appetite. I'd be furious if he poked any real fun at my size and then he'd feel guilty, and honestly, I think we may have to put a lid on some of the teasing until after the baby comes. I don't have the energy for it.

Oh, I laugh at myself here!

I laugh because Richard and me not teasing each other is just not Richard and me. Teasing is the real us and I know it. The same way I know that loving someone for real means that sometimes the only way we can show it is by teasing, since we are lucky enough to have someone to tease at all.

But if, in the next trimester, I fail to see the humor in something Richard says, like when he tried to make me laugh by saying it's okay if I eat for two as long as he can drink for three, and I fly off the handle or say something I need to apologize for, or if Richard does, it's okay because I know we *are* trying our best. I think this is the feeling Richard was trying to get at when he'd patted the sofa and asked me to sit down.

Safely on the other side.

"Whatever I can do to help," Miss Stephanie said to Richard on Skype, settling a little farther into the throw pillows behind her.

It was the first time we'd used Skype together and it was a little unnerving. She must have seen my eyes taking everything in because she said, "Welcome to a typical San Diego bungalow." But there was nothing typical about it to me. My eyes traveled from one elegance to another— from the beautifully draped shawl over the back of her overstuffed armchair to the turquoise picture frame with a photo of Richard and me standing in first position, holding hands. We were in our late teens. I leaned in closer, straining to see.

For once, she wasn't offering help with "our" baby—she'd already sent oodles of baby clothes, a car seat, even baby's first tutu. No, she was referring to the fundraiser Richard was whipping up fast.

A few evenings earlier, I looked down from the middle stair to see Richard slip his feet into his tap shoes without having to force them. I crept down farther. Turning on the light in the studio, he walked in, stopped, tapped his right toe against the wood, then his left. He walked over, looked into the mirror, pointed at himself and started to tap, gently at first, then with more punch. And that's how I left him, as if the door to his cage had been opened and he was safely on the other side, ready to quench the air with tap-beat.

I tiptoed back upstairs.

A sense of balance.

The word from Rivers was that Joey and his father were being held in Texas and hadn't been extradited to California yet. Apparently, the state of Texas was trying to tie the two of them to several unsolved local cases of assault.

As soon as I hung up the phone, Richard said that he wanted to go to Texas to talk to Joey himself, and in disbelief I said what sounded like a selfish thing. "You can't do that *now*." What I meant was now that he was dancing again—not that I was pregnant, but that's not how Richard heard it. I burst into tears, taking a tissue out of my waistband and blowing my nose. I saw a look of annoyance cross his face, but he quickly hid it.

Truth is, I get more confused between Richard's needs and my own lately, or what I think he can handle and what *I* can. Some days, I feel so on-edge, I know he doesn't want to be around me and I can't blame him. Unfortunately, these are usually the same days I need company the most.

"I'm afraid for you." I said.

"*I'm* afraid for me."

I was afraid for him, but I wasn't surprised, not really. On stage, there's a sense of urgency to Richard's first heel drop, and then this need to test himself further. I saw that he would face Joey in the same way he sharpens his sense of balance—by rising to an even higher toe stand, nearly falling backwards. Except he never does. It made me see how the only way Richard would be able to put the past behind him was to look directly into the eyes of his attacker and not turn away.

"And where would you see him?"

"At the Cottle County Texas Jail."

"It sounds like a bad country western song."

"Yes, ma'am," he twanged.

"Are you going to forgive him?"

"I have forgiven him," he said. But then he hesitated, "I think so, anyway. I want to."

Fatigue had started to cut me down like a tree by eight o'clock. By eleven, I was wide awake again thinking how just yesterday Richard had gotten so angry, he swore he'd never forgive what happened, and now he is absolutely sure it's the right thing to do again. I closed my eyes and smiled to my unborn child and to myself. "That's because both choices take the same amount of courage."

Richard had taken thousands of selfies to document the progression of his recovery—the black turning to blue turning to yellow, and then fading away to reveal raw skin underneath, and finally, each thick, raised scar zigzagging his calf. "Physical scars," he labeled the file. "The mental ones would break the internet," he said, trying to laugh, but his expression changed. A gloom fell over him. We looked at each other, both knowing we couldn't go too far down that road, not at a fundraiser. A fundraiser has to be cheerful. A fundraiser has to be "*up*."

He'd also superimposed newspaper clippings as background images. Scrolling through, I noticed his face come alive in a way that made me remember how, after his mother died, he'd fallen into a slump so low I thought nothing would lift him out of it. Until he'd show me the photos he'd taken of her and the same smile would light up his face. I wanted his images to have the same effect on our audience, reminding everyone to turn their focus outward, away from themselves, and that's what I said. "Even if all the photos are selfies," I said, the irony catching us both by surprise.

"Yeah, they're selfies…" He paused. "But they aren't vain." A few seconds flew by. "Are they?"

And you know how every so often you feel like you're caught between two truths at once? I kicked his shin lightly, like in the old days, to sort of skirt the question (we both knew it), and when he didn't flinch, moan, or complain, I said, "I think that's the most obvious sign of your recovery yet."

Every once in a while he still limps, but only when he's really tired.

And yesterday he donated his cane to Lenny's office. "Good riddance," he said tossing it into the closet.

In living color.

"We don't just want you to help," Richard said moving his face closer to the screen, "we want you to dance." He'd drawn yellow tap shoes around the frame of his screen and Miss Stephanie was staring at us from inside it, trying to take in what Richard was proposing.

"It's a lot to ask, I know," I said. "You're so insanely busy and everything," thinking how on earth she could make room for everyone in her old life when there are just as many in her new. She had students, family, Rivers, and the wedding they were now planning. It was an unreasonable expectation.

"No, I'm sanely busy," she said, thoughtfully and with a smile. "I do what I love. But I'm afraid my performance years are behind me." I could hear it, the question every dancer asks themselves eventually: *Is the best of my discipline over?*

Of course, looking back I can see how my reluctance had nothing to do with Miss Stephanie's sudden lack of confidence and everything to do with my own.

"What are you talking about? You look great!" Richard said.

"People want to see young, new energy."

"People want to see *you*. New gets old."

"Oh, stop," she said. I was holding my breath to hear what she'd say. Her face brightened. "Well, if you think it's a good idea?"

"Of course it's a good idea," Richard said. "Everyone will come if you dance."

And there it was. I knew he meant well, but I felt the sting run up my arms. I couldn't tie my own slippers or curb my eating and I was, I hate to say it again, jealous. That's right, green as tomatillos, this time because my teacher was still fit as a fiddle.

But that wasn't all of it. I couldn't imagine a performance happening at the Star Struck that I couldn't be part of. I felt left out. I'd grown so used to confiding in Miss Stephanie, I almost felt like admitting how jealous I was, but for once I couldn't. The bucket of crabs I watched the day my dad drove us to the coast came to mind, and I knew exactly why. I couldn't rely on my mentor for everything. For once, I was going to have to make my way over the bucket rim without her guidance nudging me forward.

Alone, I'd walked off along the sand to get away from my parents, stopping to watch a fisherman stick his hand into a bucket full of crabs. "Why don't they escape?" I asked. "They ain't too smart," he said, not bothering to look up. I watched as they scratched and scratched at the sides of the plastic bucket, climbing over each other to get to the top. As soon as one almost made it over the rim, the others pulled it back down. If they were smart, I thought, they'd make a chain, claw-to-claw, filing up and out over the rim until the last crab was safely on the other side.

I was glad there was no mirror above Richard's laptop. I would have hated to see my own eyes turn such a shade of green, my claws worn down to nothing like that.

"I don't leap anymore," Miss Stephanie was saying, "or jump."

"Since this isn't the Olympics, that hardly matters," Richard said.

"Well, I suppose I could come up with something," she said, and by the look on her face, I knew it would have taken a nuclear bomb to keep her away.

I thought of something else, too, something my mother said once after I'd spent the afternoon worrying if I was as pretty as the other girls in sixth grade. "Lucy," she said, popping the lid off a pint of Holy Cannoli, our favorite splurge, "Competition brings out the best in Ben & Jerry." She took a few licks off the back of her spoon, "and the worst in people."

The line.

Things were getting back to normal, or the new normal, meaning Richard was dancing again, enough for the both of us now. And though once I would have thought it the laziest, most unforgivable thing to do—to nap in the middle of the day—Lisa pointed out that I wasn't lazy. Putting her face right up to mine she said I was *working*, as in creating a life, hello? It was just another good example of her generous sensibility I would come to know well in the following months. Next to me sat a plate of greenish cookies she baked (instead of butter she used an avocado), and I couldn't help but think of the color as privately mocking the jealousy I'd had to wrestle to the ground.

Richard goes through every step of his new routine a hundred times.

After another start and stop of Travie McCoy's "Keep On Keeping On," he was at the foot of my bed staring at my stack of cookies. "You wouldn't believe how fat my ankles look from this angle," I said.

"Are you going to eat all those?" he said making it clear he had no real interest in my ankles, only in cramming cookies into his own mouth, and returning to the studio, which pleased me no end. "Thanks for coming up," I yelled. "It's kind of you to look in on me."

"Don't eat too many," he yelled over his shoulder. "You're starting to look like you belong in this town."

It hurt, I admit.

I listened to the lyrics for a while. And what I believe I heard was, "*You gotta keep on keeping on. Even with the feeling that you're gonna keep losing. You gotta come back strong.*"

And it struck me how Richard did sort of verbalize one of the things about Yucca Springs I've started to appreciate more as of late: You don't have to be thin to be accepted here. You can gain a few pounds, it's not the end of the world. "I think you, baby girl, have changed me for the better already," I said looking down at my stomach, and then at the photo of my mother on my bed stand. Aloud I said, "It seems I have two generations weighing in, one from each side."

Oh, the reason I know it's a girl is because curiosity got the better of me and I scheduled an ultrasound. Richard came with me. I remember looking in the mirror at the two of us in the waiting room, both in sweats and t-shirts, and thinking, *oh, god, now we look alike.* And just when I thought we'd waited long enough, they called my name. Watching the monitor was like peeking into a floating miracle. When the nurse said my baby *girl's* heartbeat was strong, Richard said, "Strong? Or bossy?"

Later, when I told Miss Stephanie that I was determined to be upfront with my daughter, "to make sure she doesn't hold back any part of herself," she was happy to share what she thought. "The best way to teach her, Lucy, is by living that way yourself." I knew she had more to say on the subject, more of a point to make, she just needed a minute to come out with it. "Just remember that devotion to your own discipline doesn't come from a selfish place like some people might—no scratch that—*will* imply down the line. It comes from the opposite. Your passion is a *gift* to your daughter."

I knew that what she was saying is that in order to feel whole, and to show my daughter how to feel the same, I'd likely always need to rely on dance in the same way a farmer relies on the land.

In the seconds right after I hung up, the air stilled. *She's right,* I thought. *Pregnancy has never stopped women before.* How easy it is to think I should take it easy, but it proved too hard in the end. As soon as I heard Lenny's car drive up, Richard yell, "Bye!" and the screen door snap shut. I got right up. *Get out of bed and back into your body* came the command, fast and direct, coming at me even as I threw back the covers.

As soon as I was in the studio, I looked long and hard at myself in the mirror, something I was careful not to do when teaching for fear I'd lose concentration. The body I saw was curvier, yes, but still lovely, something my ballet-eyes had been too stingy communicating as of late. I lifted my chin. "Hello," I said as kindly as when I try to make a new student feel comfortable.

"Energy begets energy," was one of Miss Stephanie's favorite sayings, sometimes pinching our nose first if one of us whined about how tired we were. But it's true. That afternoon, I felt tired going in, and nothing but energized coming out. I'd let myself come pretty close to believing that dance was fleeting and motherhood is lasting. But as soon as I started moving, I realized that dance, *movement*, is for life. It's pregnancy that is fleeting.

And motherhood?

"A huge part of life, but not all." I did not feel the least bit guilty or uneasy saying this. I pointed at myself and spoke sternly: "You will have to be careful about the choreography, though. You can't cross the line. The first rule of performance is *know your audience.*"

Our audience (or most of the people we know) holds on to the status quo about so many things, marriage *before* children still at the top of the list. "You will need them to like you, Lucy. Not fear what you have to say about women, babies, marriage, or hope."

And by hope, this time (I think) I mean *love.*

Not romantic love. Support, affection, encouragement, being there for someone no matter what. But wait. These qualities *are* romantic love, aren't they? My mother's words rush back at me: *Well, you'd think so, wouldn't you?*

Miss Stephanie had said something about crossing this very same line: "Oh, don't get me started about *that*," she said to someone on the line. "Because lines are generally invisible until it's too late. And the need to stay this side of them is not only true for women in Yucca Springs, but true for all women, everywhere. I'm sorry to say it, but it's true!" Then she slammed down the phone.

I hate to think what would have become of me if she hadn't moved to town and said all the things I needed to hear just about every time she opened her mouth.

When I finished my workout and turned down the music, I felt my daughter kick. "Wasn't that great?" I said rubbing my stomach, wondering what I'd been so worried about.

But later, in the deep of night, I was reminded of what.

In my dream, the parents of my young students came to our fundraiser dressed as pioneers, the men in suspenders, the women in bonnets and aprons, all of them thinking and one of them shouting, "Over my dead body is my daughter taking ballet from *you!*" I can still see the accusing look on their faces, they had grown strong on fault and blame. Their fingers were stiff from pointing. I wanted to yell, "My daughter is a gift, and I won't feel guilty about her." And, ever so slowly, I did yell that.

Before anyone could object, there was a screech from outside. A harsh sound.

I woke, startled. The hawk soared past the window in a brown flare.

Seconds later, a cardinal landed on my sill, tiny reddish wings thumped against the glass. I feared she thought she could fly straight through. She kept flapping her folded wings.

I ran to the window. There was another sound, softer this time. But whether it escaped from my frantic throat or hers, I have no idea.

Fifteen

"Talk about dance? Dance is not something to talk about. Dance is to dance."
~Peter Saint James

Why?

THE COTTLE COUNTY TEXAS JAIL IS NOT THE KIND OF place that makes it easy for a visitor to get out of the car. Richard's hands were pressed against the dashboard to stop them from shaking. "He's nearly hyperventilating," Rivers said. He put the phone up to Richard's ear so I could talk to him.

"Richard? Are you okay?"

His voice was trembling, "I d-don't think I can go through with this."

"You don't have to. You can turn around and come right back home."

No one had been able to talk him out of driving to Texas. Not even Joey when, according to Rivers, his first reaction to Richard's request was, "I ain't talking to that chicken hawk." But after a few more days, he changed his mind and agreed to see Richard, but wouldn't say why.

The next few days of waiting were tense for Richard. He never budged from his decision to go, but he lost his nerve, gained it back, then lost it again.

Now, I know you don't have to necessarily like someone to forgive them—and you don't have to be a parent yourself to want to help someone worse off than you in the parent department—but during those long, drawn-out days until Rivers came by to pick Richard up, I came to see how by going to Texas, Richard was acting like a parent in the greater sense of the word. And so was Rivers by offering to drive him.

The first time I saw this fatherly trait in Richard, we were only seven. Miss Stephanie wanted to spotlight dance styles from around the world. She rented a Bollywood film where the opening scene showed all these little boys diving into a river to collect coins tourists were tossing in. I couldn't imagine swimming in such filthy water, but when I asked Richard if he'd jump in he said "sure," not even needing to think about it first. He said he'd give the boys his pullover to dry off. I remember thinking what a kind thing to say that was, to be willing to give the shirt off your back.

"You just need time, that's all, Richard. Take your time. It's not like Joey is going anywhere. Wait until tomorrow maybe?" I heard Rivers clear his throat heavily, so I guess that wasn't really an option, but I said it anyway to remind Richard that he didn't have to rush.

"He'll come around," I told Rivers, explaining how Richard goes through the same transition backstage. One peek through the curtain at a full house and he starts to walk in circles, nodding to himself with his eyes closed until he's finally ready.

As told to me by Richard, as soon as he walked through a string of locked metal doors—each one locked behind him before the next one was opened—he was met by "a beast" who barked in a gravelly voice for him to store his phone and wallet in a locker. Then "another beast, but bigger" opened one more door after a loud buzzer went off. Then "a total freak" yelled "keep your hands on the table!" and leaned his back against the door with his arms crossed after ushering Richard into the visiting room where only a sliver of natural light streamed in through a narrow strip of a window high over their heads. "It was so hot, no air, not even a fan," so that sweat poured out of everyone. He almost vomited on the spot. He tried not to look over at any of the other visitors or inmates after one of them shot him the bird, and with his thumb and forefinger, made a circle and continued to slide it up and down over his erect finger. Richard lowered his head, walked to the only open bench, sat down, and after another door opened, there was Joey—older and thinner than he remembered, his eyes sunken into their sockets.

"Why are you here?" Joey wasted no time in saying.

Richard's heart was pounding so hard he could barely breathe let alone speak. "I... I... I've come to ask you the same thing."

Joey shrugged but wouldn't answer. Richard straightened up and managed to look straight into Joey's eyes and hold his gaze. Joey leaned forward with a smirk on his face, tapped his finger on the crumbly table and said, dead serious, "you're a bum-driller."

"A wha...?" He paused. "Well, that's one way to put it. I've heard worse." And somehow he found the words he came hundreds of miles to say. "But here's the thing, so are you."

Joey stared back for a long, stricken moment, fear darting in every direction from his eyes. He started to scratch hard behind one ear, then behind the other, his whole face filling with rage. But no matter how much he tried to hold it back, "I could see all this pain in his eyes trying to twist itself out," Richard said, "as if his body couldn't hold on to one more lie and then something inside of him caved, he couldn't collect himself."

And without any other baiting from Richard, the whole truth started to pour out of Joey, fast as his first admission to Miss Stephanie. It was as if Joey needed to, once and for all, rip himself open in order to reveal what was underneath. He spoke in nearly a whisper about how he got in trouble for "it" the first time in Yucca Springs. "Though he didn't say with who, and I wasn't about to ask," Richard said. Looking both ways before speaking again, almost excited now in his telling, Joey told how his dad had been in Texas for a while, but when he came back to Yucca Springs and found out that his wife, Joey's stepmother, had agreed to let Joey take a dance class, he beat her up so bad she ran off and they never saw her again. They'd moved to Texas soon after, where Joey was forced into conversion therapy. "The shrink kept saying fags aren't born this way, God don't make us this way and I was only fourteen so I believed it, see. When my dad caught me at it again he beat me with a dog chain and took me to the hardcore."

"Hardcore?" Richard asked holding back tears.

"They hook your balls up to wires like Frankenstein," he bent his head back, looking straight up at the fluorescent lights. "My dad said I better change or he'd kill me. And he would have, he sure as shit would have."

"Your father is lying. They are all lying. You are made like this. And it's okay."

Joey straightened up and said, as if reciting, "To be a man I have to fight for my country, fight for my race." He scratched behind his ear again. "So I started going out with him until we found some fag or wet-back or darkie to kick around."

Richard said later how he couldn't understand the tie between patriotism and race, or homosexuals and Mexicans, or whatever. And Rivers said it's impossible to understand—haters hate, it's the only feeling they work on, and when it builds up so that they can't control it, they want to beat up the next victim, it hardly matters why. "Problem is, they don't generally feel any less angry after, so that's when they tend to turn on each other."

Staring at his hands, Joey went on. "We drove up to Yucca Springs to get his stuff out of storage out at Sparky's, see, and that's when we saw that poster hanging in the window at Papa's Barbecue." When Richard asked what poster was he talking about, Joey said, "You and that nigger kid in the girly pose. My dad started yelling that you were the one who'd made me this way."

"Me?"

He put his hands on the table and straightened his arms, "He always gotta blame someone!"

"But why Charles?"

As if the answer was obvious as the nose on his face, shutting down any further discussion, like Richard was stupid for even asking such a crazy thing, he yelled, "'cause he's a nigger!"

"It was like a sledgehammer hit me between the eyes," Richard said. "I half-expected the roof tiles to come down." And he was about to stand when Joey raised his right arm in a fist and yelled at the top of his lungs, "They will not replace us!"

"I didn't even want to ask who else he meant by *they*," Richard said. He turned to the guard "who was Black, so like, whoa," and as calmly as he could, he asked, "Would you let me out of here, please?" Before he walked out, he turned back to Joey and quickly said, "I forgive you anyway."

After Richard made me promise that neither one of us would ever tell Charles what Joey had yelled, he said, "The thing is, I could have ended up like him. Hating myself. Hating everyone. If my mother hadn't stuck up for me and protected me from my father, if she hadn't signed me up for dance classes because I sure as hell couldn't throw a football, it could have been me sitting there in a jumpsuit."

I said I didn't believe that was true. When I called him later to check in, he said that while driving away from the jail he saw Joey's future pass by before his eyes: Every day, hatred spewed in the yard with other men, older men, who also hate themselves.

Mounds of hatred passed between them in the chow hall.

And nothing but hate-drivel before turning in.

As soon as Richard returned home, we went about our days routinely, doing all the things that made our lives ours. In the studio, I'd play music I thought was perfect and Richard would tell me what was wrong with it. Or I'd come up with a new sequence and he'd watch and say something like, "you *could* do it that way," then mimic the moves before slapping down a few steps of his own, much better than mine. And I'd say, "Isn't that what I just did?"

Most evenings Lenny would come over and he and Richard would cook something up together, or Lenny would cook and Richard would drink wine and tell him what he could do better, too. I was happy just to watch my two friends try to make pizza dough from scratch, flour all over the floor, serrated packets of yeast on the counter.

Things were good. We were full of hope.

And by hope, I definitely mean love this time.

Because Richard and Lenny together? Like watching yeast bubble.

⤙⤚

I wasn't much help with the fundraiser details. I didn't have the oomph.

After Lenny left for the evening (Richard had started to spend nights at the Star Struck again so he could rehearse late into the night), I'd open my door a crack to listen to his tapping, remembering when I'd stay up late, half the night sometimes, working on a new piece until the sun rose and the noisy Towhee toddled on the roof.

But as soon as Richard's steps grew tired and a little wobbly before they stopped and he started to pace, anxiously—partly due to the long hours of rehearsing because Richard always thinks his work needs another pinch of something, like my mother making her tomato sauce. And partly because he filled his every free moment with getting the word out, distracting himself, which allowed him to imagine (briefly) that men like Joey are unconnected to his real life. I'd walk halfway down the stairs to see him staring out the window again, his eyes searching the night as if for someone hiding out there. So I'd yell down something like "I'm here if you need me," just so he wouldn't feel alone.

Crawling back into bed, I'd plump up my pillows and make myself go sort of still inside. I have a strong desire to rid myself of extra stress lately, trying to make peaceful room for my daughter.

As far as planning, I know Richard knew that no matter how many hours he put in, the best part of the fundraiser would likely be accidental—some unexpected thing, a surprise to him as well as to the audience.

I say this because of something else that made a huge impression on me back when we were researching all the hateful websites. Richard puts on a good face, but I know the larger issue for him now is that there is so much hatred spreading like oil, denser by the day. And though I still like to think Richard can outrun the slick in his dreams, I sometimes fear that in real life he might start to hold back rather than give more of himself because of what haters might do to him again. And there is nothing I can do or say to help him get over this any sooner.

"After trauma, anxiety is a huge part of the healing process," Lenny said when I shared my thoughts on this, taking his sunglasses off to blow on each lens before wiping them with the edge of his shirt as if trying to make me feel more assured by such an ordinary effort, but I sensed he was as concerned as I was. "People feel dwarfed by the experience, lost in a world that feels too threatening. But our boy won't get trapped by it." We both agreed that Richard wasn't wired for endless anxiety. "But I know how you feel. When he stares out the window at two o'clock in the morning, I feel helpless as a newborn."

Sixteen

*"There is a bit of insanity in dancing that does
everybody a great deal of good."*
~Edwin Denby

The sun rises.

ON MONDAY, THERE WAS A NEW WOMAN IN CLASS FROM
Samoa, of all places. She walked through the door slowly,
but I never got the feeling it was because she is bigger than
most people, only that she comes from such a hot place in
the middle of the Pacific, an island where wooden huts sit
right over the ocean, and slowly is just how people walk
due to the humidity. But after she started swaying back
and forth, moving her hips in a circular motion like some
holy version of femininity, it didn't take long to see how
when she danced there was nothing slow about her midriff
movement. Nothing slow whatsoever. It made me catch
my breath.

Her name is Talia. I think she is a Goddess. Her
movement strikes your heart before it even reaches your
brain, and I've never met anyone so big (she had to come in
the door sideways) who is as light-footed. When I popped
out of class to use the loo, Richard waved me over. "We'll
have to reinforce the floor," he said, real concern in his voice.

I was thrilled to have Talia in class, but it went further
than that. I had to think about it, but a few days later I

said to Richard, "She's one of those rare people you trust right away. " Later, when I thought even more about why I felt this the moment we met, I considered all the people who are moving to Yucca Springs lately with lots of money and airs to match. But Talia has the nature of someone whose had to work physically hard to earn her place in the world, and I can identify with that.

"I've danced hula since the day I could walk," she said sitting on the floor next to me, tucking her calves, round as cantaloupes, under her skirt. There was a short silence and then. "I got the sugar," is how she put it, which as Lenny wrote in her file, meant she was diabetic and suffering from peripheral edema caused by bad diet and excessive salt and sugar intake. "It's so hard to give up salt pork and a Coke for whole grains, fruits, and vegetables," she said. "But I try."

"I never realized how amazing the hula is," I said to Miss Stephanie. "It's like serenity and energy coming together at once."

"Like the sun rising."

All my thoughts turned to what she just said. I could see it, the horizon coming to life at the most fundamental level. Such a basic, clean line illuminated.

Everyone in class was spellbound by Talia. By her eyes that are huge twinkling discs. By her fleshy cheeks and jet-black braid wound into a knot on the top of her head. By her long flowy skirts—folds of lemon yellow, lime green, coral pink, purple, all the colors of the rainbow worn by women in our Grubstake Parade maybe, but not out and about on a daily basis, not around here anyway. By the way she places her hand in front of her mouth, trying to hide her laughter because she naturally wants to laugh off her missteps more than the rest of us. By what she does after, rubbing one hand over the folds of stomach as if she is trying to buff away the mistake. It's the funniest thing.

The first time she made the connection between a *plié* and the way she squats on her heels, saying how everything about ballet switched for her after that, "Ballet go from baloney to spit-roasted chicken, like that!" I thought how cute that was, that her craving to learn is as big as her appetite.

Everyone wants to talk to her, but no one gets to hog her affection for long. She's too maternal for playing favorites. After a minute or two she scoots them away, swatting their behinds.

She came to our next class with a lei made of plastic orchids from Walmart. "Where you find a real lei in the middle of the desert, eh?" she said handing it to me. It was lovely, I thought, without being over the top. "Even a candy lei is better, but Mr. Lenny say stay away from sweets. So I do." She put the lei over my head, but she shook hers, as though trying to feel okay about fake orchids, but not quite able to. "One thing should always be real," she said. "Flowers."

As the others started to trickle in, we chatted about the hula studio she left behind in Pago Pago, which sounded so exotic to me, but her face didn't light up or even change expression, she just wrinkled her nose and dropped her shoulders up and down. I thought she was like me in this way. When I'm having one of my tired-of-the-same-place days, I wrinkle my nose too. It made me see how we all get tired of home sometimes—same old, same old.

I felt my baby kick just then. *Had she heard me?* I wondered.

Next, we talked about her sons who came to this country to serve in the military, about my baby on the way, and how she had her first at fifteen. "Catholic, that's why," she said. She had nine other children after that. Nine! Six of them living in California. How she lives with her oldest daughter in Desert Hot Springs. She even showed me the bottom of her feet, covered with thick brown calluses— better than the best dance shoe ever, we agreed. She must have sensed that I was the perfect person to show your feet to. I've always been drawn to how to treat calluses, like how to use super glue to hold them together after they split down the middle. Things like that.

Talia is by far the oldest friend I'd ever made. I feel like we both have a strong desire to know someone completely different from ourselves. "Talia is so unlike my own mother," I said to Miss Stephanie.

"And yet there's something about her that makes you think of Peggy anyway," she replied. "So you tell me, how different does that make her, really?"

The best place on earth!

Our fundraiser was a huge success!

Try to imagine Richard—looking out the window at the line of cars waiting to park in our lot, with more traffic backed up along Twenty-Nine Palms in both directions— full of the forgiveness he worked so hard for, full of himself, and enough carbohydrates to fire up a furnace.

And just as fired-up about our grand re-opening, with a full-class schedule that includes hula taught by Talia and karate taught by her son, a new Bose Digital Music System we just *had* to have (according to you know who), baby-proofed cabinets, draws and outlets, a new loveseat for the lobby, and even a swamp cooler for the hottest days now that pretty much everyone agrees that global warming is more than just finger pointing.

Still, while the director in me wants my partner to have everything he thinks we need, pregnant me is in no position to provide it. My last trip to Baby Cubby Consignment was *it*. I'm just holding my breath that I can pay the Visa bill.

Lenny said he'd gladly match the donations, fueling Richard even more.

Imagine, too, you are sitting on a folding chair or a floor-pillow, the lighting just perfect—not so dark that you can't see the high heels Mrs. Powers "forgot" to take off at the door or Nancy Prusso in a long fancy dress like it was prom or something, sitting next to Lisy wearing her Rancho Mirage Royal Academy of Dance T-shirt (I fumed!)—but dark enough so there's a hint of romance in the air. "Strong feelings necessitate soft lighting," Miss Stephanie said turning down the lights.

So, can you picture it? People so into the good mood of the event that they don't mind putting a twenty into the jar even though they swore they'd put in only a ten? The atmosphere so intimate that it's easy for people to forget about who they are the rest of the time and whatever they thought they were so upset about, namely, men sleeping with men, unwed pregnant ballerinas, immigrants stealing their jobs, you name it.

The house lights go down. Richard springs up.

The first dance belonged to Richard, not only because he deserved the honor, he loves to be the first at anything. Ready to dance his heart out, it's like having a front row seat to a growth spurt—one man maturing into someone more confident and whole; it was difficult to believe he had ever been weakened. He was wearing black jeans, a new tight white T-shirt that I was sure had Lycra in it, and the sweeping effect of eager dancing against the projected images of his recovery process, step by steadfast step, was incredible. "Calvin Klein meets Stomp," he yelled out and everyone clapped like crazy. We wiped tears from our eyes, but he was also making us laugh. It wasn't manipulative, just two sides of emotion given the same weight. This can happen under the direction of a skilled performer who knows it's the perfect opportunity to draw people in to cold, hard, truths while they are seated on warm, soft pillows, surrounded by the love and support of familiar faces.

Even if their love and support... is a little limited at times.

And there is more generosity than we ever expected, even from women who go way back with my mother, and not exactly as friends, yet suddenly they are tossing in the dollar bills. You could practically hear the money stacking up.

It was a surprise, really.

Then again, Miss Stephanie was our star promoter, and there is no better social media than Miss Stephanie. She weaves an everlasting web.

Days before the performance, she traipsed and twittered all over town, reminding everyone how much beauty, discipline, and culture the Star Struck has brought to Yucca Springs over the years. "I'm determined to break up the logjam of rumors so no one knows *what* to believe," she said to Richard and me. And that's what she did, wading right into the muddy waters of hearsay, forcing everyone to acknowledge how we all want to be treated with compassion and respect.

And people listened, boy did they.

"It's like she's running for mayor," Lenny said.

"Nothing has really changed about the world," she said over dinner her first night back in town, Lenny, Richard, Rivers, Lisa, her, me, crowded around a picnic table at *Pie For The People* because Richard said the only thing that would calm his nerves was carbs. "The best social network is being *social*," she said. "We still need to look into each other's eyes to effectively change minds, behaviors, and most of all," she clapped her hands together, "studio enrollment."

Unsurprisingly, Mr. Lawson was the only person who was less than respectful, running out to tell Miss Stephanie that her car was parked over the line as soon as she arrived. She replied by saying that allowing her to park in the shade was the least he could do for a weary traveler, to which he replied he had Bill's Towing on speed dial.

"I'd hoped he'd evolved a little by now," she said. That caused Lisa to say that she thinks men like him peak in high school and develop backwards from there. We all laughed so hard, soda gushed out of Richard's nose. And I nearly, well, never mind. (Pregnancy talk can get too personal. I'm trying to be more discreet.)

By and large, though, everyone welcomed Miss Stephanie back to town with open arms. The end of her three-day "campaign" left a lingering trace of communal spirit in the air. Her opinion makes people think twice, it's always been this way. You are ruined for the run-of-the-mill point of view once you listen to Miss Stephanie.

"Still, she was smart to move away," Lisa said after Rivers and Miss Stephanie excused themselves, leaving earlier than the four of us.

"Why?" I said.

"Because she's..." she thought for a moment. "She's like a bite of good taste for people who don't necessarily want a steady diet of it," which made me catch my breath, Richard shriek, and Lenny found the statement so funny he had to grab the table to keep from falling backward in his chair.

The best part about Miss Stephanie's networking was that just by hinting at how much she knew—meaning how many husbands had put the moves on her, how many parents skipped out on paying her, "but I would never resort to coercion," she said, smiling—she filled every square inch of the Star Struck.

"She worked this town over like a pro," Rivers said, partly in fun, but he meant it, "with major agenda with no one but her grasping what the agenda *is*." He said it was the same tactic dictators use to overtake a country, which really made me think. "It can take politicians years to understand how to do what she does instinctively," he said. "If they ever learn at all."

She even convinced the Ladies Auxiliary of the Sportsman's Club to make three hundred cupcakes for our bake sale, once she convinced them that dance was the most physical sport in the world. To emphasize her point, she dropped into a Russian split, rolled to her stomach, and lifted herself up using only one arm before demonstrating, on point from fifth position, a petit allegro into a series of grand battements. "It was the least I could do to insure enough Red Velvets," she said yawning, as if saying what she was about to say next already bored her to pieces, "They're all perfectly nice women. If nice is all you care about."

Oh, and I should mention how Miss Stephanie is pretty close to dancing in your lap if you sit in the front row, so a few men, because they are men, started coming two hours early. More and more people were coming and going from the lobby after they'd thrown their pillows down, or staked their spot with a lawn chair, taking time to look at all the new photos Richard had enlarged and hung in rows right up to the ceiling.

"People want to be their best around Miss Stephanie," Richard said, noticing how most women wore their Sunday best pantsuits.

Before Richard danced, in the rear of the studio, Lenny stood on a plywood platform (donated from Parker's Lumber) set down arm to arm on our old sofa. As soon as he turned on the work light he'd borrowed from the Building Department (one of the staff herniated a disc last year and couldn't say no to Lenny), a shaft of dust-bunnied light lit up the stage area, suddenly golden. Richard slid the makeshift curtain open and walked to the center of the stage. A collective gasp went out, and one "go Richard!" from Mike.

Suddenly, Mr. Lawson's schnauzer started barking right outside the window. Lenny hopped down off the couch and shut the window so fast everyone starting clapping. "And I haven't even started dancing yet," Richard said jokingly, except he started nodding vaguely to give the appearance of having everything under control—his head turning one way, then so far to the other that it looked as if he didn't quite know how to continue, hushing everyone into an uneasy silence.

A few more seconds went by before he tipped his head back and smiled, his voice poised, "I'm not a victim." He paused, "Well, maybe a little." People laughed timidly, but it was perfect. We all relaxed. "And I'm not one to dwell on the past, and I'm certainly not one to want sympathy from anyone (Lenny winked at me), but I wanted to choreograph this piece even before visiting the man in jail who hurt Charles and me. After hearing how much my attacker struggled since he was a kid and how much he'll have to overcome in order to be h-h-healthy (later he told me he almost said *human*), made me realize what a great life I have here in Yucca Springs." The audience was wrapped (rapt!) around his little finger. "But also how much I've had to overcome. I had no idea how to begin because haters are so difficult to understand on one hand, and so uncomplicated on the other. And then it dawned on me when I was in Texas and I picked up a newspaper, and there was an article I'm sure most of the men in the diner missed on their way to the sports page." There was a chuckle, mostly from the women. "The story was about a boy much younger than me who'd been beaten up by two men who told authorities they did it to show the kid that gays are not welcome in their county." People shook their heads. "It was a tiny article with no picture of the boy or the two men who beat him. And it revealed to me that there are only two kinds of gay men in the world: the ones who've been attacked and the ones who are afraid of being attacked."

The audience drew in one long breath before about a hundred pounds of pity came down on everyone.

It may have been a bit much all at once.

"But this evening is not about the pain I've been through, but about recovery!" A shared exhale overflowed. I had to give Richard credit, he knew what he was doing. His timing had always been impeccable. He has this little thing he does with his mouth when he's setting his audience up like this, a little pucker of his lips that straightens out when he's through. Miss Stephanie blew him air kisses, one with her right hand, one with her left, in quick succession. "And not just my recovery, or Charles' because the word on him is that he's playing football for the Chicago Maroons and dancing on the Ramble Dance Team."

Everyone cheered! (Well, not everyone. I noticed one couple trying to hold their disapproval in check.)

While Richard was speaking, Talia's hands moved in front of her face as if she was trying to help Richard through the words. "Fa'afafine," she said jutting a hip forward and raising her eyebrows, as if shimmying away any idea to the contrary. Most mornings she arrives early for class now, and one morning we sat on the floor as she explained how, in Samoa, people believe there is no such thing as being "gay" or "homosexual." *Fa'afafine* is simply a third gender, well accepted and "celebrated in my culture," she said, just as a stripe of sunlight washed over the tattoo of a gecko slithering up her thigh. No one could have choreographed the effect any better.

"Here's to firsts!" Wade yelled out from the audience, sitting in front of Mike. He leaned back with his elbows on Mike's knees, openly out of the closet for the first time that I knew of. He looked younger, calmer—a more comfortable version of himself. Earlier he'd told me, in a hushed voice after pulling me aside softly by the arm, that coming to my class had helped him get over himself. He'd finally been able to break through the guilt and fear that had repressed him since grade school. I wasn't sure how I'd accomplished this, other than once the spine is loosened, all sorts of tensions dissolve. Regardless, I was grateful he'd taken the time to tell me. He looked on top of the world, despite a few doubtful stares.

But I don't think people stared the way bullies stare with hate in their eyes–just how people stare sometimes when something is new to them and they just aren't sure how to process it yet. Like the time I was standing in line at Vons and there were two men from out of town holding hands and it was just such a surprise for old Mrs. Peters who had lived in Yucca Springs all her life. And yet, she's the first one to offer the men a dime when they come up ten cents short, likely because their hand-holding wasn't really such a shock after all, like something that would haunt her forever. It was just her first time seeing such a couple up close. Her kindness helped me to see that I was going to be Mrs. Peters one day, and I'd be lucky to age so tolerantly.

Richard went on. "What tonight is really about is the recovery of the Star Struck." Miss Stephanie grabbed my hand and squeezed. "Lucy has been the most generous friend over the last year, and with your help, it's high time she and I both get seriously back to work. So tonight we're dancing for anyone with love in their hearts and a few dollars to give." Someone cleared their throat, but genuinely. "And for any one of you who has ever made a mistake."

People looked at each other. Then, at once, they turned to look at me. I stood, stunned, holding my lower back like Sophia Petrillo. Surely he didn't mean me, did he? I couldn't believe he was being so insensitive at a time like this. I saw one smirk I'd rather forget. I slunk backward a few steps, glaring at Richard from the back of the room. *Mean thing to do!*

"No, wait, I don't mean Lucy," Richard yelled but it was too late. "I mean anyone who has ever posted lies and rumors. And other mistakes. Like we've all made, which, in the last couple of days, Miss Stephanie may have pointed out to many of you."

The room went stock-still.

"Uh oh," Miss Stephanie whispered, "talk about climate change." And then, "Nonsense!" she cried, as she walked to the front of the crowd. ("I didn't know what else to say," Richard apologized to her later, "it just popped out." Triggering Miss Stephanie to say, "Now, that's a slight exaggeration. It didn't just pop out, it exploded." Two seconds later, *she* apologized.) "Mistakes mean we are still at least *trying.*" We were rescued, as if everyone knew that this is the woman we should be listening to anyway, this is who we've come to see. People stood and applauded like crazy.

"I've never felt warmer toward the people of this town than in the last few days," she went on. The kindness everyone has showed me made me see that even if I wasn't born in Yucca Springs, I will die grateful I've lived and worked in the best community of people anywhere!"

"That's right!" The woman from Art Pottery yelled, in a tone that implied how on earth Miss Stephanie could have ever moved away (still, I will always have a soft spot for this woman, she worked like mad to get my mother's ceramic-angel tree topper done before our last Christmas together), causing Miss Stephanie to smile her most patient smile, never once forgetting her real reason for returning to help us.

"In fact," Miss Stephanie went on, "if a total stranger were to stop me on the street and ask me where I'm from, I wouldn't even think about where I was born. I would automatically say, Yucca Springs!" The crowd went wild. I think every one of us was reminded that Yucca Springs might not be perfect, but it's the only home most of us will ever know. People were more than happy to jump into the high spirit of the evening again, willing to settle for being less than perfect, just not for anything slighter.

Later, in private, Miss Stephanie said, "I can read these people. It's a simple matter of knowing their language is all."

"I think you could get the Santa Ana winds to blow from the west," I said.

As soon as the fundraiser was over, Miss Stephanie shouted to everyone waving goodbye on the sidewalk, "Yucca Springs is the best place on earth to live!" her arms folded around my waist and Richard's.

Minutes later, with Rivers in the passenger seat, she blew out of town, thirty miles over the speed limit.

But before she blew out of town ... dim the lights, please.

It's the little things: smooth entrances and exits, panties matched to costume, a well-organized finale where everyone knows who bows, in which order, and for how long. Every pause, every spotlight, every fade to black, timed just right.

"Otherwise, the hour will feel like eternity," Richard said to Talia at one of our last-minute rehearsals. She looked at him like he was silly, but then I realized what she was really trying to say was *calm down*. Otherwise he would have driven us all crazy.

By far the most important element is the music selection. Songs can be so deep-seated that it's impossible to rid the body of their first effect. And that's what we wanted, *effect*.

So when Lisa chose "Holding Back the Years" by Simply Red for our duet, I was a little skeptical. It wasn't a song I remembered well, and it felt a little sad. I feared that if our song was a downer the donations wouldn't add up.

The lyrics say something about the wishes of pater hoping for the arm of mater that get them both sooner or later, but they keep holding on, holding on, holding on, which sound weird at first. But once I looked up the definition of *pater* and *mater* I was totally on board. "But seriously," I said, with, I admit, a ton of stored up resentment, "I think we maters should run the world and paters should run the house, see how that goes for a while."

"You so funny," Talia said slapping her knee. Hu whistled through her teeth, like she thought maybe I was being disrespectful, I couldn't tell for sure. Leslie just rolled her eyes.

Luckily the song was slow enough for someone with twenty plus added pounds (I'd stopped weighing myself) to gracefully make her way through. Though, clearly, it was still too fast for Lynette, Leslie, and Hu who had decided not to perform after all. I'd put together a simple sequence for them, a series of crosswalks in a circle, but who was I kidding? It would be cute for children to pull off, but 50/50 whether people would love adults for trying or drop their heads in pity. When I asked if they'd rather run the ticket sales at the door and the bake sale inside of it, I could tell they were as relieved as I was. "Some of us," Leslie said, "really would just rather pull on an apron and spread out the cupcakes—it's liberating." And for the time it took to find enough platters for the job, Lynette and Leslie and Hu were overjoyed. They'd become friends outside of class and it was good to feel like the spark for bringing them together. We all need a shoulder to lean on.

One morning I'd gone upstairs to fetch something, and just as I was about to come back down, I overheard Leslie say to Hu, "Well, you *say* he's supportive, but when I hear you talk to him, you don't sound like yourself." It was such an intimate yet dicey thing to say, I sat down on the top step to give them their privacy.

"What you mean?" Hu said.

"Like when you agreed with him that Richard is weird, when you don't feel that way. You love Richard."

Hu was quiet for a moment. The silence sent chills up my spine. "I don't want to make him mad."

"So what if he does get mad, if it's how you really feel? At this age, you look down the barrel of truth and decide one of two things, to tell your version of it, or someone else's."

I picked at a hole in my sweatpants, afraid to make a sound.

"I don't have to be right all the time. Like you."

"No, but does that mean you have to be invisible?"

Hu turned and limped away. A few seconds later, she turned back to say, "You coming?"

I have a photograph of her taken that day, around an hour after that exchange. Her arms are clasped around Leslie's back. She is peeking out from under Leslie's right shoulder and they are both smiling. The look on their faces told me things about friendship I was just beginning to understand, that there can be genuine honesty between us if we are fortunate enough to find genuine people.

I think there are just some conversations we are meant to overhear.

Do I need to dim the lights myself?

But where was Lisa? We couldn't go on without Lisa. "She is exactly one half of our duet!" I cried.

Leading up to the fundraiser—when the sun started to heat up the roof, walls, and floorboards—no matter how hot and tired we felt after class, Lisa and I rehearsed. As the fans swayed the curtains and sunlight fell in longer and longer lengths across the floor, I pushed myself through. My belly grew larger by the day it seemed, but my legs remained strong and firm. I felt fit and healthy, and I'd stopped being surprised by how pregnant I looked, trying hard to silence my life-long desire for a classic ballet body.

With nearly all of the details taken care of, Richard now poked at things that didn't need fixing, like saying that by asking only the women to run the bake sale, I sounded sexist.

"Okay," I said, "here's what I know about sugar-loving Yucca Springs. A good bake sale can bring in a bundle, so if you know someone better to both man the moneybox and make sure no one steals a cupcake, have at it." It's amazing how quickly he agreed with me after that.

Wade said from the get go that no way was he going to perform anything—ever, period. "Bread is my contribution, Lucy, bread I can do." He donated six dozen demi-loaves of banana bread.

"But Wade," I said, "all you have to do is stand in the middle and tug at Lisa and me as we pull against you from either side." I think Lisa and I were pretty much the same size by then, though maybe she weighed a little more. Not that I cared or anything.

"Huh?" Wade said.

"Just act as if you're a shady presence trying to keep us down."

"I'm sorry. What?"

"Like you are trying to defy Mother Nature."

"Come again?"

"And you'll need to wear black to appear alarming. It also hides you against the curtain."

"I have no idea what you are talking about."

"And you can sit in the audience until your cue."

"No."

"I'll cry, if I must."

I have no clear memory if I actually did have to resort to crying. But if I had to guess...

Talia had learned the lyrics to "Holding Back The Years," so that's how we ended our duet, with her singing and holding Lisa in one arm and me in the other, as if her maternal muscle gave us the strength to overcome our Biggest Fear (played by Wade, finally, and for the few seconds he was on stage. I think he actually enjoyed it, surprised, *rapt*, by how exciting it felt).

The choreography was Lisa's idea. She wanted to tell the story of how fear can hold us back. How women tend to internalize clues from people and the media about what defines "appropriate" behavior for females and how, in turn, all the "shoulds" keep us from pursuing our dreams. And I was dying to say how women can have a career and a baby and flourish at both because I was sick to death of people asking me how I'd possibly manage a work/life balance—that silly thing everyone says now like we are the first generation ever to have babies while still having to work hard at everything else.

Lisa said she came up with the idea after she'd scolded Hu for calling me the "B" word, jokingly, behind my back. I blinked. I couldn't believe Hu would say such a thing. "Oh that's nothing," Lisa said, "there are plenty of ranchers who won't let me operate on their livestock. There's still a high price to pay for having no dick and plenty of balls." I had to run upstairs to change. Laughter that side-splitting was a close call for me even before I was pregnant.

As soon as I came back down, I said, "Did I tell you that new pastor from the First Church of God stopped me on the sidewalk, and had the nerve to ask me how I could be an example for young girls now that I would never get ahead. I still can't figure out what exactly he thinks I should get ahead *of*."

"He's threatened by you. You're not following his flock, or any flock. You're okay with life being a big question mark, you don't need pat answers. You're fine with not knowing the outcome before you jump in."

"I am?" I was taken aback. Her picture of me took me by surprise. "In my choreography, maybe, but in my personal life? I'm not so sure. I think it's more like I jumped in without thinking. And now I have no choice but to deal with..." I rubbed my belly, "the future best I can."

"Which *is* a choice, don't you see? And that's why you make him so nervous. How's he going to rule the roost if people go at life their own way? No sheep, no flock. No flock, no *power*, though he's happy to call it *God*. No power, no money in the collection box." She smiled over the top of her water bottle.

"And the worst part was the anger in his voice. My mother had an expression for the way he talked to me, she'd say it was below the belt."

"That makes sense. Since below the belt is where our wombs are. Wombs are the last frontier. Men will never gain complete control without them."

Light poured in from every direction. "You're really something," I said.

"I've dissected a cow, intestines twenty times long as its body. *That's* something. Untangling the guts of religion is easy."

We just never know when something someone says or does will have an effect on us. Her words sparked through me to the ends of my fingers. It was then, in my mind's eye, that I saw us both pulling with all our might, Lisa and me, but neither of us pulling the other off center, we were not competing. We were equal give and take, steady balance, reciprocal sides of risk and beauty.

Even if we had to explain all this to everyone later.

Like how Talia's daughter had to ask why Lisa kept pulling if she was on my side, and I had to explain that we were two wings pulling together, not away. And how Lisa had shown this generosity to me more than once, though no part of me was about to say when the first time was (but that did not keep me from thinking about Billy, remembering him distinctly even). But people have seen so many cat fights on TV and in the movies they think women always need to compete with each other, so that's what she thought she saw. So I said, "I'm tired of people implying that having a baby and a career is too much," which had nothing to do with her question, but the adrenaline rush must have set me off.

But before we even got that far into the evening, like I said, we couldn't find Lisa.

"She outside," Talia said giving me a friendly little shove toward the back door. "She scared."

Lisa was outside the door, huddled on the bottom step smoking a cigarette, a puff blowing out the side of her mouth. When she saw me, she raised her eyebrows in an apologetic way. "I only smoke when I'm this nervous," she sighed. "Did I ever tell you about the time in high school when I just couldn't go through with it, but I had to. So I went out there and, sure enough, I chain-stepped off the foot of the stage."

"No. You did not tell me. And I can't believe you are telling me now."

"It was years ago. Except it feels like yesterday. Actually, it feels like right now."

"If you don't stand up this instant, the memory of giving up this time will hunt you down like a dog in heat and ruin your life forever!"

Before I could take it back, a change came over her. "Step aside," she said stomping out her cigarette. "I'm going in."

It was the major reason why our duet was such a success, according to Miss Stephanie. "We could feel how determined you both were."

We were determined. We pulled harder than we ever accomplished in rehearsal without one of us falling over, wanting people to sense how women find ways to balance it all—men, babies, work, all of it. We manage somehow, we just do. *Our legs may burn, but they don't cave!*

Also, by way of Talia's strong arms, we wanted to remind people that if someone older and wiser is willing to take your hand and guide you, it's a good idea to let them.

Earlier, in silent preparation, I'd taken myself through pretty much every recital since I was a girl. With a catch in my throat, from our first to our last, right on through to when the nurse wheeled Charles away. While I was at it, I even let the rousing images of Billy float up—the longing, the kissing, the stroking... before asking *Sina*, Talia's Goddess of Love (I learned about in our latest "talk story") to help me get over the pull he still had on my emotions. I willed myself to bring up all sorts of bad feelings and resentments so that I could rein them in, not wanting anything unexpected to well up while I was on stage. After fiddling with the hem of my skirt for another minute, postponing the moment when I would have to leave the bathroom, I managed to stand, open the stall, and shoot for the door without stopping to examine myself in the mirror. "This is it," I whispered to Lisa as soon as I saw her.

When I stepped into the spotlight, I didn't pause to feel the eyes on me. I laid down on the floor, sure to fix my skirt so that my leg muscles were exposed, as Richard had directed. And once I thought about it, I understood what he meant. The audience needed to *see* feminine muscle (oiled for effect) reach for the trust and support that was extended.

Enter Lisa.

She circled me with *piqué* turns before offering her hand. After shying away, suddenly I couldn't stay away. I reached for her, but then I stopped, shot away (battu, *bah-tew*), before turning to look her directly in the eyes as my contractions increased (dance contractions) and for a few hushed seconds, it looked like Lisa was saying with her eyes, *trust me.*

And I said with mine, *I trust you, sister, I do!*

Again, I'm not saying the audience got it.

But at least they felt *some*thing.

Then, wait, what's this?

Mid-way through our duet, there's a commotion in the reception area. I remember hearing a noise, but it didn't distract the audience. I don't remember anyone turning around.

Later we learned that Karen had slinked in to insert her own brochures into each row of our brand new, three-story, clear-acrylic flyer stand.

Hu saw her first. She was sitting at the baked goods table working on cupcakes by flashlight, trying to make the crushed ones look sellable. Leslie had her head down counting the crumpled singles and Lynette was lost in another Red Velvet so neither of them noticed Karen come in. Hu nudged Leslie soon as she saw how sneaky Karen was acting. "Just what," Hu rose and said, "you think you doing?" Suddenly Karen was lying flat on the floor, Hu's tiny feet pinning her down until Lenny could escort her from the studio. Just before she was fully out the door, she shot Hu a flip of her finger. "What kind of yogi flips the birdie?" Hu hissed, the veins above her temples standing out, her eyes locked with Karen's.

Leslie said she's never seen Hu get so angry. It all happened in a matter of seconds and no one from the audience seemed to notice.

"It's just what small towns are like," Miss Stephanie said stretching her arms toward the ceiling. "They can seem friendly from afar, but once you get down inside the crannies," she stopped stretching to look around the curtain, "the stakes are high. The competition is brutal. People want to be the only one."

Lisa and I took turns bowing to our standing ovation before Lisa ran backstage and I ran forward to dim the lights (Richard forgot) a little more, as per Miss Stephanie's instructions.

Talia walked forward, removed her outer robe, transitioning from wise mother-of-our-duet to even wiser mother-of-the-Pacific where even grandmothers are allowed to show considerable skin. Everyone gasped, but her rippling folds weren't meant to titillate, only to help people see how, in other places of the world, dancing is for all shapes and sizes. The shell horn blew, the drums started to throb, and after bending slightly over from the waist to allow her daughter to place a red and yellow feathered headdress on her head that must have been two feet high, her hips started to move under a soft cascade of the flowy skirt. Before long, the room was mesmerized.

Another thing Talia shared with me about Samoa was how many problems they have: too many drugs, not enough jobs, people drink too much. "It sounds a lot like here," I said. And I was trying to remember another thing she'd said that I found moving, but I couldn't put my finger on it until I noticed her son start to sway his own hips with his baby girl on his shoulders, reducing my insides to mush, and that's when I remembered: "My family tree has many branches," after Hu asked her if she wanted to return to Samoa one day. "My father is from Tonga. My mother from Australia, and my new grandbaby is American, her mother part German and also part French," adding the sound she likes to make when she's excited, *"ioe"* (which sounds like 'ee'). "So maybe I stay," which sort of answered Hu's question, but not really.

I kept looking at the audience to see what everyone thought. Some of the women started to talk to each other, softly but eagerly, and I knew Talia's class would be a huge success, packed with women dying to break out. *I have flaps. I have folds. Why should I hide them?*

Somewhere a real lei was found. Talia's son removed the headdress and placed the lei over his mother's head carefully. It fell over her chest like a wreath, giving off this dreamy perfume. "She owns this room," Richard whispered. "Look at Mr. Prusso. He'd like to climb her like a tree."

The applause went on and on until Talia modestly lowered her forehead while her dangling earrings kept right on swinging. She lifted her chin to announce in her sweet but no-nonsense voice, "I hope you take my class." Then she backed away from the spotlight slowly, and walked off with her back to us, her hips swinging side to side like nobody's business, the wood under her feet sounding stressed for the first time.

And did we ever learn a thing or two about self-promotion by watching her work the room during intermission.

Eat the damn cupcakes.

Richard stood on the platform with Lenny, clapped his hands twice, and announced that the finale was about to begin. Talia yelled *ioe!* Richard climbed down, ran from the lobby to the bathroom, *click, click, click,* shutting off all the lights—the relief of having made it through the evening unmistakable in the spring in his step. He nearly tripped over two frosting-induced boys who were racing around the studio.

Famished, I twirled toward the cupcakes, stealing a quick reflection of myself in the glass. I thought I was over being so hard on myself, but a lump of guilt rose in my throat. The more rambunctious of the two boys ran past me, bored now, and tried to crawl into his mother's lap, Sara, Lynette's daughter. I got the feeling by the way she was eyeing me, that she saw me take a long ravenous look at a cupcake and then turn my back on it. She scooted her son off her lap, marched right up and said, "You are not fat. You are expecting. Though expecting isn't the right word. I've never liked that word. You are nurturing. That is what you are doing. Now, eat the damn cupcake."

Sometimes the best advice is the most straightforward.

Cue the lights.

And there it was. The song to set your soul on fire: "Stand by Me." There is a lot of desire in the song, for sure. Especially the *darlin' darlin'* near the end.

I couldn't help but wonder if Miss Stephanie's stomach felt as nervous as mine. (Though it might have been the three cupcakes I nurturing-ly wolfed down.)

Sweet mother of Samoa! I couldn't believe what I was seeing. Rivers walked out on stage hand in hand with Miss Stephanie. Is he Miss Stephanie's... what, exactly? Partner? Prop? His smile beamed. "I bet she can probably get him to do just about anything by now," Lisa whispered.

Lenny turned up the spotlight and Rivers showed a lot of pride in his footwork, even more in the way he looked at Miss Stephanie. When he ran his lips over the tips of her fingers, I think every woman in the room would have run off with him on the spot if they could have. Together they glided across the floor, delivering a smooth chain step.

But best of all, absolutely the best, was the way Rivers looked at Miss Stephanie when he said, "Stand by me, oh stand by me."

Lifts are tricky for both dancers, and a successful one is half the battle of a *pas de deux*. The woman fears being dropped, the man of dropping her. If done right, it can seem like no great shakes, but in a split second, the move can either bring the house down or turn it into a deafening gasp. So when Rivers nearly dropped Miss Stephanie as they attempted a fish dive—the easiest lift because the woman's nearness to the ground lets both dancers feel more comfortable—everyone inhaled as if it was the last breath they would ever take. Without meaning to, I shook my head in disbelief. Love can't be *this* blind. Can it?

Rivers seemed unaffected by the slip, paused for a moment, cleared his throat and tried again. This time it was flawless, creating a lovely line of downward diagonal Miss Stephanie contrasted by upward arch of Miss Stephanie. Everyone stood and clapped. Why I had, for an instant, doubted Miss Stephanie is beyond me. I looked directly into her eyes. She didn't lower hers or look away. Instead, her pupils lit up, as if it wasn't a question for her, standing by another even if the mountains *should* crumble to the sea.

Rapt! I am rapt by the beauty and confidence of my teacher. I use the word once more because I felt like an awestruck little girl again, staring with wonder at what I wanted to do. I smiled at her in perfect appreciation.

Now Richard jumped up and buffalo-stepped towards Rivers. *Wait, are you in on this too?* How funny the two of them looked as they waltzed together off the floor, taking turns looking back at Miss Stephanie who was smiling with her hands on her hips like the real Ginger Rogers: *Boys, I can do everything you do, only backwards and in high heels. With an underwire cutting into my sides.*

Nothing about the liveliness of the piece changed after the men exited, but everything from that point happened a hundred times more impressively. Miss Stephanie raised her arms into second position, priming to give what everyone was waiting for, and in seconds, her leg extended to its highest position just as she rotated her palm upward as if to stress the grace and skill involved in holding a perpendicular line to the floor. She was everything you think of when you think of ballet—everything you need to know about technique, about practicing endlessly. It was even more satisfying because of her nearness, so close we could hear her breath draw in and exhale, see each step come off light from the floor. Every line was sharp yet supple and she used weight shifts in ways I hadn't even thought of. I was holding my breath to see what came next. She was so accomplished and strong and confident I... I...

I wanted to cry.

I put my hand to my mouth and nearly did.

"Out of... joy!" I whispered to Lisa who noticed how upset I was.

"No one cries out of pure joy," Lisa said as if she could read my mind.

She was right. Miss Stephanie had shown me a whole new level of competence to reach for. When she was finished, I had to run to the bathroom and hold a wet washcloth to my forehead. I still feel my own possibility through her. And later, once we were alone, I told her so.

She put her nose to my nose and took my hands in hers. "You are so accomplished already, Lucy. Don't you dare let that mean little voice in your head tell you otherwise. It's a leech, that voice. It'll suck every last drop of joy out of dancing if you let it."

"Okay," I said trying to sound convincing, *convinced*.

"It's good to have examples of how you want to live your life, and it's good to want to be like someone you look up to. But I want you to know something, you inspire *me*. And if I've been any kind of good example, than you will have to trust that you will keep challenging yourself for the same reason I do, because it makes you happy. A dancer doesn't quit because she has a baby or can't afford to eat in restaurants or buy new clothes, a dancer quits when she starts to believe that uncertainty isn't supposed to be part of the process." Then she said it again, as if to call even more attention to the fact. "Uncertainty will always be a part of it, a big part. I need you to remember this because it's too easy to forget sometimes."

She always points me toward the heart of the matter.

When I was very young, I danced all around our house. I danced around my mother fanning herself. I danced around her complaining that we couldn't afford air-conditioning. I danced around her touchiness once the needle on the thermometer hit one-hundred degrees. I danced until I fell on the rug in a heap of exhausted giggling. I was doing other things that summer too, like riding my bike and swimming in the community pool. My mother said I was always looking for somewhere to run off to. But that's not what I was doing. I felt so afraid and fidgety all the time. Dancing relieved all that. Even then, I danced because I was looking for somewhere to calm me, somewhere to *stay*.

Finally, I said, "How did you persuade Rivers to perform with you?"

She gladly dove in. "I reminded him that he may have noticed something about me by now, that I generally get what I want. The next morning, I found this taped to my bathroom mirror." She took out a little folded up piece of paper from her purse that said, *Count on getting what you want. Count on me.*

"That's when I knew," she said.

"That's so romantic," I said.

"There's still no substitute for good old-fashioned romance," she said.

Or good old-fashioned tears, I thought. Pure this time, definitely.

Later, when I asked Rivers if he'd been more nervous about learning the choreography or turning down Miss Stephanie, he said, "What do you think?"

Ahh.

After Miss Stephanie's solo, Rivers reappeared on stage again, and as soon as I saw her flick a nod in his direction, I knew they were preparing for a shoulder sit. I couldn't cover my eyes or I'd never forgive myself. I scanned the room looking for Richard. He was on the platform next to Lenny. He gave me a thumbs up, remembering, I'm sure, how many times we'd done the lift together, Miss Stephanie calling out, "Don't lean forward!"

With River's hands on her waist, Miss Stephanie did a deep *plié*, and whoosh, my whole life passed in front of my eyes. And I'm sorry, but what I did next is unforgivable. In my defense, I was in total reflex mode. I ran to the foot of the stage and extended my arms. I wanted *not* to, but once a spotter, always a spotter.

Miss Stephanie laughed. Everyone laughed. I think most people thought my action was planned. Embarrassed, I sat back down, and from behind Sara tapped me on the shoulder. "I wanted to do the same thing," she whispered. I thought that was the sweetest thing to say, if a little ruined by her son saying, "Yeah, mom, but you *didn't*."

As soon as Miss Stephanie's toes touched the floor, a mutual *ahh* fell over the room. And not enough can ever be said of the mutual *ahh*.

For the purpose of fundraising, expressly.

A true finale.

Richard wanted everyone to change back into our costumes for the finale.

"Sorry," I said shaking my head, "My side seam ribbed out. It isn't pretty."

Just before I'd walked over to survey the baked goods, I saw a slim, stylish man slip in without saying a word. He looked about thirty, wore a black button down shirt, distressed jeans, and I detected a bit of makeup around his eyes, grey shadow and liner. But what really stood out were his loafers, deep yellow suede. From the moment he arrived, Hu eyed him curiously. She drummed her fingers on the table, stood up abruptly, looked him straight in the eye and said, "you buy?" In seconds, she'd sold him a cupcake.

"Like a hawk zeroing in for the kill, " Lynette whispered.

Lynette, Leslie, and Hu had been discussing two Japanese tourists who'd also found their way in. Their hiking clothes looked new and expensive, like they'd shopped at the Eddie Bauer outlet store at Desert Hills before hitting the trails in Joshua Tree. "Half-pants-half-shorts? Is this what tourists think they need to take a walk through a canyon nowadays?" Leslie said.

"I think they look smart," Hu said.

"Imitating the country who blew them to smithereens? How smart can they be?"

Lynette piped in. "I hear they rebuilt those cities. You can't even tell they were blown-up."

"Oh, they rebuilt them, alright," Leslie scoffed, "one ATM at a time."

As if wanting to steer the subject away from any conflict, private or worldly, Lynette said, "The Chamber of Commerce wants us to call them visitors now, not tourists."

"Oh, yeah?" Leslie said yawning. "I can't keep up."

I was having so much fun listening to the three of them, but I kept stealing glimpses of the man in yellow shoes, the sight of which worried me. I wanted to say as much to Lenny who was trying to talk to the Japanese couple the best he could. There was a lot of smiling and nodding and picture taking. I found Richard instead, just before the man walked up to tap Richard's shoulder. He extended his hand.

Richard hesitated. He squinted, trying to remember, just as I'd tried to remember but couldn't quite. "Do I know you?"

"I'm Benjamin."

Everything went still for a minute. Then we all started talking at once. "I couldn't wait another fifteen years to come back here," Benjamin said, "not after I read about what happened to you." He looked down at his loafers. We all looked down at his loafers. "You started a fashion trend, you know."

"I did read something about it," Richard said blushing, digging his hands deeper into his pockets.

Within minutes, Richard was wearing the yellow loafers.

—⁓⁓⁓—

In stocking feet, Benjamin walked out to speak to the audience. "I haven't been in a dance studio since my dad yanked me out of this one." A hush rolled through the audience, what compassion would sound like if it echoed, I thought. "Since then, I've been to other schools and even more schools of thought, but no one has ever made learning as much fun as Richard."

"I don't believe this evening could get any better," Miss Stephanie whispered in my ear.

Benjamin went on to say how, before moving to San Francisco, he'd been living in Washington State, documenting a river's rebirth—how, in the early 1900's, dams were built as sources of power for nearby cities "in the greenest country you've ever seen," and how the dams provide power but not fish ladders, which devastated the salmon populations. The Elwha Act, signed by Congress, drove the removal of the dams and he'd been proud to be part of the dismantling.

I noticed a few men who looked as though they just had to be a part of work like that, and I had a long history with the look in their eyes, remembering the same hunger in my father's—the mere mention of faraway places hitting him smack between the eyes like a blow.

"But even in the wilderness, not many days went by when I didn't think of how Richard helped save me from... from so much I won't go into, not here, not tonight. But seeing him again makes me see how it's always worth it to take a risk, be yourself, and do the work that you love."

Everyone clapped.

Talia sashayed in wearing another floral skirt, as beautiful as the last, and tried to pick Benjamin up in a hug, but his socks slipped on the wood. He tumbled to the floor in a sprawl. After he peeled himself up, red-faced, he left the stage and slinked back to his seat. Talia's son ruffled the top of his head soon as he sat. "That happens a lot when men meet my mom, " he said with a laugh. "Just ask my dad."

⁓ↄ✿ↄ⁓

All week leading up to the performance, I had mixed feelings but I went along with Richard's idea for a finale, even after Miss Stephanie turned her nose up at the music and said, "Are you sure you want to reduce the evening to overtly sexual overtones?"

"We could always take our bow to the soprano part of the Messiah," he said, holding her glance.

She blinked first, a clear sign of conciliation.

I thought some of the moves might be a little out of the question for me, certainly, but as I sat there watching the others, chewing my cuticles off, I couldn't help myself, I had to join in. I did ask if maybe there was a slightly less suggestive way of moving my rear end from side to side.

"I've seen you do this move a million times," Richard said with almost no sense of humor. "It's a new era. The world has a place for pregnant women who want to shake their booties."

"Yeah, but…" I looked down.

"So, what's the problem?" he said. "Everyone calls you Lucy-Goosey already."

"I'm going to count to ten," I said and turned away. In a few seconds, I turned back. "Yeah, well, *being* Lucy-Goosey has made me realize that it takes far more concentration than you can imagine to not to pee on myself when I wiggle my ass."

No one thought that was as funny as I did, but they walked over sympathetically, one by one, to place their hands on my shoulder.

After the third run through, I had it down. I watched myself do the latest dance moves, trying to find a reason a nurturing woman should not roll sensually up her spine with her hands on her bottom. And you know what? I couldn't find one. I pressed my index finger to my behind like there was a spark at the tip of my finger. *Tsssss.* Richard gave me a hug.

Talia burst out laughing. She'd stripped down to baggy boxers and a big white Playtex bra. When we hugged, our bellies bumped in the middle. "Oh, this bad. And so much fun!" she said squatting right down until her rear end hit the floor.

"Gravity is a good reminder of just how low we can go," I said laughing, trying to squat as low, holding my belly with both hands now, protectively.

I did notice Miss Stephanie danced a softer, less suggestive version of the choreography. I also noticed Richard noticing her doing so. "Are you kidding me?" he said, riled a bit.

"This is my interpretation of the choreography," she said, more seriously this time. She was trying to be a good sport, but her tone lingered in the air longer this time, warning as a siren. Richard heard it as much as I did and we both knew no matter what he said now, it wouldn't matter, even if he wanted it to. And he didn't want it to, not really. There was just something about the skillfulness in the way she did the moves that went beyond dancehall, and always would. There is nothing indelicate about Miss Stephanie's hip thrust.

"One in a thousand chances I'll remember all these moves," Lisa said revved up.

"Are you sure it's not too in-your-face?" I said, but I knew what Richard's answer would be. And I knew he was right.

<hr />

And then, drama!

Seconds before we actually had to go on stage again, I split out my fanny seam. Talia quickly tied one of her scarves around my waist, but my confidence started to fail. Miss Stephanie swooped in with a red dress in her arms, the kind of dress that would leap through the air on the cover of a magazine, spilling over the side of a dancer's legs high off the ground. "I was saving this for later," she said, "but I think you could use it now." It was lovely. And as soon as it slid over my body, I *felt* lovely, the kind of lovely that can revive your confidence in a second. Lisa leaned in to kiss my cheek. We held hands and waited in a line before walking out. *Up and over, together, as one.*

I wasn't hoping for a miracle. I was hoping for rent money. And I don't remember much else about being backstage just before the finale, but Talia's quick thinking, Miss Stephanie's dress, and Lisa's encouraging kiss?

These are miracles I do remember.

~•ᴔᴕᴕ~

When people were leaving, they said it was the most fun ever, one of our best performances yet!

I stood watching their smiling faces, a few awkward tries at shimmying when women thanked Talia, all the people who wanted to shake Richard's hand on the way out the door. I watched it all—the hugs, the mingling, the schmoozing, the cupcakes and banana breads going, going, gone, the gallon mayonnaise jars full of cash. But everything stopped affecting me the way I wanted it to once I checked the signup sheet for upcoming classes. Hula was full beyond capacity, we'd have to add a class. Tap was overflowing, too. My eye kept peering towards the columns for Pre-Ballet through Advanced, but only a handful of names were written down, including Lisa's.

I wasn't afraid new students would never find their way to the Star Struck—new families move here every day. So for once I let hope tug at me from one direction while worry pulled from the other, and I was content to call it *uncertainty*. And leave it at that. I stepped back from the registration table. In a circular motion, I began to rub my belly. "Now, what?" I said calmly. And I did feel calm. Maybe I was relieved how well the evening went. Maybe it was something about Richard's recovery. Maybe I'd never know. People were much too interested in Benjamin and

Talia and Miss Stephanie to pay much attention to me, thank goodness. So I stood fast and smiled at everyone.

I held my uncertainty close as cloth covering me. And I smiled at everyone.

And I thanked them for coming.

I told myself that the best part of the evening was that we could, and *did*, put the worst of the past behind us. I remembered what Miss Stephanie said, how I would always find a way to dance, and how her words had called to mind a *Sex In The City* episode where Keri tells Charlotte (in the bathroom at her wedding) not to miss the real thing while *waiting* for the real thing.

The room had grown hot under the heat of the work lights so that Lenny left both doors open. I noticed the wisteria had climbed voraciously over and through the cracked cement wall. Blue flowers hung in firm clusters. When I turned around, Talia was standing there. "As soon as I got to this country, I had cataract surgery."

I had no idea what she was getting at, but it didn't matter. Her stories always give me pause simply because she is Talia.

"So now I see everything. Like that vine you are staring at? I think that vine is just like you. Nothing can stop it."

I had a sense of the floor underneath me not quite level for a moment. "I don't know. I feel like I've sort of lost my center..." I said.

She took my hands in hers which instantly made me feel more grounded. "You know what I always want to say when you tell me to hold my center? That no one can hold it forever. We get pulled down. Then we get back up. That's what I would tell you, if you needed an old Samoan woman to tell you anything. But you don't. So I say nothing."

And now, for reasons that have everything to do with finding your twining way up no matter what, wisteria comes to mind a lot.

Boogie Shoes.

The studio vibrated with the beat.

"That's our cue!" Lisa cried. We'd slipped on boogie shoes of one kind or another, all spray-painted yellow: galoshes, slippers, sneakers. And, thanks to Benjamin, Richard got to wear the real deal.

Pfffffft. Blown fuse.

"I think the Gods are trying to tell me something," Talia said. "Like maybe I should stick to hula." Everyone burst out laughing.

Lenny had thought of everything. He lit the Coleman. But there was no saving the sound. So Talia started to sing:

> *"Oie, I want to put on my, my, my, my, my*
> *Boogie shoes to boogie with you, oie!"*

And she began to dance.

So, hula, or our best imitation/simulation hula is what we ended with. I whispered to Miss Stephanie that I thought maybe Talia had asked her Tagaloa God to cut the juice, and it was the only time I had ever seen Miss Stephanie struggle to be herself. And it hit me: Other than Richard and me, she is the only one who knows where the fuse box is, and Rivers was nowhere to be seen.

Then the Coleman sizzled out of fuel. "If only I'd remembered to fill it," Lenny said nervously.

Richard shook his head, taken over by his disappointment, but only for a second, before he bust out with all of his best moves and, so help me, so did I. Claps rose up from the audience and everyone stood. Our bodies, mere shadows by then, came alive. So freeing! I knew that I would never stop dancing any more than Talia would or Richard or Miss Stephanie, backing off stage quietly on tiptoe.

Talia stopped singing. We bowed and left the stage. When I looked back over my shoulder, all that glowed was our old battery-powered clock. And someone was peeling it off the wall.

Just to recall how gently Miss Stephanie held the clock until she'd tucked it safely into her dance bag makes the tiny hairs on my arms stand up.

Stumbles every day, and just as many falls.

Once, I thought ballet was the highest discipline and that all other disciplines looked up to it, but the need for me to think like this has passed. Richard claimed this freedom long before I did, I see it in his photographs, how he frames everything into its own uniqueness. And so, for the first time since I was five, I am open to taking other styles. I signed up for beginning hula.

And if I flounder while teaching, I let someone catch me until I am steady again. My class is full of excellent spotters. They extend themselves freely, they don't hold back.

And when I start to feel there will never be enough time in a day to be both a good mother and a good teacher, I try to think back to Lisa's and my first duet and how what I really wanted to say was that it has always felt this way—it's nothing new to feel lost and overwhelmed, or that we've fallen flat. Talia is right. Our job is to catch ourselves, and others, as needed.

What I mean to say is, I'm more sure of myself every day.

I think so, anyway.

And since I've never had to forgive a real villain, like Richard has, the next best thing is to try to forgive my father. I've even decided to thank him for something he taught me, which is...

I will need to think more about this.

Okay, I've thought of something. "Dad? You had a good memory. And a dancer needs a good memory, mind and muscle. So, thank you."

And if things like that don't put my worries into perspective, I hand them over to Richard for the day. He just tosses them out with the recycling anyway, at least that's what he tells me. Then he figures out how to make things better in ways I never thought of and I pretty much slap my temple every time, thinking, *Why on earth didn't I think of that?*

And if he's not around, I find a way to toss them out myself.

⌁

The spirit of the finale remained long after everyone had gone.

Before going to bed, I read a text from Richard: *Just so you know, you danced like nobody's business tonight.*

Reply: *Just so YOU know, it might have been a good thing the lights went out or we might have been closed down by the censor police.*

I felt a kick. *Grand Battement.*
Then three soft taps, but brisk. *Allegro.*
I took a deep breath, held it in, let it out.
Actually, it felt like we both did.

⌐∘∘∘⌐

Demi pointe: supporting your body on the balls of your feet with your heels raised. I have to do a lot of them now, not to improve my *relevé*, but to relieve the cramps in my calves. After ten of them this morning, the name Demi came to me, pronounced *deh*-mee, emphasis on the first syllable. Unlike the actress with all the young boyfriends once Bruce Willis was out of the picture.

All along, I've been ninety-nine percent sure I'd name my daughter Stephanie, but now that the time is near, I still can't say the name without proper reverence and title.

Except for the one time. I remember it because it was one of those moments when you really need to trust yourself: It was a hot afternoon, one of the hottest on record. And later, when the sun was just beginning to disappear under the San Bernardino Mountains, the hour when all the sluggishness that prevents you from doing anything productive cools into what feels like a promise, I made myself one. "As soon as the sun completely fades, I'm going to make up my mind about a name."

The air darkened. I was just about to settle on Stephanie, I even said the word aloud, *Stephanie*, when the very next sound to rush out of my mouth was "Demi." The feeling was like leaping onto stage when, for a split second, everything stops.

Middle name? *Jeté* (zhuh-TAY).

Because life is a big leap.

~ecvov~

"Demi Jeté," I announced to Miss Stephanie, a little reluctantly.

"It's like giving her two legs up before she's even born," she said clearly thrilled, not at all disappointed. Right then, all of my love for her sort of gathered itself up into a smooth tight weave and fell over me softly. And while I don't know how I will ever repay her for all of the warmth she's given me over the years, I will always try.

My need to see *Demi Jeté* in writing was so strong that I went so far as to write it on a paper napkin. After adding the accent mark, I wanted to share it with Richard right away.

"I don't want to disturb your workout, but," I caught my breath. His face was intent and sweaty, but there was something different about his eyes. Looking at him, I saw a young man bothered by my interruption. But only a year ago, I would have seen more of an exasperated *boy*. I showed him the piece of paper. "What do you think?"

"What do *I* think?"

I braced myself. I knew he'd been thinking a lot about a name, too.

"I think she'll never live it down. I think it's too uppity for people around here to pronounce. I think they'll nickname her DJ if you're not insistent."

"DJ?" Oh, I did not like the sound of that.

He shifted his weight from one foot to the other, striking a toe tap before resting his heel to the floor. "*I'd* call her Rikki."

"Rikki?"

He lifted his chin and gave me a big smile. "Rikki Royale."

The name appeared before my eyes like a bouquet tossed mid-leap onto stage, both outcomes hurled at me at once: *Oh! Such lovely flowers! But where will I land?*

I didn't know what to make of it. The only thing that kept me from objecting was an even stronger surprise, *tap tap tap*, from deep inside my belly. Then three more taps, stronger still. Clearly my future was already being choreographed.

And just like that, in time but not late (never!), my past arrived: Miss Stephanie walked around the room, shifting our gangly legs and arms into elegant lines, gently but firmly; instructing how graceful lines are not honed by looking in the mirror, but by paying attention to how they feel. "As we know, all dances are made of lines. Without sensing the line," she said, "all we have is a picture. And we are *not* pictures. So, class?" she looked to us. "When our pose of greatest strength makes itself known from within, this is not where our best line ends but . . .?"

We take great joy in our answer. "Where it all begins!"

The End

Acknowledgments

I've never felt that I could write my books, such a solitary endeavor, without the love and overflowing support of my husband, Larry. Everything begins and ends with you, my love. For this one, he also helped me to better understand the difference between criminal cases better than anyone else. He might be the most patient man I've ever met.

Phil Bevis is a truly generous publisher who has greatly improved this book from the beginning and has helped everything about the process make more sense to me. Every writer needs someone who believes in them. Thank you for taking a chance on my work. And for working tirelessly to make beautiful books happen, my deepest appreciation.

Thank you to everyone at Chatwin Books, especially my copy editor Megan Gray, Helen Ruth for her sharp-eyed assistance, Julie Greene who helps so much with publicity and marketing, and all the other wise people of the team. Much gratitude!

Writers would be too lonesome without good friends to keep them company, encourage and commiserate. There really is no other way to get through the long, solitary process. Thank you my intimates, you know who you are. I would be lost without you, it's as plain as that. And most of all, Sheila, my great artist friend in New York who gives so much support, so often. Our friendship has shown me that two serious artists who meet at an artist's colony can become a kind of sacred twosome for life. And to my sister, Lou Ann, who still seems to love me no matter what. I often wonder if any of you will pick up this book and recognize just how much you have touched me along the way.

To all of my incredible dance students past, present, and future who have taught me in every way possible how to be a better teacher. I've finally found my truest calling and it is: There is so much to teach young dancers other than technique and choreography.

And one last: to all of the programmers for the many organizations, clubs, conferences, salons, and fund-raising events who have hired me in the past and who hire me still. Every day I depend on your invitations so that I can continue to bring my words to life through my speaking voice. Thank you for putting your hearts into choosing your speakers. For me, as a literary speaker, your efforts have been life-changing.

www.ingramcontent.com/pod-product-compliance
Lightning Source LLC
Chambersburg PA
CBHW031622100726
47898CB00006B/1902